VENGEANCE SERIES

KAYLEA CROSS

EXPLOSIVE VENGEANCE

Copyright © 2019
by Kaylea Cross

* * * * *

Cover Art and Print Formatting:
Sweet 'N Spicy Designs
Developmental edits: Deborah Nemeth
Line Edits: Joan Nichols
Digital Formatting: LK Campbell

* * * * *

ISBN: 978-1698158600

Dedication

To all my readers who love strong heroines! Thank you for following along on my Valkyries' adventures with me.

Author's Note

Here we are at Chloe's story! She was maybe the most fun heroine of mine ever to write, and I hope you'll fall in love with her in this book. Never a dull moment with her around.

Happy reading!

Kaylea Cross

Chapter One

C hloe Wilson tugged at the hem of her pearl gray suit jacket and checked to make sure her hair was still securely wound into a tidy bun at the back of her head before turning the corner and entering security camera coverage of the target building. Pausing on the sidewalk outside the entrance in the cool October night air, she adjusted her black-framed fake glasses, her stage makeup disguising her true appearance.

Let's do this.

To ensure this meeting happened in total privacy, it was after hours. Situated in the center of Paris's business district, the building was all but deserted now, only a single security guard stationed at the front desk in the lobby.

She used her security pass to scan herself in. The guard glanced up from his work to study her for a second, then went back to looking at whatever he was reading as she passed by on the way to the elevator.

The meeting room was on the nineteenth floor, the floor-to-ceiling windows framing an incredible view of the lights of Paris. Her target was already waiting for her in the private conference room next to his office. Like everything else Dominic Dubois owned, this place was sleek, expensive, and paid for with dirty money made from the criminal empire he and his brother ran.

"Ah, Gabrielle. Right on time." A fit, attractive man in his early thirties, Dominic rose in his custom-made suit and walked to the antique sideboard to help himself to a drink. "Brandy?"

"No, thank you." She set her briefcase on the table and sat. This was their third meeting, so she knew the layout of this entire floor—including all security measures, entry and exit points—by heart. There were no cameras in here. Because Dominic Dubois carried out his most private business transactions here. Things he didn't want a record of or anyone else to know about. Which was perfect for her.

He didn't realize the biggest threat to him and his empire was in the room with him right now.

Chloe held his stare, a sense of triumph rising inside her. The Valkyrie Program might not exist anymore but she was still running ops on her own because they needed to be done and she had enough money put away to live on for the time being. This was *her* time now. She'd chosen to spend it delivering the kind of karma to evil people that the universe wouldn't, spreading out her targets with time and distance to mitigate the chance of being identified and captured.

Sipping his brandy, Dubois leaned back against the sideboard and crossed his ankles, completely oblivious to what was about to happen. "You've got the documents ready?"

The fake contract authorizing the sale of twelve women he had smuggled into France several days ago, mostly from French northern Africa. Chloe didn't know where they were and she needed to find out if she was going to have a chance at saving them.

"Yes." A rush of power surged through her as she watched him coolly, maintaining the ice queen business-woman persona she'd used to infiltrate his organization to get to this point. She'd only attended a handful of meetings in person because she hated them and preferred to work anonymously, but also because it minimized the risk of her cover being blown. It added to her mystique, and Dubois ate it up.

He stared at her for a long moment, expression unreadable, then pushed up from the sideboard and crossed to the door behind her. The sound of the lock turning put her on instant alert as he turned to face her.

His dark brown gaze was shrewd. Cold as he measured her. "Remind me, Gabrielle. How long have you been working for Monsieur Roche?" Her fake boss who supposedly loved buying women sold into slavery, and then dispersing them across the globe to brothels and clients who paid top dollar.

She kept her expression passive, all the while reviewing her contingency plans for the best exfil option if this went sideways. Dominic was clearly suspicious. What did he know? "Three months." Her cover had been set up with the help of a female friend united in their cause to rid the world of scum like the man before her—men who got rich off the suffering of the women they sold like farm animals into a fate worse than death.

"Three months," he mused. "And yet, in all that time, my people haven't been able to find out much at all about you. Until now." His stare hardened. "Chloe."

It took everything she had not to show her reaction to hearing her real name. Inside, cold spread through her gut. How did he know her name? *How*? She frowned at him in confusion, maintaining her cool. "My name is Gabrielle."

His mouth twisted. "Liar." He whipped a hand into his jacket and came up with a pistol.

Chloe exploded out of the chair and hurled it at his

head. He barely had time to raise his arms to protect himself before it slammed into him, knocking him sideways. Chloe was on him the moment he hit the floor, wrenching his wrist up and back. He let out a yelp of shock and pain as the weapon tumbled to the carpet.

His gaze shot to hers in astonishment but she was already jamming a needle into the side of his neck. His eyes widened. "You—"

He never finished that sentence. The dosage in the syringe was powerful, already making him slump over. He wouldn't lose consciousness, would remain aware of his surroundings, but unable to move.

"You've been a very bad boy," she murmured, straightening to slip the syringe back into her interior jacket pocket. "But guess what? The party's over now."

Dominic Dubois was a waste of oxygen and needed to be disposed of. Despite the things he'd done—including keeping a personal sex slave from each new shipment of women he arranged, before selling her once the initial thrill was gone for him—corruption within the law enforcement and legal systems ensured he evaded justice at every turn.

No more. Tonight, Dominic would pay the ultimate price for all the evil and suffering he'd caused.

She dragged him from the room to the elevator reserved for his private use. The one without security cameras so no one else knew who he came and went with— or who he was smuggling in and out of the building. This freaking idiot might think he knew who she was, but he clearly didn't, or he never would have met with her alone.

She pressed his limp palm to the biometric scanner next to the door, shoved his face into the screen for the retinal scan, then hauled him inside and rode down to the private parking area beneath the ground level. He made a garbled sound, lying in a crumpled heap at her feet.

Chloe drove him home in his own vehicle, leaving a

voice text for her contact on the way. "Compromised. Picking up precious cargo at target house. Meet me at the place in one hour."

The luxury townhome Dominic kept was in the Arrondissement de Passy, one of the wealthiest areas in all of Paris. This was his private domain, where even his security was not permitted access. She parked in the garage, entered the code she'd memorized into the security system, and dragged him into the spacious, spotless kitchen before getting to work.

By the time the drug wore off he was bound and pinned spread eagle to the wall, and she was back in her usual wardrobe of tight black cargo pants and long-sleeve shirt, her hair pulled into a long ponytail at the nape of her neck. The charges were in place, and she'd pulled the precious human cargo from the upstairs bedroom that served as the woman's prison for the past several weeks.

"Can you talk yet?" she asked him in a bored tone.

Though she was anything but bored. She was pumped, and more than ready to end this evil, privileged asshole's reign of terror for good.

Dubois blinked several times, agitation clear on his face as he tugged at the nylon ropes keeping him immobilized. A worm, wriggling on a hook. "What the fuck do you want?" A tremor of fear shook his voice.

"I'm so glad you asked." She stepped up to him, stopping close enough to smell his expensive cologne, and put her face inches from his. "I want to destroy you, Dominic. I'm going to take everything from you. Starting with the money you've made off selling women."

He bared his teeth, looked like he might spit at her, so she slapped him across the face, cracking his head to the side. "Fuck you," he spat, his eyes promising murder. "I'll fucking *kill* you for this."

She laughed in his face. "I'm not the one dying tonight. Now. How do you know my name?"

"I know *everything*," he spat.

Nope. He couldn't. Unfortunately, she didn't have time to interrogate him about that further. The clock was ticking. She needed to get this done and be out of here within the next twelve minutes if she was going to make it to the RV point in time with the captive she'd just freed.

Turning her back on him, she strode to the island where she'd left her tablet, then spun back around to face him. "I've got your secret stash account information right here. You're going to give me your password, so I can transfer the money in it to me."

He gave a derisive laugh. "I'm not telling you shit, bitch."

"No?" She drew her silenced pistol, aimed at his thigh, and fired.

He screamed as the bullet ripped into his leg, writhed in his bonds and snarled more threats at her.

She gave him a cool stare, unmoved by his pain. He deserved to suffer. "I've got a full mag here, Dom. I'm fully prepared to use every shot and then some to get this done if necessary. It's up to you. How many holes do you want punched in your oily hide?"

"Fuck you," he gasped out. "Fuck you, you—"

Chloe drew her knife from the scabbard on her thigh and hurled it at him.

A high-pitched scream rent the air as the knife buried to the hilt in the wall an inch beneath his spread groin. His eyes were so wide the whites showed around his irises, full of terror and shock as he stared first down at it, then back up at her. "You're fucking crazy," he choked out.

He wasn't the first to say so, and he wouldn't be the last. He also wasn't wrong. "Yeah, I am. So, we doing this? Or shall I keep going?"

His chest was heaving now, his face sweaty and pale, looking like he was going to be sick as blood dripped down his pants and onto the spotless marble floor. "You won't get to keep the money long enough to use it," he snarled, his eyes glazed with fury and pain. "You'll be dead before you can spend a single Euro."

"Yeah, yeah." She'd heard threats like that before. She raised an eyebrow, then her pistol, taking aim at his other thigh. "Password."

He gave it, then snarled a stream of obscenities and threats. Chloe tuned them all out as she made the transfer, satisfied only when the thirteen million landed in the account she'd set up specifically for this transaction.

"Pleasure doing business with you." She tucked the tablet into a pocket on her thigh and looked over her shoulder at the woman huddled in the far corner of the kitchen. "Kaya, you can open your eyes now. It's done."

She waited until those wide, dark eyes focused on her, the terror in them twisting her heart. But Chloe wanted Dubois to see this next bit. Wanted him to see this woman he'd kept as a slave walk free while he was powerless to stop it. "I need you to go pack one small bag, quickly, and come right back down. Do you understand?" she said to Kaya.

That frightened gaze remained locked on Chloe. But she nodded. "*Oui*." She pushed to her feet, shaking, then shot a panicked look at Dubois and fled upstairs.

"You can't take her," he rasped out, still bleeding all over his pretty floor. "She's *mine*."

The man was delusional. Beyond any chance of redemption, in this life or the next—if there was such a thing. He was about to die, and that's what he was worried about? "She was never yours, you fucking psychopath. And she'll never be yours again. Her or any other woman. Because you're about to die for what you've done." She stalked over to yank the knife out of the wall, paused with the blade against his groin and enjoyed the flash of stark terror in his eyes.

Kaya reappeared a minute later, a tiny bag in hand, her

gaze darting between Chloe and Dubois. Chloe gave her a reassuring smile. "Time to go." Kaya had been terrorized far too much already. She didn't need to see the rest of this.

But before she left Dubois to his fate, she couldn't resist one last parting shot. She took a moment to rake her gaze over the length of him, helpless and bleeding on the wall. "No one's going to protect you this time. You've been playing with fire for way too long, and now you're finally going to get burned. See you in hell, asshole."

His threats and shouts of rage followed them into the garage. Chloe put Kaya in the front passenger seat of his Audi, then reversed out into the street and shut the remote garage door. "Close your eyes," she told Kaya as they drove away. "You're safe now."

When the woman did, Chloe slipped the small detonator out of her hip pocket and pressed the button.

The resounding thud of the explosion reverberated in her chest. She glanced up at the rearview mirror to check her work.

The windows on the main floor were aglow with flames, smoke already pouring through the shattered windows. On either side of the townhouse, the only damage to the neighboring buildings was some broken glass.

Perfect, she'd calculated it just right. No one else would be hurt. The fire crews would arrive shortly to prevent the fire from spreading to the other buildings, but the heat of the incendiary material she'd used would ensure Dominic Dubois was little more than ash by then.

Kaya wrenched around in her seat to look out the back window, then stared at Chloe. "You…killed him," she whispered, her voice shaking.

"Yes." And she wasn't sorry. "You're safe now. I'm taking you to a friend who will look after you. She runs an organization that takes care of women escaping from this kind of situation."

Kaya sniffed and wiped at her eyes, her voice rough. "You did this for me?"

Chloe gripped the steering wheel tighter, wanting to kill Dubois all over again for what he'd done to all the women like Kaya. "For you and all the others he hurt." She was doing the world a service by ridding it of cockroaches like him.

"Why?"

"Because someone has to." She'd seen a lot of trafficking during her sanctioned ops over the years—drugs, weapons and people—and most of the assholes responsible for buying and selling other human beings had gone unpunished or overlooked because they didn't warrant a spot on the government's list of priority targets. Chloe was doing her small part to balance the scales.

She ditched the Audi several blocks from the meeting spot, wiped it down as an added precaution, then took Kaya's arm and walked her to the RV point. Fleur was already there, her light auburn hair pulled back in a braid as she waited with a worried expression and a warm coat for Kaya.

Chloe had met the government social worker by chance a year ago here in Paris while on another job. After Fleur had vented her frustration with the lack of action by the government against human traffickers over dinner one night, Chloe had checked out her background and vetted her carefully before approaching her about a secret alliance. Now Fleur IDd the victims in need of rescue, and Chloe handled the rest of the details before handing them over to her friend for safekeeping.

Since then they'd saved over thirty women and teenage girls together, but it wasn't enough.

It would never be enough.

"Are you both all right?" Fleur asked, scanning them both anxiously.

"I'm fine, but I think Kaya's a little shaken up." She

bundled the young woman into the coat, then pressed a wad of cash into her palm and took Kaya's chin in her hand. Fleur would get her medical care and a safe place to stay immediately. "You're going to be okay. You haven't done anything wrong, and you have nothing to hide or be ashamed of. If anyone questions you, you just tell them the truth. Understand?"

Kaya swallowed and nodded, the fading bruises on her cheeks and beneath her left eye filling Chloe with rage. Dubois's death had been too quick. He should have suffered more. "Thank you."

"It was my pleasure." She turned to Fleur, who looked ready to start wringing her hands, and grinned. Foreign it might be, but it was nice to have someone care about her. "Good to see you, my friend. If anything comes up, you know how to reach me. I'll be in touch."

"Yes, yes, now go and get out of here." She threw her arms around Chloe in a quick, fierce hug. "You're going to give me an ulcer one day, you know that."

Chloe made a face. "Then stop worrying about me."

Fleur pulled back, shook her head. "Somebody needs to."

Touched but embarrassed at the mushy sentiment, Chloe pushed her toward the waiting vehicle. "Go. Take good care of her."

"I will." She ushered Kaya to the car.

Chloe watched until the Renault disappeared around the corner into the night before hurrying to her own getaway vehicle. When she reached the next block, she reached into her coat pocket and hit the second detonator. The Audi's engine exploded behind her. Chloe didn't look back.

Killing Dominic put a lot of heat on her, but the thing that had her worried was that he had known her name.

That should have been impossible, and it meant she had a major problem. Because the only way he could have found out was if someone from within the Valkyrie Program itself had tipped him off.

Paris had been her permanent base since the Program shut down, but it was no longer safe for her. She had to get out of the city for a while, and determine who the hell had sold her out.

Chapter Two

"So we have an agreement, then?" the man asked him.

Guillaume Dubois set his wineglass down on the table and considered his options for a moment. They were seated in a private booth in one of the most exclusive restaurants in all of Paris. He was a regular here, and the staff always afforded him the utmost discretion when he was here for business. "If you drop the price by ten percent."

The man's smile slipped. "That's not possible."

"It is if you want to do business with me." He injected a hint of steel into his tone, just enough to remind the man who he was dealing with.

Anger glinted in the man's eyes. "You're not like your brother."

"No, and that's why I'm as successful as I am." Dom was too flashy. Guillaume preferred to keep things quiet, secret. He couldn't count the number of times he'd been forced to step in and clean up his younger brother's messes in order to save their business and reputations.

Still, he loved his brother and would do everything in his power to protect him.

The man considered him for a long moment, visibly uncomfortable under the weight of Guillaume's unflinching stare. "Fine. I'll sell you the product at the figure you named." The man held up his glass in salute with a tight smile. "To the first of many successful business ventures."

I don't think so. Guillaume knew this man's type and had already heard things about him that made additional deals too risky. After this one was done, Guillaume would ensure the man met with a fatal accident.

Still, he returned the salute, took a sip and endured the small talk that always followed the conclusion of the business transaction. While he smiled and nodded and paid lip service to what the man said, he was actually thinking of this new shipment of weapons, how much he could get for them, and where he could send them for maximum profit. There were so many conflicts around the globe right now. It amounted to a gold rush for a man careful and connected enough to handle the risks involved.

He held up a hand to stop his dinner companion from speaking when Guillaume's head of security discreetly interrupted. "Sir, you have an important phone call."

Jean-Pierre would only interrupt him if it were an emergency. "Thank you." He smiled at his dinner companion, a rich executive who had arranged transport for the women his brother Dominic was about to buy. "Will you excuse me for a moment?"

He took the cell phone from Jean-Pierre, who followed him outside onto the balcony of the five-star restaurant overlooking the Seine. When he saw the name on call display, he frowned and dialed the number back. "Inspector Berdine. How can I help you this evening?"

"Monsieur Dubois, I'm afraid I have some difficult news for you."

Guillaume paused at the railing, a sense of trepidation building in his chest. It couldn't be his wife or the girls. He'd just talked to them prior to arriving at the restaurant. They were all home, safe. "What is it?"

"There's been an explosion at your brother's town-house here in Paris."

Guillaume whipped around, snapped his fingers at Jean-Pierre and gestured for him to hand over his personal phone. "Is he all right?"

"We don't know."

He gulped in a breath. "How bad is the damage?"

"Bad."

Guillaume quickly brought up a local newscast on Jean-Pierre's phone, currently broadcasting a breaking story. The picture showed fire crews in front of Dom's townhome as flames and smoke poured out of the lower floor windows.

He swallowed. This hadn't been an accident. Not with the lifestyle his brother led. "Was my brother inside?"

"We're not sure. A neighbor reported seeing his car leave just seconds before the explosion, but we have been unable to reach him so far."

"I'll call him." He handed Jean-Pierre's phone back. "Keep me updated?" he said to the inspector.

"Of course."

Guillaume dialed his brother, left a voice message and then texted him for good measure. *Are you all right?* He was concerned, but not overly worried if Dom had left prior to the explosion. What had caused it?

His brother's head of security had no answers. Dom had apparently held a private meeting at his office a little over an hour before the explosion. No security had been involved, and Dom's home alarm hadn't been triggered afterward.

Unable to shake the worry, Guillaume finished his dinner, then paid the bill and started for his car without having heard from his brother. His phone rang just as he was getting into the backseat. Not Dom. Berdine. "Inspector. You have an update?"

"The fire's out, and the investigative team is starting their work. But...I'm afraid they found a body in the kitchen."

Guillaume's heart leapt into his throat. "Not Dominic, though. You said he was seen driving away prior to the explosion." Although it made no sense that his brother would kill someone in his own house. Zero.

"Unfortunately, the remains are in such a state that they will require dental analysis to determine their identity. But from the positioning of the victim, he or she was bound at the time of their death. We also found your brother's car several kilometers away, blown up at the side of the road. A forensics team is trying to pull prints but it's likely not possible."

Dammit. Guillaume rubbed at his forehead, his mind spinning. This didn't bode well. He'd warned Dom again and again to be careful to distance himself from the...seedier side of their business, but his brother couldn't seem to do it. Dom was addicted to the rush of it, especially with the women and drugs. Guillaume would have to pull him from it. "I've reached out to him but he hasn't responded."

"His cell phone has been turned off."

Guillaume's insides clenched. Dom never went anywhere without his phone, and he never shut it right off. What if the body was Dom's?

Ice slid through him. "I'll come down to the morgue. I'll pay privately to have the dental analysis done immediately. Find me someone and tell them to name their price. I need answers."

"I've alrcady made inquiries."

Guillaume couldn't go home now. He texted his wife

to say he had a late meeting so she wouldn't worry, then had Jean-Pierre drive him to the hospital where the remains were waiting. Berdine met him there, but refused to grant him access to the body because it was in such bad condition.

He sat in the hallway for nearly four hours waiting for the private forensics team to process the dental records. Berdine finally exited the exam room and walked toward him, his expression grave.

And Guillaume knew.

He shot out of his chair, his heart threatening to explode. "Who is it? It's not Dom. Tell me it's not Dom."

Berdine stopped several feet away and shook his head. "I'm so sorry, Guillaume."

"No!" He bellowed it, grief and denial punching through him. He took several staggering steps up the hallway then pivoted and paced back the other way, raking his hands through his hair as the horrible finality hit home. "No, no, *no…*"

His only brother was dead. Tied up and burned to ash in his own house, without any alarms being triggered. How was that possible? *How?*

He lurched toward the door his brother's body lay behind. Berdine blocked his way. "No. I can't let you see him like this. It's best if you don't see him."

Guillaume stared up at him, struggling to hold his grief inside. He was going to be sick. "I can't… I can't accept this," he croaked, his voice breaking.

Berdine gently took him by the shoulders and steered him back into a chair. Guillaume collapsed into it like a doll. And then he broke.

Painful, ragged sobs burst out of him, each one searing his chest, his lungs. He buried his face in his hands and cried for his little brother, a charred corpse lying in the room across the hall.

I failed him. I failed him!

Jean-Pierre got him into the car. Guillaume alternated between a fog of shock and piercing grief on the drive to his home. His young daughters were asleep in bed but his wife was there to meet him at the door, her heartbreak written all over her face. Without a word she enveloped him in a comforting embrace that made him break down again.

Once he had regained control, he sent her to bed and immediately locked himself in his office with Jean-Pierre. "I want to know who Dom met with," he bit out, rage beginning to burn through the terrible, suffocating pain. "Get me all the surveillance footage from his office and townhouse. Get me whatever I need to find out who did this."

In less than an hour, Guillaume had his suspect.

He stared in shock at the attractive woman captured in the security feed. The only footage they'd been able to get was when she'd first entered the building. Gabrielle Boucher, representative of the wealthy Monsieur Roche, who Dominic's company had done several business deals with over the past few months—buying and selling women in the skin trade.

There was barely any background on her, making her ten times as suspicious.

But there was more. So much more.

Dom had kept a woman in his townhome. A captive he'd bought off a skin trader in a recent shipment from North Africa. She was missing. And Dom's main business account had been drained just minutes prior to his death.

Gabrielle. She'd done this. She'd taken Dom's money and then taken the woman and killed him. Now the captive woman was out there somewhere too, about to tell what Dom had done.

Shaken, sick to his stomach that his brother was gone, Guillaume swallowed the bile burning the back of his throat and spoke to Jean-Pierre. "Find her. Find her and bring her to me."

"Yes, sir." New orders in hand, Jean-Pierre left the room to begin the hunt.

Guillaume sucked in a painful breath and continued to stare at the woman's image on screen, memorizing her features. The only consolation in all of this is that Dom had died fast. He'd likely suffered before dying, but in the actual moment of his death, he wouldn't have known what hit him.

But the same couldn't be said for the woman who had killed him.

"Gabrielle Boucher" would suffer for what she'd done. Once Guillaume got back what she'd stolen from them, he would double his profit by selling her to the most sadistic bastard in the skin trade.

In the end, she would beg for death, but find no mercy.

****

After reading her sister's text, Megan rushed from the stables and into the manor house. She loped up the stairs and hurried to the bedroom at the end of the hall that now served as her sister's office.

As expected, Amber was seated before a bank of monitors, her precious laptop, Lady Ada, front and center on the desk, her chocolate-brown hair swept over one shoulder.

"Have you got something?" Megan asked. After being separated as kids and funneled into the Valkyrie Program, they'd finally been reunited a few months ago. She appreciated every moment they spent together now, united in this common cause.

"Think so. Come take a look."

Her heart beat faster. They'd been searching for the other remaining Valkyries together for the past several weeks. They'd managed to rescue one other so far—Kiyomi, who was staying here at the manor with them. But there were others, and time was running out.

Megan stood behind her sister as Amber pulled up a news story on one screen and security footage on another. "What am I looking at?" A burning house, and a train station.

"A Paris businessman with suspected ties to the criminal underworld was just blown up in his own house. It's the fourth incident of its kind over as many months. All of them involving men connected with organized crime, and all of them small, controlled explosions with no collateral damage."

"Is it Chloe?" She desperately wanted it to be Chloe, a fellow Valkyrie trained as a demolitions expert. It had been so many years since Megan had seen her former friend and roommate—she wanted to bring Chloe in safely.

"Odds are high it's her. If it is, she's been taking out risky targets."

"Chloe always loved breaking the rules." A memory surfaced, something she hadn't thought about in a long, long time.

Exhausted from a long day of training, Megan groaned as she flopped onto her bunk. Her hand touched something beneath the pillow. Sitting up, she lifted it to reveal a giant candy bar—and it was her favorite kind.

Immediately she rolled over to peer over the edge of her bed at Chloe, stretched out below on the bottom bunk. "You know we can't have that in here. It's contraband."

"Yeah. So?" The crinkle of a wrapper sounded as Chloe ripped open her own.

"So we'll get in trouble."

"Only if we get caught. And we're not going to get caught, because you're not gonna say anything."

Megan chewed her lip. Her stomach growled, the

thought of sinking her teeth into the chocolate pure torture, making her mouth water.

"Come on, live a little. Be a rebel with me, Itch."

Megan smiled at the nickname. She was Itch, because she was always restless and itching to be on the move. Chloe was Twitch, because she was...well, twitchy, and high-octane. Sometimes she thought Chloe was actually a little crazy, yet there was talk that Chloe might be put into the demolitions program. A terrifying thought.

A partially-unwrapped chocolate bar appeared at the side of her mattress. Chloe waved it around. "Come on. Cheers me."

Laughing under her breath, Megan tapped her bar to Chloe's. "Okay. Race you." They had to make them disappear fast in case there was a lights-out inspection.

"Game on." The bar disappeared back to the lower bunk. "Ready? Go."

They wolfed down the huge chocolate bars. Megan barely tasted hers, didn't even enjoy it really, because she was too worried about one of their instructors coming in for an unannounced inspection.

Footsteps in the hall outside their room made her freeze. "Shit, they're coming," she said around a mouthful of chocolate.

"So hurry up and hide the wrapper."

Megan nearly choked getting the last bite down her throat, then quickly shoved the wrapper under her mattress and flopped down on her back just as a key turned in the lock. The instructor came in, did the inspection, and left without incident.

Smiling up at the ceiling in the darkness after the door closed, Megan reached a hand down over the edge of her bunk. "You're a bad influence."

"I know. You're welcome." Chloe curled her pinkie around Megan's in a finger shake, then let go. "Night, Itch."

"Night, Twitch."

"Take a look at this," Amber said, pulling Megan back to the present as she typed in some commands and shifted aside to give Megan a better view. "I've been using a new facial recognition program and got a hit."

Megan leaned closer to the second screen showing a paused surveillance video Amber must have hacked into. The things her sister could do with a computer were downright scary.

"Watch right…here," Amber said, freezing the screen on a shot of people standing on the platform. She zoomed in on a woman standing in a long, gray trench, a black knit cap on her head, a blond ponytail trailing down her back. "Recent chatter says this matches the description of the woman seen leaving the victim's office earlier tonight. And it looks a lot like—"

"Chloe," Megan breathed, setting her hand on the screen as if she could reach out and touch her old friend. Her throat tightened, and for a second she struggled to control the punch of emotion that hit her. "When was this?"

"A few minutes ago, in a station in central Paris. She bought a ticket to Strasbourg. Train leaves in eighty-one minutes."

That didn't give them much time. Certainly not enough to get to Paris before the train left. "How long does it take for the train to get to Strasbourg?"

"Two hours, give or take."

So, around three-and-a-half hours total. Still not enough to arrange and hop on a private flight to get them there in time. "We'll have to intercept her in Strasbourg."

But how? They couldn't involve the police or any other law enforcement because they didn't know who was targeting the remaining Valkyries. If only they had someone in Paris they could have step in—

A light bulb lit up in her brain. "I got it!"

Megan dashed from the room before her sister could answer, racing downstairs. She found her boyfriend Tyler in the study having a beer with Jesse and the master of Laidlaw Hall, her dear friend Marcus. All three men looked at her as she burst into the room.

"I need you to call your friend back," she blurted to Tyler without preamble. "The one you talked to this morning."

He blinked at her with those sexy slate blue eyes. "What, Heath?"

He was still in Paris for another day or two. "Yes. Right now. Come on." She grabbed his hand, pulled him out of the chair and dragged him from the room, gesturing for the others to follow. "We think we've found Chloe but we need someone to follow her so we don't lose her. Her train leaves Paris for Strasbourg in a little over an hour. Can you get him to follow her?"

"You want *Heath* to follow her?" He sounded incredulous.

"Yes." He and Tyler were pretty much best friends after working together as security contractors in various hotspots and combat zones throughout South Asia, Africa and the Middle East. "It's our best shot. He's former AFSOC, so he's trained—"

"Not for something like this, and it's not fair to him if I can't tell him what's really going on."

"Tyler, we *need* him. Plus he's got some security clearance. And as a former PJ, he cares about helping people. He's perfect." She towed him up the stairs to the office where Amber was still working her magic, then turned the puppy dog eyes on him, aware of Jesse entering the room and Marcus's cane thudding on the floor in the hallway. "We can't afford to lose her when we're finally so close, and after this hit she'll be in even more danger. Please?"

Thankfully Tyler was used to her by now, and he was

quick on the uptake. He also knew how hard it was to track a Valkyrie, let alone capture one. If they lost Chloe now, they might not get another shot.

He sighed and turned to her sister. "Amber, show me what you've got."

It took him all of two minutes to get a read on the situation. After briefly discussing it with everyone in the room, he pulled out his phone, then hesitated. "I hate doing this to him," he said to her. "But we can't afford to lose her."

"No, we can't. So hurry."

Tyler glanced at Jesse, former MARSOC-turned-hitman, now a part of their team. "What do you think?"

"You trust him?" Jesse asked.

"With my life." He said it immediately, without any hesitation.

Jesse nodded, absently stroking a hand over Amber's hair. "Then make the call."

Chapter Three

Escape.

That's what Heath had needed, and he planned to make the most of this leave in Paris between security contracting jobs. Escape from the grind of being in a combat zone for months at a time. From the sheer, mind-numbing boredom during downtime, then the toll of frequent bursts of high-alert status when they went outside the wire.

Escape from the ghosts that never truly let him rest. Friends he'd lost on the battlefield, whose faces remained sharp in his mind whenever he tried to sleep.

He took a pull of ice-cold beer from the bottle, set it down with a sigh and picked up his cutlery to dig into the crepe filled with Nutella and bananas. It was late and the café was mostly empty. He'd always heard the food in Paris was second to none, and so far, he'd have to agree. This place around the corner from his rental was open until three in the morning and he liked this time of night because it was peaceful, without too many people around.

After spending the past two days shaking off the dust

of East Africa in the French capital, he was in full vacay mode. He'd already seen the Eiffel Tower and been to the Louvre. Over the next few days he planned to see some of the Napoleonic sites, and visit the famous catacombs that were essentially underground ossuaries full of the bones of six million Parisians.

During his years in the Air Force and then as a security contractor, he'd spent more time in Africa, the Middle East and South Asia than he had in all of Europe combined, and he wanted to rectify that during his time off between jobs. He had less than three weeks this time, and he was going to make the most of it.

He stuffed another bite of crepe in his mouth, frowned when his cell phone rang. Who would be calling him at this hour? His aunt was getting up there in years and was starting to get forgetful, but she still had enough wits to know it was the middle of the night over here.

But it wasn't his aunt, or any of his cousins back home calling. It was his buddy Ty, from the UK. "Hey, what's up?"

"Hey, man. Where are you?"

"Just grabbing a bite to eat. Something up?"

"Yes."

Heath blinked and stilled at the serious tone, his loaded fork poised partway to his mouth. "Okay. Something wrong?"

"Are you in your room?"

"No, I'm at a café around the corner. Why?"

"Your line isn't secure, and I need this conversation to be as secure as possible."

Wow. Okay then. What the hell was going on? Was Ty in trouble?

"Hang on." He set down his fork and stood. "Gimme two minutes and I'll be in my room." He drained the last swallow of his beer before hurrying away.

"I'll talk while you're walking."

"Sure." Concern started to build inside him. What the hell was so important that Ty would call him now and needed a secure place to talk? "Are you okay?"

"I'm good. But we've got a situation, and you're the closest person I know who can help."

Heath frowned and picked up the pace, digging his key out of his pocket. "Who's *we*?"

"Megan and I. We need a favor."

"Uh...okay," he said slowly as he let himself into the building and jogged up the stairs to the second floor. He hadn't met Megan yet, and Ty had been annoyingly vague about the girl he'd lost his mind over. So this must be one hell of a favor. "I'm almost there. One sec."

He unlocked the door, did a quick visual check out of habit to make sure everything was as it should be, then locked it behind him. "I'm in. Now what's going on?" His phone might not be encrypted, but he was alone and not under surveillance of any kind, so this was as secure as he could make this conversation.

"There's a woman about to get on a train from Paris to Strasbourg. She's an...old friend of Megan's."

"Uh huh," he said, still unsure where this was going or why it concerned him.

"She's in trouble."

Heath stilled. "What kind of trouble?"

"The kind where dangerous people might come after her."

"What kind of dangerous people?"

"Organized criminals."

Like gangs? Terrorists? Heath hated how vague his buddy was being. But if Ty wasn't spilling the details because the line was unsecured, then he had his reasons. "And you want me to do what about that?"

"I need you to find her and follow her."

He blinked. "To Strasbourg?"

"Yes. And wherever she goes after that."

Oh, no. "Look, man, I—"

"We're too far away to get to her in time. I'm sending you a picture of her right now."

Heath's phone dinged with an incoming message two seconds later. He glanced at the screen. "I see her." A good-looking blonde with a serious expression and big brown eyes gazed back at him. Late twenties or early thirties, maybe.

Dammit. Ty knew his weakness—that Heath was a sucker for a woman in distress and wouldn't be able to turn away.

"Her name's Chloe Wilson, and she's leaving Paris on that train in under an hour. Can you get there in time and follow her?"

Heath shoved out a breath. Did he really want to get involved in whatever this was? It was on the tip of his tongue to refuse, but how could he do that when Ty had saved his ass not four months ago when that sniper in Afghanistan had a bead on him? If not for Ty, he'd have died up on that mountain ridge. Besides, it sounded like this girl was in trouble. "I assume there's a reason you can't just involve the cops?"

"Yes. Will you do it?"

You can't refuse. You owe him. You owe him huge.

Heath rubbed a hand over his face. This was not how he'd seen the rest of his night going, but he wasn't going to turn Ty down or leave a woman in trouble out there on her own. Ty could have guilted him into it, but hadn't. "All right. I'll try to catch her in time."

Ty's relieved sigh filled the line. "Thanks, man. I'll send you the station and train details. When you get to Strasbourg, if there are any other updates, contact me at this number. As soon as she stops moving, we'll fly over to meet you to take over."

"And then you'll read me in on what's going on?"

"Absolutely. We'll catch up. I really want you to meet

Megan."

Ty had even asked Heath to be his best man when he and Megan tied the knot. That was some crazy shit right there, Ty talking marriage when they'd only been together a couple months. Heath wanted to meet this girl. "All right."

Even though he had a not-so-great feeling about all this, he got his ass off the couch and hurried to his room to pack a backpack. "I'm not armed." He hadn't thought he'd need to be on this trip, and getting a concealed carry permit here wasn't easy. Pepper spray didn't cut it when shit went south.

"Understood, and I don't think it'll be an issue. We just need you to watch and follow her. I'll reimburse you for expenses when I see you."

"Whatever, man, I'm not gonna take your money." Not from the guy who'd saved his life. "Anything else?"

"Yeah." Ty was silent a second. "Don't get too close, and don't let her know you're following her. If she's spooked, she'll disappear. Like, gone. But keep her safe. It's important."

He was getting that. "Okay, I copy."

"Good luck. I'll talk to you soon."

"Yeah." Heath ended the call and frowned at the phone. Good luck? Did he need it?

A moment later a message popped up on his phone, giving the train station and platform info. It was halfway across the city from him, so he'd better haul ass if he was going to make it.

He slid his phone into his pocket and hurriedly packed the rest of what he needed, mentally shifting gears to get in the right head space. So his holiday was being cut short. He'd wanted to see more of France anyway, and this way he'd be helping out his friend and the mystery girl in potential danger Ty was so concerned about.

But as soon as Heath saw his buddy, he was going to

find out exactly what the hell was going on here.

****

Chewing a stick of her favorite spearmint gum, Chloe slouched down in her train seat and tugged the brim of the ball cap down lower on her forehead as she darted a glance across the aisle. The train had left the station in Paris twenty minutes ago and she'd been on full alert every second since, even though it didn't look like it.

She could have rented a car and driven out of Paris, but she'd opted for the train because of speed and to vary her means of transportation so as not to follow a certain pattern that would make her easier to catch. A trade-off: increased risk balanced out by speed. It was a two-hour trip to Strasbourg. Given what she'd just done and who she'd just killed, she couldn't put Paris behind her fast enough.

Her face was completely bare now, not a drop of makeup on. She was dressed ultra-casually in a pair of stretchy black leggings and a long, cozy grey tunic with a coat over top, her ponytail threaded through the hole in the back of the cap. The backpack with the Canadian flag patch at her feet added to her appearance—just another unthreatening tourist trekking her way through France.

The cap not only shadowed her face and concealed her ears, making it harder for anyone to recognize her in surveillance video, it also hid her eye movements from anyone watching.

And at least one person on this train was definitely watching.

He was seated across the aisle, two seats ahead, facing her. A good-looking, clean-cut guy with short, dark brown hair and a nice body. At the moment he was reading a magazine printed in English. His bearing, body language and watchfulness spoke of either military or law enforcement background, and that put her instantly on alert.

She'd spotted him on the platform just a few minutes prior to boarding. Their eyes had met briefly—his were a bright, piercing blue—before he'd looked away. Several times after that he'd glanced at her when he thought she wasn't looking.

At first, she'd wondered if he was here to arrest her. Then she'd wondered if he was actually harmless and might be thinking about hitting on her. But after they'd boarded, he'd walked past her to his seat without a word. He was still paying attention to her now, although he was being subtle about it. It put her on edge.

Dominic's brother would know about the explosion. Might even know that Dominic was dead already. They would have surveillance footage from the office building—both tonight and on her previous visit. Even with the stage makeup she'd worn before, it was possible someone had tracked her to the station.

Could this guy be one of Dubois' men? Or National Police maybe?

She couldn't decide if he was a threat or not, but she wasn't ruling it out. The Dubois brothers had eyes and ears all over Paris and half the country because their dirty fingers were in all sorts of pies.

Well, Guillaume's were. Dom didn't have any fingers left.

The thought had her fighting a savage smile. As far as she was concerned, one less evil, misogynist son of a bitch taking up precious oxygen was cause for celebration. The risk was worth it. She was used to being on the move anyway, staying at least one step ahead of anyone hunting her. Besides, Kaya was safe now, on her way to a new life with Fleur's help. Chloe took major satisfaction in that.

Keeping part of her attention on the man across the aisle, she shifted down in her seat and tucked her gum high up under the side of her upper lip with her tongue.

Folding her arms, she dropped her chin to her chest and pretended to go to sleep.

A few minutes later, the hottie across the aisle glanced over. He stared at her for a second, then went back to reading.

Huh. Maybe she was just being paranoid. Maybe he wasn't a threat at all.

But being paranoid was why she was still breathing.

Chloe continued watching him covertly as the minutes ticked past. He had a gruff edge to him, in his body language and his don't-talk-to-me expression. He diligently read the whole magazine, then set it aside and pulled out his phone. He didn't appear to be texting anyone, just scrolling through whatever he was looking at on the screen. Every so often he would glance over at her, moving only his eyes, the looks so subtle someone without training would have missed it.

Why are you watching me?

She feigned sleep until a voice over the speakers finally announced they were approaching Strasbourg. Gruff hottie put away his phone and tucked his magazine into his backpack, his open jacket giving her a perfect view of the muscular contours of his chest beneath his snug shirt.

She narrowed her eyes and resumed chewing her gum. He might be nice to look at, but if he was a threat, she'd take him out without hesitation.

Before the train stopped, she was up and out of her seat, making her way to the door at the far end of the car. A quick glance to the side showed him up and heading toward her. He was pretending not to look at her, but he was edging past people to get closer.

I don't think so.

The conductor had barely begun to open the door when she shoved through it and hurried along the platform, watching all her angles for any sign of a threat. Gruff hottie was still behind her, walking fast to keep her in his sights, but not chasing her.

See ya.

Chloe ducked around the corner, chose a different route to double back with, and sure enough, found him now on the platform looking around for her.

She ducked into the closest ladies' room. In a locked stall, she pulled out some things from her backpack to change her appearance. Wearing light makeup and different clothes, she checked her reflection in the mirror to make sure the wig was on straight, then exited the washroom and doubled back with a group of passengers exiting the station.

Gruff hottie was standing on the platform, looking left and right. His gaze swept past her, then he began walking at a hurried pace through the terminal, searching for someone.

Her. She knew it.

Chloe followed, keeping a safe distance while he checked outside the building, scanned the parking lot. When he turned back and headed for the side of the terminal to check there, she made her move.

Slipping around the corner of the building from the other side, she chose a shadowy spot away from any people or cameras, and waited, knife in hand. Rapid footsteps approached to her right moments later.

Gruff hottie.

The second he was within reach, she pounced.

Grabbing him by the shoulders, she spun him around and slammed his back into the brick wall behind him before he could react.

Those blue, blue eyes locked on her face in pissed-off astonishment as she pressed the edge of her blade to his groin and growled, "Who the fuck are you, and why are you following me?"

Chapter Four

W hat the *hell*?!

"*Whoa.*" Heath grabbed her wrist and locked his fingers around it to prevent her from doing severe damage to his junk with that KA-BAR, staring down at the woman snarling in his face. Jesus Christ. He barely recognized her. When the hell had she had time to change into a disguise?

"Talk," she growled, the prick of the blade against his inner thigh telling him she meant business. From the way she gripped it she knew how to use it, and would do some serious damage if she didn't like what he said.

Holy shit. He was an expert in CSAR missions, had saved dozens of lives in the line of duty. Rescuing people was his specialty, but from the glint in those narrowed brown eyes, she sure as hell didn't look like she was in need of—or wanted—rescue.

"I'm not going to hurt you," he ground out.

"That's right, because I've got a knife to your balls. Now what's your name?" she demanded.

"Heath Barrett, and I'm here to help you. Now lose the

knife." He could snap her wrist and disarm her, but there was serious risk she'd slice him up pretty bad in the process, and the glint in her eye said she knew it.

"Help me?"

"To make sure you're safe, because you're in some sort of trouble. My friend sent me to follow you to make sure nothing happened to you," he told her, keeping his voice low and calm because the position of that blade made him damn nervous. One wrong move and he could find himself castrated—or bleeding out alone on this sidewalk.

"Who sent you?" She was stronger than she looked. Even with his grip on her slender wrist, she wasn't budging. The sharp point of the blade pricked the juncture of his thigh and groin, and it took everything he had not to snap her wrist right then and there. A few more ounces of pressure and she could slice through his jeans, thigh, and even sever his inguinal artery.

"My buddy Ty Bergstrom. He called and asked me to make sure you're safe." Ty had always teased him that his white-knight complex would get him in trouble one day. Ironic that it happened when Heath was trying to help him out.

"Who does he work for?" Chloe pressed harder on the tip of the blade, breaking his skin. "*Talk,* or I start cutting."

Shit, Heath wasn't sure who Ty worked for at the moment. And Ty had conveniently neglected to mention she might have a knife. "No one, but he used to be a security contractor with me, and before that he was military. You're an old friend of his girlfriend, Megan."

She stilled, her expression changing ever so slightly. "Megan who?"

"I don't know her last name, but you guys were roommates or something." College maybe? Hell if he knew, but now he wanted to, because if he *had* known he would have protected his balls better.

His explanation meant something to her because she stiffened, her eyes no longer narrowed but still cool, filled with suspicion and doubt.

He upped the pressure on her wrist as warm beads of blood dripped down his inner thigh. His temper surged. "Chloe. Lower the damn knife and put it away. I'm not here to hurt you." Well, he didn't *want* to hurt her, but if she didn't move that blade away from his nuts in the next few seconds, he might be forced to snap her wrist.

Rather than reassure her, his words made her brows crash together in a fierce frown. "Did he give you my name, or did she?" She didn't move. Didn't flinch as he squeezed her wrist harder, though it had to hurt.

Don't make me hurt you. "He did when he contacted me an hour before your train left, and said to follow you and keep you safe. That's it."

"Keep me *safe*? You're not even armed," she said in disgust. "And I'm supposed to believe you would hop on a train in the middle of the night to watch over a total stranger?" She snorted. "What does Megan look like?"

Heath didn't need a weapon to protect her, he could do enough damage with his hands and feet when necessary, but clearly, he'd better keep talking or this could get ugly quick. And keep her safe from what? Ty had been so damn vague about it. Heath should have pressed him harder for more details. "I dunno, I've never met her. She and Ty have only been together for a couple months."

"He's such a good buddy that you'd drop everything to do this favor for him, and you've never met his girlfriend?" she pressed.

"Yeah, because I've been in northern Africa on a security contracting job until a few days ago." He pushed down on her wrist, his patience running thin. "Now lose the damn *knife*."

She studied him for a tense moment, then twisted her

wrist against his hold, moving the blade away from his groin. He let go, relief washing through him when she slid the knife back into a holster hidden beneath her waistband. She did it without looking, and so smoothly it was clear she'd done it a time or two—or a thousand—before.

Then she stepped back, just out of reach, her left foot slightly in front of her right, weight on the balls of her feet and her hands curled slightly at her sides. A fighter's stance, and it made him wonder again exactly how much and what kind of training she had. Why hadn't Ty told him? He'd said to be subtle because she'd ghost on Heath if she noticed him following, but hell, he hadn't expected any of *this*.

"And just where were you planning on following me to?" she asked, cocking her head slightly. Not backing down, but no longer feeling threatened. He wasn't sure if he should feel insulted or not.

"To wherever you were going." Who was she? What was the real story here?

"And then what?"

"Then I let Ty and Megan know where you are." And oh, he couldn't wait to talk to Ty. He had a few choice words for his buddy for leaving out some important fucking details.

"What do they want with me?"

"They want to talk to you about something in person. I'm not sure what, Ty didn't say."

"Yeah, well, we'll see about that." Before he could move, she snatched his phone from his pocket. Heath bit back an annoyed retort as she considered him a moment longer, then came out of fighting stance and took a step back. "All right, you're coming with me."

Heath shot her an incredulous look. *You gotta be shitting me.* She'd held him at knifepoint, stolen his phone, and he was just supposed to go with her now to wherever she was going and pretend he was okay with it?

36

She lifted a dark blond eyebrow. "What's the matter, you scared?"

"No," he bit out, even though yeah, she was kinda scary and made his balls shrivel.

One side of her mouth curved up, somewhere between a challenge and a taunt. "If I'd wanted to kill you, you'd already be dead. I'm not letting you out of my sight until I can verify your story, and I'm not doing that here. So come on. We gotta go." She darted a glance around them, then gave an impatient jerk of her head. "Now."

He bit back the defensive retort that immediately sprang to his tongue. She might have gotten the drop on him initially because he hadn't expected any kind of threat from her, but he could hold his own and wasn't as easy a target as she seemed to think, his bleeding inner thigh not-withstanding.

For a few seconds he considered saying screw this and walking away. But a promise was a promise. He owed Ty and had given him his word that he'd watch Chloe, and he would, whether she was nuts and dangerous or not. Besides, now he wanted answers. "Where are we going?" he said with a scowl.

"You'll find out soon enough. Move." She gestured toward the parking lot, her hand near her waist, ready to draw her blade again.

Heath started for the lot, biting back a retort and shaking his head at himself. He'd thought this favor would help even things out on the debt scale with Ty? Not freaking likely.

You owe me for this, you tight-lipped bastard. Big time.

Chloe directed him to the rental car section of the parking lot. He kept a wary eye on her, having a newfound respect for her abilities and vowing to remain vigilant about watching his back until this little detour in his holiday was over. And that couldn't come soon enough, because there was obviously a lot more going on than he realized.

Question was, how much did Ty really know?

Heath had come here to protect a woman in danger, but from where he stood, the real danger was Chloe herself.

****

She's so hot, but she almost cut my balls off.

Heath still couldn't quite wrap his head around that. Over an hour later he had no further information about the situation he was now stuck in.

He'd been forced to ride shotgun from the train station, watching Chloe's every move as she drove them to this rental townhouse outside the city limits. She still had his phone. She'd checked it over, then switched it off completely before beginning the drive, he guessed because she was paranoid that someone was tracking his movements.

The ride had been tense. They hadn't said a single word to each other since leaving the station, and it was seriously grating on his nerves. She didn't seem bothered by it, totally absorbed in what she was doing, driving in circles, he could only assume to see if they were being followed.

He had a real bad feeling about this. She was no helpless civilian in need of protection, that was for sure, so if she was under threat, it had to be pretty major.

"The house is a few blocks east of here," she finally said as she parked along the curb and turned off the engine. With that she reached into the backseat for her backpack and climbed out of the car.

The one-story cottage looked to be at least a hundred years old, the exterior covered in a pale yellow plaster. "Stay here," she whispered as they reached the back of it.

Since there was no point in arguing, he stood to one side, on alert as she unlocked the back door, staring in surprise when she drew a weapon from beneath her tunic and eased inside. A pistol? How the hell had she gotten that on the damn train, and what else was she armed with that he didn't know about?

She came back a minute later, her weapon no longer visible, wig gone and wearing what she had been on the train, minus the hat. Her golden blond hair spilled down her back in a long ponytail. It amazed him how fast she'd made herself practically unrecognizable back at the station. Spooky and impressive at the same time. Was she a spy?

"All right," she told him. "You can come in." The moment he crossed the threshold she shut the door and locked it.

He retreated to the living room and watched her from the safety of the sofa. She paced around the kitchen, chomping on her gum, snapping it now and again as she switched his phone back on and checked for whatever she was looking for.

All of a sudden, she stopped, faced him and strode toward him with an unreadable look that had him instantly on his feet and on guard. "All right. Call Ty and put him on speaker," she said, thrusting his phone at him. "Tell him I want to talk to Megan personally."

Jaw tight, Heath held her gaze and took the phone. He got why she'd be suspicious of his story, but Jesus. He hadn't done a single thing to make her feel threatened. Other than...following her and...being a big guy and a complete stranger to her.

He heaved an irritated sigh. "Fine." This whole thing was bullshit and he wanted it resolved as badly as she did.

He dialed the number Ty had texted him from and put it on speaker while Chloe watched him like a bug under a magnifying glass, arms folded across her chest. "Hey, it's me," he said when Ty picked up, "and you're on speaker because Chloe wants to hear this and then talk to Megan."

"You got her?" Ty asked when he answered.

"Sort of." Not the way Ty imagined, however. More like she had *him*.

Heath shook his head, his annoyance burning through his forced calm. "What the *hell*, man? I followed your girlfriend's friend, thinking I was doing a good deed by keeping an eye on her because that's how you painted it, and not only was she *not* happy to see me, she nearly sliced my junk off with a freaking KA-BAR."

Ty laughed. "Oh, shit."

Heath glared at Chloe, who was grinning now as she chewed her gum. "Yeah, oh, shit is right. A little more info or some warning would've been nice. Care to tell me what's really going on now?"

"Brother, that's a long story and I'll fill you in later, but just know I'm sorry for all this and that I owe you big time."

"Yeah, *big* time," Heath agreed, still watching Chloe. Ty hadn't sounded that surprised about the KA-BAR bit. Asshole. "Anyway, we're at a place outside Strasbourg, and no one else followed us. Can you put Megan on so I'm not in the hot seat anymore?"

"One sec."

Heath stood there holding his phone like an idiot while they waited for Megan to come on the line. Chloe hadn't moved, and though she'd lost the grin, her big brown eyes held mingled curiosity and amusement as she watched him.

"I'm here," a female voice said a moment later, and Chloe's expression sobered. "Your end secure?"

Chloe's face gave nothing away. "No."

"Understood. You like Wagner?"

Something flared in her eyes. "Yes."

"You know what to do."

40

Before Heath could make sense of the odd conversation, Chloe swiped the phone from him and ended the call. Pulling another phone from her hip pocket, she texted someone.

What was she up to now? Why wouldn't anyone tell him what the fuck was going on here? "Can I have my phone back now?" he said, a bite to his tone.

She kept typing. "Nope." She stopped, scanned the screen, and when it buzzed with an incoming message moments later, she tapped a button.

The first few bars of a classical song he vaguely recognized filled the silence.

Chloe froze, surprise flickering across her face before she masked it and stopped the song.

"What? What does it mean?" All clear? Danger? Jesus, he hadn't felt this clueless since he'd been captured in SERE school.

Those big brown eyes swept over him from head to toe and back again, as though she was seeing him for the first time. "Stay here and don't move," she ordered. Tossing him his phone, she pivoted and marched from the room, her phone to her ear.

Chapter Five

Wagner's "Ride of the Valkyries." That was the song the woman claiming to be Megan had sent.

Chloe's heart raced as she hurried to the bedroom, waiting for the call to connect. All the signs said this was real. Megan's name. The timing of Megan finding her. The song. Even the guy waiting in the other room.

It had been years. So many years since she'd heard her friend's voice, and she didn't want an audience for this conversation.

"Hey," the same woman answered.

Megan. Was it really Megan? "Your end secure?"

"Yes."

"When did you graduate?"

"May nineteenth."

Same day as Chloe. "Who was with you when you got your mark?" Chloe asked.

"You."

Damn right. That rite of passage was branded every bit as much on her mind as it was on her left hip. "Motto?"

"Lima Uniform Delta."

Loyal Unto Death. Damn straight. "Nickname?"

"Itchy. But you called me Itch, and I called you Twitch."

A wide smile broke over Chloe's face, her throat thickening with an unexpected surge of emotion. "Itch, is it really you?" Her voice was a bit rough.

Megan laughed softly. "Yeah, Twitch, it's me. God, this is surreal. How are you, sistah?"

"I'm…hanging in there," Chloe said with a stunned laugh. "How the hell did you find me? And who's this guy you sent?" He wasn't an operative like them, that much was certain.

"It wasn't easy. We've been trying for months to track you down."

"We?"

"Yes. I've got so much to tell you, but it'll have to wait until it's in person. I've got access to a private plane and can be there in a few hours. That cool with you?"

"Sure." But if Megan had found her, then it was a good damn thing Chloe had gotten out of Paris when she had. Dubois would have looked at the security footage from Dom's office and the train station by now. He'd have people after her. "And the guy is?"

"Heath Barrett, my boyfriend's best friend. I haven't met him yet, but they served together as security contractors for a few years."

Chloe's eyebrows went up at the first part. "Yeah, tell me about the boyfriend part."

Another laugh. "Like I said, there's a lot to fill you in on."

"Apparently." She had a hard time imagining Megan getting that serious with a guy. It was dangerous.

"Heath's former AFSOC," Megan added.

Ahh. That helped explain the calm head he'd kept during the whole knife thing. "What did he do for them?"

"Pararescue."

"Really." Well, wasn't that interesting. He had SOF training, yet he hadn't hurt her, even with the knife to his groin. "Ty didn't tell him what I am."

"No."

"So he thought I was a civilian."

"Yes."

Yikes. That explained a lot. Now Chloe felt kinda bad for what she'd done. Poor guy had honestly been trying to help her for whatever reason. She hadn't realized there were any men like that left in the world. "I may have pulled my blade on him. And I may have nicked him in a sensitive spot when he didn't talk fast enough."

Megan chuckled. "Poor Heath. I'm sure he'll get over it. Eventually."

Chloe frowned. "Well now I feel bad."

"Don't worry about that. I want to know about you. Is the job you were on finished? Or is there more?"

"I'll talk to you when you get here." Even with an encrypted phone she wasn't going to risk saying anything too sensitive.

"Understood. We're working on something big, Twitch. Really big, and I want to bring you in on it. Do me a favor and look up a major news story from London back in September. You'll know it when you see it."

"Okay, I will."

"No, now."

Chloe laughed. Some things never changed. "Still bossy. Okay, hang on." When Megan got something in her head, she was like a bulldog until it was dealt with.

Pulling her tablet out of her backpack, Chloe booted it up and searched for major news stories in London back in September. "All right, I see two busted terror plots, a couple murders, lots of political stuff, and an unsolved mystery concerning a bunch of dead guys in a sewer. Which one do you want me to read about?"

"Guess."

It wasn't a hard decision. "Okay, sewers it is."

She quickly read the first story she pulled up on it. Five lines in, she could see why Megan had wanted her to read about it. Everything about the situation described screamed Valkyrie involvement. All the dead guys were connected to the Russian mafia. No one had a clue who'd done it, and investigators suspected organized criminals.

Chloe smirked. "You've been busy."

"You could say that. But the point is, it wasn't just me this time. There are others. We've got a damn good team here, and I want you to be part of it."

Chloe was intrigued enough to meet with her to discuss it further—and to make sure this wasn't some kind of trick or trap. She was ninety-eight-percent sure it wasn't, but that two-percent suspicion had kept her alive through some dangerous times. "I look forward to hearing more about it." She glanced at her watch. "When will you be here?"

"Three hours, give or take. I'm bringing Ty."

"Sounds good." She paused. "One thing though, Itch."

"Yeah?"

"No matter what you're going to tell me, I can't come in right now. I've got something I need to take care of first." She needed to get this shipment of trafficked women to safety. She'd also killed a lot of high-profile people and had a long list of enemies that would love to come after her. So she had to play this carefully.

"Maybe you'll tell me about it later," Megan said.

"Maybe." She shut down her tablet and put it away. "I'd better get back out there and keep Heath company." Gruff hottie was understandably confused and not happy with her. "Maybe I'll kiss his owie better."

"If he lets you, sure. But no more knives to the gonads, okay? He's Tyler's closest friend."

"No promises," she said with a grin. "See you soon."

Chloe tucked her phone away, excited and happier than she had been in months. No, years.

When she walked out of the room, she found Heath standing in front of the open fridge, his back to her. She leaned a shoulder against the doorjamb and took a moment to admire the sight of him, all broad shoulders, strong back and tight ass in those jeans he filled out real nice. The man was nicely put together, fit and hard in all the right places. "Just make yourself at home."

He shot her a scowl over his shoulder. His broad, muscular shoulder. Yum. "I'm hungry. I was in the middle of eating my dinner at a nice café when I got the call from Ty. And what the hell is this?" He gestured to the contents. "Seriously? What adult woman has nothing but a case of energy drinks—which is shit for your body, by the way—and a box full of Pop Tarts in their fridge."

"I like caffeine. And Pop Tarts give me energy." She didn't care if it was bad for her, the chances of her living long enough to die of diet-related issues was pretty much nil.

He gave her a sardonic look. "Based on what I've already seen, more energy's the last thing you need."

Oh, that was cold. So very chilly.

She walked over to him, enjoying the way he straightened, his expression turning back to gruff. "I need your phone again."

He edged away from her with a suspicious scowl, turning his body as if to shield his phone in his pocket. "What for?"

She smothered a laugh. "Because I need it, that's why."

He narrowed his eyes. "What are you going to do with it?"

With an impatient sigh, she held out her hand. "Quit being a baby and just hand it over."

"No."

"Fine." She pounced.

He jolted as she jumped on him and wound her legs around his waist, turning even as he snatched the phone from his pocket and held it high over his head, out of her reach.

Undeterred, Chloe clamped a hand on his shoulder and boosted upward to grab the phone. "Hand it over," she ordered, trying to pry it from his grasp and enjoying herself a whole lot. He felt *nice* and smelled good too.

"Get off me," he snapped, turning around in a circle and pushing at her shoulder with his free hand. He was way bigger and stronger than her, so he wasn't trying very hard. Almost like he was afraid of hurting her if he exerted too much force.

Awww. Sweet, but totally naïve. The man was also cut, built of solid muscle. *Very* nice. "Just give me the damn phone, Barrett," she said, trying not to giggle. She'd hurt his pride enough already.

He twisted his upper body away from her, transferred the phone to his other hand and whipped it behind his back to keep it from her. But she was ready. She dove for it, seized it before he could firm his grip, and snagged it.

"Ha!" she crowed in triumph and hopped off him, dancing out of reach before he could grab her.

Heath heaved a sigh and folded his arms, his expression dark. "You better give it back."

"Uh-huh." She took the SIM card out of it, snapped it in half, then tossed the phone on the floor and raised her boot.

His gasp of horror cut through the room. "No—"

She slammed the heel of her boot into it, crushing it on the wooden floorboards.

He made a wounded sound before nailing her with a fulminating glare. "Are you *serious*? What the hell is *wrong* with you?"

Ignoring him, she crossed to her backpack on the

47

kitchen table, took out a burner and tossed it to him. "Here."

Those gorgeous blue eyes shot sparks at her as he caught it. "Knifing me in the groin wasn't enough when I've just been trying to make sure you're okay? You had to crush my phone on top of it?"

She shrugged, refusing to feel guilty. "Had to be done. Couldn't risk that someone else was tracking us or listening in." She walked around him to the fridge and pulled out a can of energy drink. "Want one?" she asked.

"No," he growled, jaw tight.

He was even sexier when he was annoyed. "So, how much do you know about all this?" she asked, casually crossing one ankle over the other as she took a sip.

"Nothing. Okay? I know *nothing*, and I gotta tell you, I'm pissed the hell off."

Can't say I blame you. Roles reversed, she'd be pissed too. "Well, let's hope we both get the answers we're looking for once Megan and Ty get here in a few hours."

"Yeah, let's," he muttered darkly, and turned away to rummage through the cupboards. "You got anything else to eat here resembling actual food? Crackers? Peanut butter or something?"

"I dunno. Maybe. The owner stocks it for me whenever I stay, but this was pretty last-minute setup, so I doubt she had time." She watched him look through the cupboards. "You should just have a Pop Tart."

"I'm not eating a damn Pop Tart," he snarled. He pulled a loaf of bread out of the cupboard above the toaster, followed by a half-empty jar of peanut butter, and proceeded to make himself a sandwich, a scowl stamped on his face.

It was no hardship to watch him. "Nothing else to say?" she asked as he found a knife and began slapping the peanut butter on the bread.

"Nope. I'm staying put until I talk to Ty face to face,

and then I'm outta here."

"Hmm, too bad."

"What?" he snapped, looking up at her.

"I said, too bad." He intrigued her enough that she wanted to know more about him. For instance, what had made him into such a Boy Scout that he would drop everything and race to hop on a train just to help a woman he didn't even know?

Also, the gruff thing he had going on was hella sexy on him.

"Whatever," he muttered, still annoyed.

"So, you were a PJ, huh?"

His stare burned with irritation. "Yeah. And?"

"I like PJs. PJs are awesome."

He snorted and bit into his sad little sandwich. "Whatever. I bet I'm the first one you've met."

"True. But it explains a lot," she added. She'd learned about all military SOF branches during her early training. PJs were a rare breed. There weren't that many of them around.

His scowl deepened as he chewed. "What does?"

She shrugged. "Why you did the favor for Ty. You like saving people." She could picture it easily. Him in his ACUs, weapon in hand as he jumped out of a helo and raced for the wounded patient he was tasked with saving. The image was enough to make any woman sigh.

And damned if it didn't make her stony heart flutter a little. That kind of selflessness and bravery was rare in this world.

He didn't answer, just took another big bite. "You and Megan went to school together?" he asked after he swallowed it.

"You could say that, yeah."

"Did you work together after?"

"No. I work alone. We all do."

His eyes narrowed a bit. "We?"

She took another sip of the energy drink, ignoring the question. The man really didn't know anything about Valkyries. "Favorite superhero?"

He blinked. "What? Why?"

"Why not? It's not a trick question. You got a favorite, or not?"

"Falcon."

"Ah, of course. Former PJ."

He bit into the sandwich, suspicion lurking in his gaze. "You?"

"Black Widow."

"Why does that not surprise me," he muttered around the bite.

"She's a total badass. I like badass women. And men," she added with a waggle of her eyebrows. PJs were badass in an incredibly selfless, heroic way.

He stared at her, last bite of sandwich poised partway to his mouth. "Are you *flirting* with me right now?"

She laughed at his incredulous tone. Messing with him was fun. But she'd bet getting in his pants would be *more* fun. "If I was flirting, you'd know it." It had been way too long since she'd had any fun, and this guy was one of the good ones. She darted a look at his ass. "You got one of those green feet tats back there?"

If she wasn't mistaken, his eyes widened a fraction before the scowl came back. "Maybe." He shoved the last bite into his mouth.

"Can I see it?"

He blinked, might have choked a little. "*No.*"

She tutted in disappointment and decided to ease up a bit. Having fun was one thing, but he'd had a tough night so she could cut him some slack. "What about hobbies? What do you like to do when you're not saving people?"

"Sports. Rock climbing mostly." His tone was equal parts resentful and exasperated.

Rock climbing? So there was a little bit of an adrenaline junkie in him after all. "I like to throw knives. I'm pretty good at it." She almost laughed at the shock on his face. "But my favorite thing is blowing shit up." She lived for that.

He stopped chewing, holding her gaze. "I can't tell if you're being serious or not."

She smiled. "Oh, I am." At first, she'd resented being stuck with him, but now she had to admit she could've done way worse. She liked him. Was definitely attracted to him.

That made things interesting. They had another three hours or more alone together before anyone else showed up. Might as well enjoy them.

Draining the last of her energy drink, she put the can into the recycling bin, then crossed to the sofa a few yards away, aware of his eyes following her every move. She liked it, and the reluctant male interest in his gaze, probably more than she should.

Stretching out on her back on the cushions to give him a good long look at her, Chloe tucked a hand behind her head, then looked him up and down once and gave him a naughty smile. "So. What should we do to amuse ourselves for the next few hours?"

Chapter Six

Guillaume rubbed at his tired, burning eyes and leaned back in his leather chair in his home office. "Nothing else?" he said into his cell. There had to be some new intel about Dom's killer by now.

"Not yet," Jean-Pierre answered.

His heart sank. "Keep looking. I want everyone we have put on this." It was nine in the morning now. He hadn't slept all night. How could he, when Dom's body—what was left of it—was still at the hospital morgue?

"When is the service?"

"Friday afternoon." He couldn't believe he was planning a funeral for his brother instead of closing business deals with him. Dom had been a handful to control, but over the last few years he'd become so much more stable and reliable—except when it came to the women. "The mayor's office offered security for it but I want you to handle it personally. There will be politicians there, some celebrities." In light of how Dom had died, security needed to be tight. Especially since Guillaume's wife and daughters would be there. He took zero chances with his family.

"Understood. I'll start working on it now."

"Good. I'll talk to you later." He ended the call just as a knock came at his office door. He took a moment to compose himself and put on a brighter expression. "Come in."

The door opened slightly and his youngest daughter appeared holding a breakfast tray. Eleven years old, the image of her mother. "I brought you some coffee and a snack," Sophie said softly, her face screwed up in concentration as she carried it across the Aubusson carpet.

He melted, his throat tightening. "Thank you, my angel."

She set it on his desk, then paused to study him, her expression serious and full of concern. "Are you feeling any better?"

"I'm feeling much better now because of this," he lied, pulling her close and kissing the top of her head. She was so sweet, a little mother already, wanting to take care of everyone.

Dom's death had shaken him to his core. Guillaume's family should have been untouchable, but last night had proven otherwise. It stood to reason he might be a target for whoever had killed Dom. And if he was in danger, then his wife and daughters might be as well.

Raw protectiveness ripped through him as he held Sophie. He would do anything to protect them. Anyone thinking to threaten or harm them to get to him would die.

To disguise his fears, he put on a smile. "I'm just getting things organized for Uncle Dom's funeral."

"Okay, but make sure you eat. I love you." She kissed his bristly cheek and flounced from the room.

A heavy weight settled in his chest as the door shut behind her, her exit taking the life and color from the room. His whole reality had shifted in the last twelve hours. So many things needed his immediate attention.

There were deals in place that couldn't be undone. Things that needed to be overseen and finalized. Dom was supposed to have handled the upcoming shipment. Guillaume had always distanced himself from that aspect of the business because it helped maintain his image in the community, but now he had no choice. He would have to handle it personally.

But before that, he had to lay his little brother to rest.

He flipped open his laptop and brought up the security feed from Dom's office that he'd been going over with his experts. The woman on screen was some sort of operative. Had to be. She spoke perfect French, without any hint of an accent that might give them a clue as to her background, and her ID as Gabrielle checked out, though he was certain it was fake.

He rubbed a hand over his mouth, staring at her. He'd memorized that face. Every line of it. If she appeared anywhere else during their search, he would know it, regardless of whether she tried to disguise herself.

They hadn't found out anything more about her yet but she must have serious, specific training to pull off a murder like this and slip away. The British and American governments had been watching Dom occasionally over the last few years. Was she one of theirs?

The lack of information on her was frustrating, but it also made him suspicious because of something he'd heard recently. There had been rumors circulating over the past few months about a possible network of American female operatives. The program responsible for training and overseeing their operations had supposedly shut down some time ago, but he was connected enough that he heard things, and if the story was true, then it seemed like this woman fit the profile.

Was he dealing with one of the fabled Valkyries? Some people in Guillaume's circle said that Yuri Stanislav had met his end at the hand of one in London last month. That was interesting by itself, but even more interesting to Guillaume was that it seemed in Stanislav's case, that female operative hadn't been working alone—and Guillaume had heard that Valkyries *always* worked alone.

He would have to be careful moving forward, let his people find and capture her so he maintained plausible distance from the whole thing, then he could dispose of her in whatever means he wanted. "Gabrielle" was an attractive, fit woman in her prime. He could get top dollar for her on the black market. If it turned out she was a Valkyrie? He could get ten times more.

This wasn't about money, however. He had enough of that already to last him and the next three generations of Dubois descendants, and keep them all in an extremely comfortable lifestyle. No, this was about justice and revenge, and he had the resources and dirty contacts to make it happen.

"In time," he murmured as he stared at her polished image on screen. "All in good time." Right now he had to give his brother the final, dignified sendoff Dom deserved.

Twenty minutes later he was talking to his priest on the phone when Jean-Pierre walked in. One look at his head of security's face, and Guillaume knew they had a lead.

His heart rate quickened. He excused himself, ended the call, then motioned for Jean-Pierre to sit in one of the chairs positioned in front of the desk. "Well?"

"The woman might have caught a train to Strasbourg last night. Facial recognition said it's a sixty-five-percent chance it's her."

Guillaume glanced at the door, but of course, Jean-Pierre would have locked it on his way in. He never had meetings like this at home, preferring to keep all…gray area aspects of his business dealings away from his family. "Was she alone?"

"I thought so at first. But now I think not." He pulled out a tablet and brought up some images on screen. "I think she might be with this man. He boarded the same train car as her in Paris. Here on the platform in Strasbourg he follows her before he walks out of range."

A dark-haired, muscular man in a brown leather jacket. "Who is he?" He studied the image. "He's too far away to be a bodyguard. Maybe an accomplice, or someone following her?"

"We don't know yet. And we don't know where they've gone either, but we're monitoring everything we can. If this is the same woman who posed as Gabrielle, she changed her appearance with a disguise. The hat she wore made it hard to see her face, and with her ears covered it makes it more difficult to say for sure if it's her. But it's the best lead we've got at the moment."

"It's her." He'd studied her image enough now to recognize her profile and the way she moved. "Have you called in favors from our contacts?" He had everything from National Police to some military officers, intelligence officials and politicians in his pocket. Someone would be able to lend assistance.

"Yes. And thanks to new voice recognition software one of them got a possible hit an hour ago. We may have found our break." He switched screens and brought up an audio clip. "The voice matches hers, and the cell signal was intercepted near Strasbourg."

Guillaume listened as two women spoke in English. A very strange, definitely coded conversation that didn't make any sense. "She's either Canadian or American." He met Jean-Pierre's gaze. Everything he'd learned thus far said the rumors might be true. "A Valkyrie," he whispered, the hairs on his nape standing up. She had to be. Incredible as it seemed, she *had* to be.

Jean-Pierre nodded, his gaze intent. "Maybe."

No. Guillaume's gut was certain of it. "Who sent her?"

"That program was shut down completely a long time ago. It's possible she's operating on her own."

"Why did she target Dom? Because of the women?" He sneered. They were such a small part of the business. Uneducated, illiterate women who barely spoke French, looking for a better life and easily manipulated into thinking they would get it.

He was doing his country a service by keeping them out of the system. If he and Dom hadn't purchased them, they would have all landed up on welfare eventually, sucking money from French taxpayers' pockets because they were too stupid and lazy to support themselves and the fatherless children they would inevitably have. A drain on a society already sagging under the weight of the burden it bore.

"I don't know, but when we traced the other number involved with this particular call, the only thing we could find was that it originated somewhere in the UK. It was that heavily encrypted."

Guillaume grunted. Maybe the Brits had sent "Gabrielle". He didn't want MI6 sniffing around. "So she's still in Strasbourg?"

"As best we can tell."

He wanted to kill her. Instead he'd make her *wish* she was dead. "Do you have an exact location?"

"Yes." He pulled up a satellite map showing a quiet, residential neighborhood.

Righteous anger punched through him. She thought she could kill his brother and then walk away? "I want a team dispatched there immediately. Find her and bring her to me. If she's with the guy, kill him and make it look like she did it." The fewer strings, the better.

"Of course. I've already alerted our special tactics officer contact in Strasbourg. He's getting a team together now, using the story that the woman and the man she's possibly with are terrorists."

"She *is* a terrorist," he snarled. "Tell him I want a live feed to their helmet cams." He wanted to watch the operation in real time.

"I will." Jean-Pierre stood. "I'll alert you—"

"Sit down, Jean-Pierre. We'll do this here. And when the team goes in, I want to ID her myself."

Guillaume didn't care if she was deadly in her own right. He would find her, no matter how long it took. And he would make her suffer.

No one fucked with his family and lived. There was no safe place on earth for her now.

****

Well, *he* was no fun.

Chloe pouted in disappointment and stared up at the ceiling from the couch rather than look over at Heath. After her loaded innuendo she'd only been partially kidding about, Heath had merely given her a long, warning look before setting to work transferring all his contacts into his new phone.

Lame. No shock, no bulging eyes or even an interested look for her efforts. He could have at least given her something interesting to work with, but nope, he was all standoffish, cool and collected. And apparently determined to ignore her.

That kind of quiet vibe had never done anything for her before, but on him, she had to admit it was pretty damn hot. And for some reason she was even more interested now that he seemed intent on resisting her.

Since he was still ignoring her, she got up and sauntered over to the fridge. Pulling out another energy drink and a Pop Tart, she popped the top on the can and raised an eyebrow when she caught his censoring look. "What?

Keeps me sharp mentally."

He didn't comment, just went back to work on his phone.

Stretched back out on the couch a minute later, she ate her snack, being purposely noisy. She hid a grin when she earned an annoyed side-eye from him.

After she ate, she checked her phone for anything new. Megan texted to say she and Ty were on the way to their plane, and gave her an updated ETA. There was nothing from Fleur. Several news stories were talking about the explosion at Dom's place and that he was missing. No one had confirmed his death yet. But Guillaume had to know by now.

Then an alert popped up on her phone that made her sit upright. "Hey," she said to Heath, staring at the screen.

"What's wrong?" He strode over.

"We got a problem." Chloe's pulse thudded in her ears as she used an app to check the perimeter cameras surrounding the rental unit. The one on the west side of the house showed a tactical team lined up on the sidewalk across the street and two doors down.

Heath came to stand behind her, watching over her shoulder as the team of cops dressed in tactical gear approached the side door of the house. "Where's this?" he asked.

"Across the street and two houses down." Damn, they must have somehow tracked her phone's signal. If she hadn't had the encryption on it, they wouldn't have hit the wrong house.

Chloe was already on her feet when the first man in line rammed a breaching tool into the door, breaking it open. A second later the team rushed inside, weapons up.

"We gotta clear out of here right now," she said, and they both rushed to gather their stuff.

They had to be here for her. And it had to be because

of Guillaume Dubois. Nobody else in France had the resources to track her so quickly. He and his brother had been business partners. Dom had been the fuck-up of the two, with Guillaume doing everything in his power to bail his little brother out of trouble and hide his messes.

Now he was after her.

She shoved her gear into her bag, then hurried to the kitchen to gather up any trash, not wanting to leave any easy evidence behind for the forensics team if they wound up searching this place. Heath started for the back door, backpack on.

"No, this way," she said, killing the lights and hurrying to the closet door. They had to take the secret entrance or risk being seen.

Inside, she shone the beam of her penlight at the floor. "There's a hidden staircase that leads to a cellar, and that extends to the next building. We'll go out on the far side of it. Oh, and just in case…" She drew her backup weapon from her waistband and handed it to him.

He took it and edged past her, his aloofness gone, replaced by a quiet intensity that was almost electric. "I'll get the trap door."

Chloe drew her own weapon and stood back to aim the penlight at the trap door in the closet. She liked that he was quick and didn't argue or ask questions. She could feel his frustration over this situation and didn't blame him. She actually felt bad about not being able to tell him everything at this point, and hoped things could be cleared up once they saw Megan and her man.

Heath raised the trap door, weapon pointed inside the hole. He leaned down to do a visual sweep, then straightened. "Clear."

Not that she'd expected anything else, but she was glad he was being thorough. "Ready?" At his nod, Chloe stepped past him and angled her body to fit through the hole, the thin, powerful beam of light cutting through the darkness.

Heath waited until there was enough room for him, then shut the closet door and came through the opening after her. As soon as he was inside, he closed the trap door above them.

"This way," Chloe said, and hurried across the old stone floor beneath the buildings, listening for the telltale sound of footsteps on the concrete sidewalk above them.

She ducked beneath the ancient timbers acting as pillars and supports, heading for the opposite side of the cold cellar. By now the tactical team would have cleared the building across the street, and realized they'd hit the wrong one. The next step would be to check the neighboring ones. Chloe intended to be long gone before then.

The trap door on the far side didn't have any stairs up to it, and it locked from the inside. There were no boxes or crates for her to stand on and they didn't have a second to waste. "Boost me up."

Heath slid his weapon into the back of his waistband and came up behind her to wrap his arms around her hips, his grip sure and warm, sending an unexpected tingle through her. He lifted her off her feet with ease, held her steady while she reached overhead to fight with the iron peg jammed into the locking mechanism.

It was old and rusted and took several shoves to slide free, each creak of the metal making her wince. They had minutes, maybe less than five, to get out of here unseen, or things were going to get ugly. "Okay, I'm pushing the door open now." She switched off the penlight, slid it into her pocket, then eased the hatch up a few inches.

Dark and quiet greeted her on the street above. She paused there for a few moments, Heath holding her steady as she checked to make sure they were still in the clear. Thankfully there was no sign of the cops. Yet. If they even were real cops. For all she knew they could be a hit squad hired by Dubois.

"We're good, but hurry," she whispered to him, then pushed the hatch open all the way, planted her hands on either side of the opening and pushed upward. Heath boosted her up from below, making it easy for her. She moved to the side and stayed perched on one knee to draw her weapon and keep watch.

Heath's hands curled around the sides of the opening. A second later he levered his upper body through it, climbed out, then mirrored her positioning on the other side, weapon in hand as he scanned the alley.

"Still clear," she whispered. "Let's move." She closed the trap door as quietly as she could, pushed to her feet and stuck to the shadows of the buildings as she hurried to where she'd left the rental car, Heath right behind her.

"Who's after you?" he demanded in a low voice as he got into the passenger seat and shut the door, his expression tight.

"Not now," Chloe answered, checking around her before starting the engine. The street was empty but the cops would have a perimeter set up nearby, so she had to pick the right route out of here.

The heat was on, and would only get hotter. She'd managed to stay ahead of Guillaume Dubois and his many tentacles thus far, but he'd earned his ruthless reputation for a reason.

She'd taken his brother from him. He wouldn't rest until he got her.

Not that he would get the chance, because she was going to kill him first.

Chapter Seven

Heath was done with this shit. First dropping eve-rything in the middle of his holiday to help this woman, then the knife thing and his phone, and now a tactical unit might have been sent to arrest her?

With effort he tamped down his annoyance and braced a hand on the door when Chloe took a fast right, winding her way out of the residential neighborhood. As soon as she turned the corner, he spotted the police vehicles lined up behind them down the street. The start of the secure perimeter the cops would have set up prior to the team approaching the target house.

"Who's after you?" he repeated in a hard voice. He was used to rules and regulations, SOPs and chain of com-mand. This chaos was making him insane.

"Someone with a lot of power and influence," she an-swered, taking a quick left onto a main road.

It made him itch not to be behind the wheel in a situa-tion like this, but she seemed to have everything in hand, and no cops were coming after them. Yet. Maybe they were in the clear for now. "Bullshit. I've put up with everything so far, but this is *bull*shit." He was supposed to be on his hard-earned holiday right now, not on the run from the law with a crazy and infuriating woman. "Who is it?"

"Guillaume Dubois."

Heath had never heard of him.

"He's one of the wealthiest and most powerful men in France. And he didn't get that way by being a good boy and playing by the rules, if you know what I mean."

"So why's he after you?"

"That's gonna have to wait until we meet up with the others. Can you call them, by the way? We need to set up a new RV point."

"Where are we going?"

"Zurich."

What? "That's like, two hours away."

"More like just under three, actually. But it's in the opposite direction that anyone tracking me is likely to look. They'll expect me to head across into Germany, because it's closer."

Heath stared at her profile in the flicker of the streetlamps they passed. What the hell had she done? "Does Ty know what you did to land on this guy's radar?"

"Not sure, but Megan might. Call them."

Pushing out a breath, Heath pulled out his new phone, scowling as he dialed Ty. It went straight to voicemail, so he texted his friend instead. "Where in Zurich?" he asked her.

"Tell them we'll let them know when we get there."

He relayed the message, set the phone in his lap and checked the side mirror. Still no cops. Chloe seemed to have everything under control. There were no flashing lights, no wail of sirens coming after them.

"Look, I'm sorry I gave you a hard time before. Megan and Tyler will help clear things up soon."

He glanced over at her. She was gorgeous, confident

and capable, but also unsettling and intense. Heath didn't know what to make of her. While he admired her abilities, it pissed him off to be kept in the dark like this. "How does Ty know about you? From Megan?"

"Looks like."

His new phone buzzed with an incoming message. "He says they'll meet us in Zurich in three hours."

"Perfect." She smoothly merged onto the freeway. There were barely any cars on the road at this time of night. "So, why a PJ?"

The abrupt change in subject threw him for a sec. He didn't feel like talking if he wasn't getting anything back, but the alternative was spending the next three hours in a brittle silence. "I liked the job description. I didn't know about Pararescue when I first joined up, but once I heard about it, there was nothing else for me."

"Did you get through the pipeline the first try?"

He blinked, surprised that she knew about the pipeline. "No. I failed the pool section the first time." They called it Superman school for a reason, and it had taken all of his effort and mental toughness to get through that section—especially since he knew what was coming the second time around.

"That's pretty common. The water's always the great equalizer."

She made it sound like she knew that firsthand. "And you know that because?"

She shrugged. "I went through it too."

No way. He stared at her. Was she screwing with him? Why the hell would she have gone through that course? "For what?"

"For my training."

Okay. Seriously. He frowned. "Are you Israeli Special Forces?"

She laughed. "No." Then she shot him a smug grin. "Better." She faced the road once more. "But I still can't tell you everything yet. You'll just have to be patient."

He was starting to believe she wasn't kidding. About any of this. "What were you training for?" he couldn't help asking.

The hint of a smile tugged at her mouth at his persistence. "To be prepared for anything."

"Like a life of crime?" he said, a sardonic bite to his words.

She chuckled under her breath, and it sounded a little evil. "You could say that." She shifted in her seat, easing back, and he could see the tension drain from her as they drove away from Strasbourg. "I love how they call it 'water confidence'. Confidence my ass, they just throw you in the deep end and then do their best to drown you. The only way you get confidence is if you survive to pass."

"And you obviously did." He was still trying to envision it. Some instructor throwing her, feet bound together, hands bound behind her back, into the deep end of a pool and then holding her under. He didn't like the images that put in his head. Not at all.

"Not until my third try. I almost flunked out of the program because of it."

What program? Something black ops related, some intelligence agency. Nothing else made sense. It was driving him nuts, the little snippets she was giving him when he wanted to know the whole damn picture.

"Megan passed the first time. I was so pissed. Good thing I liked her."

Heath digested that in silence. Just what had these women been trained for? How had Ty gotten involved with whatever this was?

She glanced at him. "Sleep if you want. You have to be pretty tired by now."

He shot her an incredulous look. *Sleep*? "Nope."

Her grin flashed in the light from the instrument panel in the dashboard. "Don't trust me, huh?"

"Not so much, no."

She laughed, a low, sultry sound that stirred him up inside, and damned if he didn't find himself fighting an answering smile. "I deserve that."

"At least tell me who you're working for." CIA? NSA? His inner radar was pinging like crazy.

"Myself. And I'm sorry you got dragged into this. Your friend shouldn't have involved you."

She said it like he was in way over his head, and that insulted him. "I can hold my own," he bit out, his pride stinging.

"No doubt. But not against this."

He let out a frustrated sigh. "Look. We've got a long drive ahead of us, and no one can overhear us. Why are you on the run?"

She was silent so long he didn't think she would answer. Then she relented with a sigh. "Did you see the news before you came to the train station?"

"Briefly after I got there. Why?"

"Anything important being televised?"

Only one thing came to mind. "There was some kind of explosion at a house in Paris belonging to a wealthy businessman. He was missing."

"Because he's dead."

Wait. "*You* killed him?" His voice rose. He was on the run with a murderess?

She didn't deny it, and that was answer enough. "As to who's after me, I'm pretty sure it's his older brother. He's as corrupt as they come, but he covers it up with this fancy, polished veneer. He's an evil piece of shit, same as his brother was," she finished with a twist of her mouth.

"Holy shit," he muttered, running a hand down his face. "Does Ty know all this?"

"Probably. I'm betting Megan does, so…yeah, pretty sure he does."

Then why the hell would Ty have sent him to do this?

And not warn him what he was walking into? "Yeah, let's not talk anymore." He already didn't like knowing the things he did so far. He needed to maintain as much plausible deniability as possible in case they were arrested.

"Fair enough."

Heath turned on the radio, found a top forty station and left it there to fill the silence. They sped through the darkness, his mind busy dissecting everything he'd learned.

He was going to kick Ty's ass for this.

The remainder of the drive to Zurich passed without a single other word spoken between them. He'd made up his mind that she was some kind of spy.

When they were only a few kilometers away from the city, Heath's phone buzzed with a new message. "They're here," he said to Chloe. "Where are we meeting them?"

She gave him an address that he passed on, and drove them to a cottage set back from a quiet street near the freeway. "This is us," she said as she parked along the curb.

"What is it?"

"A safehouse."

Of course it was. She apparently had a network of them at her disposal.

He stood on the back doorstep watching for any sign of trouble while she punched the keycode into the door lock and went inside. Heath followed, and within moments he got another message. "They're two minutes out."

And oh, man, it couldn't go by fast enough.

A brisk knock signaled the wait was over. Heath shot off the couch when Chloe checked the back door, weapon in hand. "It's them." She opened it, the wide smile on her face transforming her from pretty to stunning. She enveloped a shorter brunette in a giant hug, then dragged her inside. "Itchy. Oh my God."

The brunette—he presumed Megan—hugged her in return, holding on for a long moment. "I can't believe you're here."

"Me either. Care to introduce me to that hunk on the doorstep?"

They separated, and Ty walked in, shutting the door behind him. He gave Chloe a smile and held out his hand. "Chloe. Nice to meet you finally. I've heard a lot about you."

She shook his hand. "I'll bet."

Ty's grin shifted to apologetic when he locked gazes with Heath. "Hey, brother. Good to see you're still in one piece."

"Ha-ha." He walked over to shake Megan's hand, his brain going a hundred miles an hour.

"And look, we brought you a new pair of jeans without any knife holes in them." Ty pulled them out of his backpack, a hint of amusement in his eyes.

Heath swiped them from him. "Thanks. Now start talking before I lose my shit."

Ty and Megan shared a look, then she took Chloe by the arm and started leading her away. "You guys go ahead and talk while we catch up elsewhere." They disappeared into the bedroom and shut the door.

Alone, Heath faced his buddy and raised his eyebrows. "Well?" It looked like Ty was trying not to laugh, but if he did Heath might deck him. "Did you know she killed a guy? It was all over the news."

Ty opened his mouth to respond but Heath stabbed a finger at his chest before he could answer. "You made me believe I was doing you a favor by looking after a woman in trouble. I assumed she was a civilian, because you didn't say otherwise. But she damn near neutered me during our first meeting, then I find myself on the run from the National Police because she's some spy or whatever who'd just killed a powerful and wealthy French businessman in his own house. What the *hell*, Ty?"

Ty held up his hands. "I know, I know, and I'm sorry

for all that. I'll explain everything. Let's sit down."

"I don't wanna sit," he growled. "Just tell me."

Ty's expression was as serious as Heath had ever seen it. Then he tipped his head toward the closed bedroom door. "They're Valkyries," he said.

Heath squinted at him. "Huh?"

"Megan and Chloe. They're government-trained assassins."

Heath barely kept his mouth from falling open. He'd heard about this a while back, but he'd never.... "You mean they were part of that program that was all over the media a few months ago? The one nobody knew about beforehand?"

Ty nodded. "The Valkyrie Program was dreamed up by the CIA. They shut it down after it was exposed when one of its members went to trial—Will Balducci."

"I remember." He'd followed the story for weeks afterward.

"But it was still running up until a few months ago, and now someone's gunning for these women. They've got a lot of enemies, as you can imagine. But whoever's targeting them is doing it from the inside."

Heath changed his mind. "I'm gonna sit down."

He walked to the couch, sank down on it and put his head in his hands, his elbows resting on his knees. This was crazy. And his best buddy had landed him right in the middle of it. "I was on vacation."

"I know, and I'm sorry about that. How long until you go back?"

"Little over two weeks. But I guess my holiday's over now, huh? There's a chance someone spotted me with her. So whoever's after her might target me too."

Ty sank down next to him. "Yeah," he said quietly. "I was hoping this wouldn't happen. But you know I wouldn't have involved you unless it was important."

Heath nodded, took a breath and sat up. "How the hell

did you get involved in all of this?"

"I got a call out of the blue from Alex Rycroft."

Heath knew the name. A former SF officer who had gone on to become a star with the NSA. "I thought he was retired."

"Technically he is. But then he got wind from a former Valkyrie he's close to about how the rest of these women are being systematically hunted down and eliminated. He formed a small taskforce and pulled some strings to get some funding, then called to bring me on board."

"Why you?"

Ty's slate blue gaze was somber. "Remember that story I told you about that girl who escaped during SERE school and scared the hell out of me by showing up at my campsite one night while I was a temporary instructor?"

"Yeah."

"That was Megan."

"Oh." His eyes widened as it sank in. "Whoa."

"Yep. Rycroft told me she was in danger and asked me to be part of the team to help find whoever was selling the Valkyries out to their enemies. After what happened between us, I owed it to her to help if I could."

"And she was okay with that?"

"Not at first. But there were other former Valkyries involved, and long story short, the villain in that scenario turned out to be her sister."

This was getting worse by the moment. "Her sister was selling them out to their enemies?"

"Some of them. The ones who'd crossed her on a team op and left her to die. She survived and went after them. Her name's Amber, by the way, and she's the reason we found Chloe in the first place. But Valkyries are still dying, and that has nothing to do with Amber now. We've been trying to locate the remaining operatives, but as you've seen, they're not easy to pin down."

He huffed out a humorless laugh. "No shit."

"Amber's a hacker. She and the others—"

"Others. How many of them are working with you?"

"Five so far. We're hoping Chloe will make six. The team's been monitoring various sources and contacts, trying to find the rest. Each Valkyrie has a specific skill set. They're cross-trained in various things, but they all have a certain area they specialize in. For instance, Megan's an expert at breaking into places and stealing things."

"And Chloe?" Though given something she'd said and how that guy in Paris had died, Heath was afraid he already knew.

"She's an explosives and demolitions expert."

But my favorite thing is blowing shit up. "Oh, shit…" The answer had startled him at the time, but he'd had no idea what he'd been dealing with. Now that he did… "She told me about Dubois on the way here, but I didn't put it all together." He rubbed his jaw, trying to make sense of everything, and grappling with the knowledge that he was now smack in the middle of it. "How did you even find her in the first place?"

"There was enough evidence to make us think she might be behind a string of professional hits over the past few months. Each target was a high-level criminal killed in a controlled explosion. Each explosion had different chemical signatures, but they were small and precise, killing only the target and no one else. Given all that, it seemed like it could be her."

"Who were the targets?"

"Human traffickers selling women into the skin trade."

Heath curled his lip, secretly impressed by Chloe's guts. People who did evil shit like that deserved to die. "Like this Dubois guy?"

Ty nodded. "Amber had picked up a potential lead on Chloe in St. Petersburg a while back. But last night in Paris was the most solid lead we've had since, and we were too far away to do anything in time. Because of the high-security level of the people after the Valkyries, I couldn't tell you any of this over an unsecured phone line. But if you hadn't stepped in, we'd have lost her, and might never have found her again." He set a hand on Heath's shoulder, squeezed tight. "I owe you, brother. We all do."

Heath didn't know what to say.

Ty nudged his shoulder. "You wanna punch me a couple times? I'll give you two free shots, but not to my face because Megan likes it the way it is."

Heath grunted. "I kinda do, yeah." He ran a hand through his hair, rubbed the back of his neck. This had been one hell of a night so far. "So what happens now?"

Ty was silent a moment, watching him. "We could use another member on the team, even if it's only temporary. A solid operator I trust with my life, and can handle himself when shit goes sideways. Even better if he's an elite combat medic. Know anyone like that?"

Ah, hell. It was impossible to stay mad at the guy, even if he'd landed Heath in the middle of this shit storm. But Heath couldn't ignore this or walk away now. Like it or not, he was at risk, and so was Ty. He had to help his friend—and the Valkyries in the other room. "Maybe."

Ty grinned. "Yeah?"

He would never turn his back on Ty. And now that he understood what was going on, he wanted to help protect the women at risk too—including Chloe.

So there was only one answer he could give. Dammit. "Yeah. I'm in."

Chapter Eight

Sitting cross-legged on the bed with Megan, Chloe smiled at her old friend, hardly able to believe this was happening. "You look amazing." All grown up, but still Itch.

"You too."

She nodded pointedly at the ring on Megan's finger. "So you and Ty are pretty serious then, I gather?" It surprised her that any Valkyrie could make that kind of promise and commitment after it had been drilled into them to never get romantically—or emotionally—attached.

"Yep." Megan practically bounced on the bed in excitement. "Oh, man, I've got so much to tell you, I don't even know where to start."

"How about you start with your sister?"

Megan's smile fell a little. "I didn't even know she existed. I had a few memories of her, but I wasn't sure if she was just a friend or a neighbor, or even an imaginary friend. We were so young when we were separated, after our parents were killed in a car accident. My mom's younger sister was named our guardian but she couldn't take us so we landed up on foster care, and then a boarding school."

"Which led to the Program."

"Right."

Megan went on to explain about how she and Ty had been recruited along with three other former Valkyries several months ago to find the person responsible for having Valkyries killed. And that the target had turned out to be her older sister, who had eliminated fellow female operatives on her kill list because they'd betrayed her and left her to die.

"To sever our bond completely, they told Amber I was dead soon after we were separated. Of course she believed them. She was too young to ever think they would lie about something like that."

"Wow." Chloe shook her head. "I knew the Program blurred the lines when it came to the law, but I never considered something like that."

"Yeah, it was a hard thing to hear, and we're still learning more things every day. Part of me always knew I was a tool to them. A weapon." She shrugged. "I guess I told myself otherwise because I wanted to believe we were more than that."

"I used to believe that too, until everything was shut down and they left us to rot, cut off and alone." Chloe hated that they had all been used, then discarded.

"I know. But I never would have found Amber otherwise." Her smile returned. "It's been a bit of a process, getting to know each other again and building trust after everything that's happened, but she's awesome. Her hacking skills and financial brain have been a huge help to the team already," Megan said with pride. "You'll love her."

"And what's the team doing?"

"We're trying to find and bring in any other Valkyries out there before it's too late, because someone's hunting us. Once the others are brought in, we're going to set everyone up with our own WITSEC-like program. We've got various funds socked away from previous ops that Amber invested for us. She and Trinity—she's the eldest of us, and kind of Rycroft's right-hand in all this—are working on it. Kiyomi and I've been helping too."

The implications of all that made Chloe's head spin. Someone was actively hunting them… "Do you know who's targeting us?"

"Not yet. Amber and Rycroft's handpicked analysts back in the States are working on it. But from what we can gather, it has to be someone who was involved with the Program."

Chloe frowned. "You think maybe someone from the inside leaked intel on me to Guillaume Dubois' network? Because it had to be him. The cops in Strasbourg—if they really were cops—found me way too fast." For all she knew, that team had been sent to kill her, not capture her.

"Maybe. Amber's searching for any chatter about it."

Something worse occurred to her. "Do you think he knows what I am?"

"It's possible. Amber and the others are on it, so if that's what happened, we'll find out and deal with it."

She hoped so. "How many of us are left?"

"Besides us and Amber, there's Trinity, Georgia, Briar, Kiyomi, and possibly four or five others out there. Once we locate the missing ones, we move to intercept and bring them to our base in the UK. After everyone's accounted for and safe, we each enter our specialized identity program and start new lives without having targets on our backs."

"But to do that, you'll need to find out who's been targeting us from the inside and end them."

"Exactly."

It was a bold mission, and Chloe approved. "I might have a potential lead on another Valkyrie."

Megan's expression sharpened with interest. "Who is she?"

"I don't know her real name. I was last in contact with her online about a group of women being smuggled from Algiers to southern France, about a month ago. She apparently got a tip about it and reached out to a friend of mine, who helps rescue female human trafficking victims. That's how we got in touch, and the way she handled everything was so slick, I wondered if she was one of us. But I can't prove it, and I haven't heard from her in a while."

"Can you reach out to her?"

"Sure, but no guarantee she'll respond. You know how it goes."

Megan grinned. "I do. But we're not operating alone anymore." She reached for Chloe's hand, curled her fingers around Chloe's. "I'm so damn glad to see you," she whispered, voice rough and her eyes a little shiny.

The back of Chloe's throat ached. "Me too, Itch." After a second she pulled her hand free and changed the subject. She craved the friendship so much it scared her a little. She didn't want to get hurt if things wound up not working out. "So, tell me more about this Heath guy you sent after me."

"Ty says he's the best. They did security contracting jobs together all over the place, and went through tight situations together. Ty loves him like a brother."

Another complication for her to worry about. "And since he's been linked to me, now he's likely under threat too."

Megan nodded with a sigh. "I know. Ty's talking to him about everything right now."

"Everything?"

"Everything. Ty trusts Heath with his life, and that

tells me everything I need to know about the guy. He deserves to know everything now that we've dragged him into this, and Ty wants to bring him on board our team anyway." She patted Chloe's knee. "We should go see them. We'll catch up more later."

Heath's piercing blue gaze locked on her the moment she stepped out of the bedroom. He was sitting on the sofa beside Ty, his expression unreadable. But those eyes. They practically saw inside her, and it was a strange, unsettling feeling to know this near stranger knew all about her and her identity and background when only a handful of others did. It was also freeing, in a way.

"So now you know," she said to him, feeling sort of naked.

He nodded once, his expression betraying no hint of judgment. "Now I know."

"And will you help us?" Megan asked, sinking onto the loveseat opposite them.

"My next contract starts in another couple weeks in Syria. I can't push it back or just drop it."

"That's assuming you're not a target now too, because if you are, you might not be able to leave," she said.

Heath acknowledged the point with a nod. "I'm in until I leave for Syria." His gaze shifted to Chloe. "What about you?"

His leaving in a matter of weeks wasn't as appealing as it should have been for someone like her. But she hadn't been interested in anyone in forever, and he… He was definitely interesting. "I'll help where I can. But I can't commit to the team yet. I've got something I need to take care of first."

"Such as?" He raised a dark eyebrow.

"There's a shipment of women coming into Marseille three days from now. I need to be there to intercept them." That's how it always worked. She showed up to verify the women were there, representing the buyer. Once she handled the money transfer—to her own offshore account—she got the women to safety and let Fleur take over.

"You mean trafficking victims," Heath said, anger bleeding into his expression.

"Yes. I intercept them, get them to safety, and then a friend of mine steps in and helps them from there."

"Why you?"

"Because Dubois and people like him behind this sort of shit are unfortunately above the law—because they pretty much own all the law enforcement and politicians around the country. They're rich, they're powerful, and they don't give a damn about anything but themselves. That's where I come in." She crossed her arms, resentment building inside her. "I operated for years on my own doing the jobs I was assigned, answering only to my handler, who's now dead. My targets were the heads of organizations. Men who ran weapons and drugs—and women."

It still sickened her, even after all this time. "Nobody ever cared about the women, or what happened to them. They only cared about the money those women brought that in turn bought more weapons and drugs, which in turn funded organized criminal and terrorist activity. Men like Dubois were a means to an end, for me and the government, funneling us to higher value targets. Men like him were never punished. Now I make sure they are." She gave him a thin smile. "I deliver the punishment they deserve."

Heath was silent a moment, watching her. Judging her?

She didn't care if he thought it was wrong. She'd seen the evil that inhabited the dark corners of the world, and refused to ignore it any longer. "If nobody else will step up to make it stop, then I will," she said with a defensive shrug.

"That's one hell of a risky mission to undertake," he said quietly.

"Maybe, but who else is gonna do it? Too many local law enforcement groups are dirty. Here in France most of them are on Dubois' payroll and can't be trusted. He has eyes and ears all over the country, and probably beyond. And it has to be me, because that's the way my friend and I have everything set up. If I don't show when the shipments arrive, those women and girls are doomed to a living hell. Not only that, I won't leave my friend to deal with this on her own."

"How much do you trust your friend?" Megan asked.

"Completely." Fleur was one-of-a-kind, and rock solid. Now that the Valkyrie Program was finished, Chloe was on her own. It was harder to get fake IDs, access certain databases. She moved around a lot. Fleur had helped her as much as possible, even stashing some of Chloe's gear—weapons and other equipment—in various places for her across Paris.

At Megan's cautious nod, Chloe focused back on Heath. His calm, serious demeanor drew her with magnetic force, and that was one hell of an eye opener because until now she'd sought out the exact opposite in guys. This man could handle himself under pressure, she'd seen it firsthand. That was damn sexy. "It might not be too late for you, but the window's closing fast."

"Not too late for what?"

"To leave. Forget you ever saw me or heard any of this." She held his stare, liking the calming effect he had on her restless energy far too much. "You might still be able to walk away, but you'd need to do it *now*."

His stare never wavered. "Like I said, I'm in until I leave."

Not only was he hot and capable, the man was selfless enough to help the others. *Damn.*

Even as she thought it, she warned herself against the

surge of repressed longing that swept through her. First time in forever that she'd been into a guy, and while she thought she'd caught a spark or two of interest from him tonight, she wasn't sure he was into her. Not that she could blame him; she *had* held a knife to his junk when they'd met.

"What if we help you with your current mission?" Ty offered. "Me, Megan and Heath. We help you and your friend rescue these women, then you come with us back to the UK."

Chloe shook her head. "This isn't over until I bring Guillaume Dubois down. He deserves to die the same way his brother did, but it would be more satisfying to expose him and bring his filthy empire toppling down on top of him first." She was under no illusions, however. Once she brought him down, someone would try to take his place. But whoever did would always look over their shoulder for her.

"If we help you do that, *then* will you come in?" Megan said.

Looking at her old friend, taking in the earnestness in her face and the hidden plea in her voice, Chloe considered it. But she wasn't going to lie and say yes. "Maybe." It was the most she could offer for now.

Megan sighed. "I guess that's the best I can hope for at this point. But just know I'm not giving up until I turn that maybe into a yes."

Chloe grinned at her. "If anyone can bring me in, Itch, it's you."

Although the magnetic man across the room might have a shot at influencing her as well. The thought caused an internal burst of disquiet.

Heath put her off-balance. In her carefully orchestrated and guarded existence, that was never a good thing.

In her world, that kind of thing could get her killed.

Chapter Nine

Guillaume held his phone to his ear as he stepped into his home office and shut the door. It was the middle of the night. He'd been waiting up for this call and didn't want to disturb his sleeping family upstairs. "What do you mean, she's not there?" he demanded.

"The target house was empty and there's no sign she's ever been here. The signal couldn't have come from this place," the cop in charge of the Strasbourg raid said.

Guillaume punched in the code to his computer with angry stabs and brought up the satellite map showing the signal they'd traced. "You read the same map I did. If the phone signal didn't come from that house, then it had to be from one damn close."

"We checked the surrounding houses too. One across the street is a rental. Someone had been in it recently, but we can't be sure if it was tonight. Forensics is working on it now. If they find any good prints, we might get a match in the database."

Guillaume doubted it. This woman was too fucking

smart for that.

"According to the owner, the renter only paid for one night. Whoever it was might have changed their mind."

Cursing under his breath, he exploded from his chair, anger pulsing hot through his veins. "It was her. You know it was."

"We had a secure perimeter set up around the entire block," the cop said in a hard tone. "If it was her, no one saw her come and go."

"That's because she's trained to be a ghost," he snapped. *Dieu*, now he had no idea where she was, or the man with her. "I assume you're checking all surveillance cameras in the area?"

"I know how to do my job. But this is a small village. We'll be lucky if we find more than one or two."

He paced around the room, thinking fast. "So where's she gone now? Germany?" If he was on the run, he would move to another country to try and evade law enforcement. And Germany was the closest border from Strasbourg. Somewhere else in France, or maybe Switzerland?

"Your guess is as good as mine," the man replied, irritation clear in his voice.

Guillaume ended the call, his mind racing. The funeral he'd hurriedly put together was tomorrow; he wouldn't be able to get much work done. The next shipment of girls Dominic had purchased was still due to arrive on schedule in Marseille. If this Gabrielle woman was a Valkyrie and knew about the shipment, she might try to stop it. She'd be stupid to come in person, but he had a feeling she might. There might be an opportunity for him to strike.

He dialed the local inspector. "Sorry to wake you."

"Not at all, my friend. What can I do for you?"

For some reason the *friend* comment irritated him more than it should have. They weren't friends. The inspector pretended to be because of Guillaume's money and influence, and that was all. He was just as likely to turn on Guillaume as the others if a better offer or the right pressure came along. "The tactical team in Strasbourg didn't find the woman."

"I verified that signal myself before talking to the commander," the inspector said, his voice shocked. "She had to have been there."

"If she was, she slipped past them without notice."

"I'll contact my source and see if he can get another lead."

"Don't bother. She'll have ditched the phone by now."

"What if—"

"Leave it alone for now," Guillaume snapped, exhausted and heartsick. His brother would be laid to rest tomorrow but his killer was still free. It was so wrong.

"All right. I'll see you at the service tomorrow."

Guillaume grunted. "After the funeral I'll be travelling to Marseille on business. You can reach me on my cell."

"I can come down and meet you there if you want. I can help facilitate the investigation."

"No." It wouldn't do to have any police involvement there when Guillaume's men would be posing as local cops to meet the shipment. Money, bribes, blackmail and threats only went so far, and he had to be careful now. He wanted Gabrielle enough to avoid using his normal contacts. If she showed in Marseille, she was his.

"All right. Let me know if you change your mind. In the meantime, give this some time. You just need to be patient."

Patient? How could he be fucking patient with something like this? His brother was dead and the woman who'd murdered him was still alive.

Too restless and upset to sleep, he spent the next few hours combing over the evidence again, trying to find another possible clue that might lead him to his target. All he needed was to be patient?

Fuck that.

Chapter Ten

"I don't know about you guys, but I'm beat. I'm heading to bed," Megan announced, pushing up off the sofa beside Chloe.

Heath had been talking with the others for over an hour and now that he had some sort of clue about what was really going on here, was even more curious about these women. They were unlike anyone he'd ever met before, and he'd met all kinds during his military and contracting careers.

Next to Heath, Ty stood and stretched his arms over his head. "Me too. See you guys in the morning."

"Yeah, and Chloe," Megan said with a half-smirk, "be nice to Heath. He's had a long day."

No shit. It felt more like a week had passed since he left Paris rather than ten hours. But now he got why Ty had asked him to get involved. This was way bigger than Heath had realized, and tough and capable as these women were, they were under threat from dangerous enemies and could use backup.

"I *have* been nice to him," Chloe replied as her friend

walked away. "Except for the nick on his thigh."

Yeah, except for that. And then crushing his phone. Though he now understood why she'd done it. "Guess I'll turn in too. I'll take the couch," he said to her.

"Or we could share my bed." She gave him another of those naughty looks and he couldn't tell if she was serious or just trying to get a reaction out of him. She scrambled his brain.

"You just met me."

She lifted a shoulder. "I'm a good judge of character."

Okay, he was way too tired for a battle of wits, and he wasn't even sure what the ground rules were here anyway. "You want to use the bathroom first?"

"You go ahead." She turned and walked toward one of the bedrooms, so he grabbed his backpack and went into the bathroom.

He opened the door after brushing his teeth, nearly jumped out of his skin to find her right there leaning against the jamb. She was so close he could see the warm amber flecks in her brown eyes, and smell the mint gum she was chewing. She'd changed into a pair of sleep shorts and a snug T-shirt that read *Cute But Psycho* across the chest.

Accurate.

And she wasn't wearing a bra, the outline of her pert breasts and nipples visible against the fabric.

"You done?"

He wrenched his gaze up to her face. "Yeah, bathroom's all yours." He turned sideways to get past her but she didn't budge. His chest brushed against her breasts on the way by, and her quiet, indrawn breath heated his blood.

He wasn't sure why she was so set on driving him crazy, but it was a relief when she shut the door. He took his backpack into the kitchen, rummaged through it to find his phone charger and adaptor to see if they worked with his stupid new phone, his head spinning. Chloe confused the hell out of him. One minute he thought she was nuts, and the next he was thinking about kissing that sassy mouth.

Maybe *he* was nuts.

He stiffened when the bathroom door opened and soft footfalls approached behind him. He rose, looked across the room as Chloe came closer. She'd pulled out her ponytail, leaving golden-blond waves tumbling around her shoulders, the ends brushing the tops of her pert, unrestrained breasts.

Not. Helping.

"You turning in?" she asked.

He nodded. "You're not?"

"Not tired."

"Yeah, energy drinks in the middle of the night will do that to you." With the amount of caffeine in her system, she should be up for days.

One side of her mouth turned up. "That's why I like 'em. I get a crap-ton done while the rest of the world is asleep." She sank onto the far sofa, patted the cushion next to her. "Come talk with me a minute."

What he should do was hit the rack, sleep, and shore up his resistance to her. Because that seemed to be fading a bit with every minute he spent in her company. What was it about her that tangled him up so much?

He took the sofa across from her rather than accept her invitation, earning a pout. "What do you want to talk about?"

She tilted her head, considering him. "You."

"What about me?"

"I'm just trying to figure out why you're sticking around after everything you learned earlier."

"Because it's the middle of the night and I'm tired."

She gave him a level look. "You know what I mean. You could try to get out now, before you get in any deeper."

He shrugged. "Ty's my best friend. I won't walk away if he needs my help."

"Admirable, but it's more than that." Those deep brown eyes continued to scrutinize him, giving him the eerie impression that she could see into his mind. "You're a Boy Scout," she murmured, having finished her analysis and come to her final conclusion.

"No I'm not," he blurted, unable to keep the defensive edge out of his tone. He'd been called that before, and though it might be true to some extent, it still annoyed him that she'd said it.

"Yes, you are. You save people. It's what you do, and now that you know what's going on, you feel obligated to help me too. But as you've seen, I'm not helpless or in need of a man to rescue me. I don't need a protector, so you can just stop with the whole white-knight routine."

It's not a routine. He bit the retort back before it could burst out of his mouth. He wouldn't rise to the bait and let her know she was getting to him. "I can't up and leave you and the others now that I know what's going on."

She sighed. "See? Boy Scout."

Well, so what if he was a bit? "I'm only going to be around for another couple weeks. You're used to working alone, but things change. What's the harm in having some backup?" Okay, part of him felt compelled to help protect Chloe as she put herself in danger for the sake of others. He didn't like that she was at risk because of it, with a dangerous enemy hot on her tail and people within the U.S. government possibly targeting her too. She needed help, whether she wanted to admit it or not.

"There's gotta be more to it than that," she argued, staring at him as if he was a riddle she was trying to solve.

He felt the same about her. "What about you?" he countered. "Why risk your life to save women you've never met?"

"Because no one else is going to."

He arched an eyebrow. "That kinda makes you a Girl Scout then, doesn't it?"

She half-smiled. "Nope. Because I don't play by the rules."

God help him, she was damn near hypnotic with that insanely sexy blend of confidence and resolve. "And what's your plan? You gonna blow something up to save them?"

Her eyes gleamed. "Only if I get lucky."

He wasn't so tired that he missed the double entendre. He leaned back into the cushions, sleep suddenly the farthest thing from his mind. "What else are you trained in?"

Amusement crept into her eyes. "A lot of handy things."

"Such as?"

Another slight upward curve of her mouth. Her lower lip was fuller than the top. A soft pink, no lipstick. He had the sudden urge to suck on it, sink his teeth into it. Mark her a tiny bit, soothe it with his tongue, then delve inside to taste her. "If you stick around long enough, I'll show you."

Only an unconscious man would miss the innuendo, the female interest in her gaze. Entranced as he was, he wasn't dropping this line of questioning yet. "How did you meet Megan?"

"When we were first sent into the Program. My first roommate washed out and was transferred to somewhere else, so they paired me with Megan." She drew her bare legs up, tucking her feet beneath her. "I was the indoc class rebel. Based on our personality and psych profiles, they thought she'd be a stabilizing or calming influence on me."

"And was she?"

She grinned. "A little. Mostly I was a really bad influence on her."

"You know, somehow I can picture that."

She lifted a shoulder. "I'm pretty proud of my rep."

"I can see that too." They shared a half-smile. "And what about your family?"

All traces of humor vanished, her expression going eerily blank, as if a mask had covered her face. "What about yours?"

He'd hit a nerve, though he wasn't sure why. What was he missing? Maybe her relatives were assholes and she didn't like talking about them. "I've got an aunt, uncle and cousins back home in Connecticut."

"No parents?"

He shook his head. "Never knew my dad. My mom died when I was young." His stomach muscles tensed at the mention of her.

"What happened?"

His initial reaction was the same as hers had been—to shut down and redirect. But he'd learned sensitive things about her, and after knowing her only for a few hours, he sensed that revealing his past was probably the best way to start earning her trust. "She was murdered."

Chloe didn't gasp or react with horror the way most people did when they found out. Her expression was calm. Watchful. "By whom?"

"Her ex-boyfriend." He didn't think of that worthless asshole often anymore, but when he did, it still sent a wave of white-hot rage through him.

Her eyes narrowed. "Bastard. Happens way too often."

It did, and though he rarely talked about this with anyone, even Ty, he found himself opening up to her about it. "She always picked guys who treated her like shit. I watched her get the shit beaten out of her on an almost weekly basis for years, until the last one she broke up with snapped and strangled her." He'd come home from school to find them loading the body bag into the back of an ambulance. The shock and pain had been so overwhelming when the social worker had told him what happened, he'd fallen to his knees there in the dirt, an inhuman sound of agony and grief ripping from his throat.

"The old 'If I can't have her, no one can'." Chloe's voice was hard. Icy.

He shook off the awful memory, forcing his mind back to the present. "Yeah. He's in jail, but he's up for parole in a couple years." How fucked up was that? He didn't deserve to be breathing, let alone have the chance at parole.

"I'd have killed him."

Heath stilled. More than her words, the deadly calm tone told him she meant it. And he believed her. "Sometimes I wish I'd had the guts to." Even at that young age, he'd fantasized about emptying a magazine into that son of a bitch's belly and leaving him to bleed out on the ground.

"You're not wired that way."

Her insight into his personality surprised him. "No." He'd taken lives in combat, but that was different. He'd done what he had to, to ensure he and his brothers-in-arms and his patients made it home. But it hadn't been enough, because some of them hadn't, and that hurt would never go away.

"And that's why you became a PJ. You couldn't save her, but you can save others."

He didn't respond, momentarily at a loss for words. Jesus, he felt uncomfortably exposed with her so deep in his head, in a place he'd only acknowledged a few years ago.

"I get it. It's why I do what I do now. In spite of all the training, in spite of all the brainwashing and ability to compartmentalize...I still feel." The halting way she said it told him it wasn't an easy admission for her. "After completing a mission, it was never killing my targets that bothered me. It was the innocent victims I hadn't saved.

So now I'm doing something about it that I couldn't do before. It might be just a drop in the bucket in the grand scheme of things, but it matters to the ones I save."

He nodded, his heart thudding in his ears. "That's exactly right." Damn, she got him in a way few others ever had. They had way more in common than he ever would have thought.

She smiled slightly, and it was different from all the others so far. This one was softer. Real. One kindred soul recognizing and connecting with another.

Heath felt that same connection form deep in his gut. An undeniable physical and emotional pull toward the woman seated across from him.

Before he could gather his thoughts, Chloe lowered her feet to the floor, stood and started toward him.

He read the heat in her eyes, read the intent there, but he still didn't move. Didn't do anything but hold that hot, bold stare, his whole body tightening as he imagined pulling her down into his lap, tangling his fingers in that gorgeous hair and tasting those sexy lips.

She paused directly in front of him, waiting a moment before bending at the waist to place her hands on either side of him on the couch. It took an act of will not to reach for her, his hands flexing on his thighs.

Her face was inches from his, the fruity scent of shampoo and a hint of mint filling his nose as her avid gaze dipped to his mouth. Heath's heart pumped faster. He shouldn't be contemplating this, didn't want any more complications in his life, but damned if he could turn away.

She inched forward, drawing the moment out, until every single heartbeat drummed in his ears. Her lips brushed his. Once. Twice, then lingered.

An electric current arced between them. Heat punched through him, along with a shocking burst of possessiveness.

Her lips were so damn soft and pliant, the slow, sensual kiss the opposite of what he'd expected from her. He was dying to grab her. Hold her close and deepen the kiss so he could taste her. Claim her in some way, and she was teasing him with the promise of what he could have if he was willing to cross the invisible line they were flirting with.

His control snapped.

Coiling one arm around her hips, he plunged his free hand into that thick, soft hair and pulled her to him, absorbing her gasp with his mouth as she ended up straddling his lap. Keeping a firm grip on her hair, he locked her body to him, those tight, firm breasts pressed to his chest, her ass snuggled against the length of his erection trapped under his fly as he kissed her. A slow, thorough kiss meant to turn her inside out.

He nibbled and sucked at her lips, stroked his tongue across them before delving inside to touch hers. Mint. She tasted like mint and bold, tempting sin.

Her quiet hum of enjoyment shot more blood to his groin, and the way she eagerly kissed him back threatened to turn him inside out in return.

Bold as he'd expected, but twice as erotic. She kept it slow, matching his pace as she caressed his tongue with hers. She didn't fight his dominant grip, if anything seemed to enjoy it, her soft murmur making him so hard he ached.

Releasing his hold on her waist, Heath slid his hand up the length of her back, pulling her breasts harder into his chest.

Chloe lifted her head to look down at him, her pretty brown eyes a little dazed as she slid her tongue across her lower lip. "Hmm, maybe not such a Boy Scout after all," she murmured in approval, and leaned back in to brush a teasing kiss across his mouth. "I like it," she whispered against his lips.

Before he could pull her back down for more she pushed at his chest, eased off his lap and rose with a smile, her cheeks flushed and her nipples beaded tight against the fabric of her shirt. "Good night."

He smothered a protest. At least one of them had the sense to stop this before it got totally out of hand. She went to his head like a drug, muddled his thoughts and destroyed his control. "Night." He mentally groaned at the sight of that shapely ass walking away from him in those short, tight shorts, leaving him hard and aching.

One kiss. One kiss and she had him strung taut as a tripwire.

Heath ran a hand over his face. Yeah, there was no way he was leaving her undefended if he could help it, even if it might cost him in the end.

For the first time in his life he was operating without a mission plan, and he didn't even care.

Chapter Eleven

Guillaume woke up early Friday morning on the leather sofa in his office when his eldest daughter shook him lightly, sunlight shining through the window above him.

"Time to get up, Papa. You have to get ready for the funeral."

"Of course. Thank you, sweetheart."

The morning passed in a blur, and then he and his family drove to the church. When he stepped out of his car the blast of a pipe organ came from inside the gothic cathedral and the pallbearers were gathered behind the hearse carrying Dom's body.

Keeping himself numb so the grief wouldn't overwhelm him, he greeted the guests, accepted condolences and walked into the church. He stopped to dip his fingers in the holy water to make the sign of the cross.

The priest met him at the entrance to the nave. "Monsieur Dubois, my sincere condolences on the loss of your brother."

Loss? It was more than a fucking *loss*. Dom had been

bound, possibly tortured, and then murdered in his own home.

Keeping his civilized veneer firmly in place, Guillaume buried the rage down deep and forced a polite smile. "Thank you, Father. It's been a trying time for us."

The priest nodded. "May God comfort you and your family at this difficult time."

He escorted his wife and daughters to the front pew. The inspector was seated behind him, offered his condolences again. All Guillaume could think about were his words last night.

Be patient.

The funeral mass seemed to take forever, and the trip to the cemetery where he endured the terrible ordeal of watching his brother being lowered into the ground almost shattered his control.

His youngest daughter reached up to take his hand as they walked toward the car. "Are you all right, Papa?"

Looking down into her innocent, beautiful little face, Guillaume's grief lessened a fraction. He smiled at her. "Yes, my angel. Just sad."

Sophie nodded, her blue eyes somber. "I am too. I miss Uncle Dom."

"Me too," he said, squeezing her as tears burned the backs of his eyes. Dom wouldn't want him to cry. He would want him to find and punish the killer.

He glanced to his right at his wife. She gave him a sad smile and reached for his hand. Guillaume grasped it, shot a wink at their other daughter, who was holding Marguerite's other hand. "I'm the luckiest man in all of France to be blessed with such precious jewels."

His wife and girls were the most valued things in the world to him. He would protect them at all cost—something he'd been unable to do for the brother he'd just laid to rest.

The inspector stopped him on the way to the car and

pulled him aside. "Did you think about what I said last night? The offer still stands."

Be patient. "Thank you. I'll be in touch." He ushered his family into the car and drove them home, Jean-Pierre following them. The reception was an agony all its own, people reminiscing about Dom, talking about how much they'd loved him.

Lies. They hadn't known Dom. Only he had. Most of these assholes were only here to enjoy the food and alcohol Guillaume was paying for.

Finally the guests began to leave, trickling out in maddeningly small groups. The inspector was one of the last. Guillaume was glad to see him go.

When everyone was gone, he locked the front door, bowed his head, and heaved a tired sigh.

"Anything I can do?" Jean-Pierre asked behind him.

Guillaume nodded. "I have something I need to take care of. I need you to follow me there."

"Of course."

He caught up with the inspector's vehicle several kilometers down a quiet, country road, and flashed his lights. The inspector slowed and pulled to the side of the road, rolling down a window as Guillaume approached, keeping his gloved hands in his pockets.

"Did I forget something?" the inspector asked with a smile. "You could have just called me. You didn't have to come all the way out here."

"Yes I did." He pulled out the silenced pistol and put a bullet through the man's forehead.

The inspector's body slumped over the steering wheel.

Guillaume bent to stare into the blank eyes. "That's me being patient," he snarled, and walked back to his car.

****

Chloe checked her messages on the drive into the closest

town on Friday night. After being cooped up in the cottage for so long to avoid detection and no new threats materializing, she'd deemed it safe to at least go out to dinner as a group.

Mostly she'd just needed to get out of there before her head exploded. Being around Heath for that long after that insanely hot make-out session had been hell on her self-control. If Megan and Ty hadn't been around, she'd have jumped him long ago.

There was a message from Fleur, under the bogus names and email addresses they'd set up to communicate with each other.

Package sent off safely. Should arrive at destination tomorrow.

Kaya. Fleur had taken her for medical care, then put her into transitional housing run by a private non-profit group in Paris that helped female trafficking victims. Kaya would be given the choice of staying in France or returning to her home country. Chloe wished her the best.

"Good news?" Heath asked from behind the wheel.

She finished typing her response, a smile on her face. "Very good. The woman I got out in Paris is okay and on her way to starting a new life."

"I didn't know you rescued a woman."

She set her phone down to look at him, that shock of awareness hitting her all over again. It was impossible not to think about the way he'd held her, the incredible rush of arousal he'd elicited when he'd seized control and kissed her, and having him so close only made her want more. He came across as aloof and gruff, but there had been nothing aloof about that. Now she wanted more, to see just how deep that hot alpha streak went.

She hadn't slept much last night, thinking about Heath and Megan and Ty's offer to help her with the Marseille op and targeting Dubois. She had to admit she could use the help, and who better to have her back than Megan and two Spec Ops trained men sworn to her cause?

After weighing the pros and cons of allowing others into her private operation, she'd finally made the decision to let the others assist her. She'd spent the morning and most of the afternoon with Megan, reconnecting and talking about the upcoming shipment Chloe was going to intercept while Ty and Heath had hung out. After that the four of them had met for a couple of hours going over logistics, and Chloe had consented to include the rest of the team back in the UK: Amber, Kiyomi and Trinity. Two other former Valkyries named Georgia and Briar were involved too, but stateside working on gathering intel.

It wasn't easy for Chloe to bring outsiders into her personal life, but Megan had been like a sister to her while they'd roomed together. She trusted her old friend, so if Megan vouched for the other women, that was good enough for Chloe. And if Megan thought Ty and Heath were up for this, then they were. They'd both been SOF, with all the training, skill set and security clearances that came with the territory. They were solid operators. It was just strange for Chloe to be working with them on an op.

"It was only the one woman," she answered. "Dominic had pilfered her from his most recent shipment of women from North Africa two months ago. He kept her locked up like a slave in his bedroom for his personal use."

The dark face Heath pulled made her like him even more. "What a fucking piece of shit."

"Yes, he was. I'm glad he's dead."

"And his brother? Is he the same?"

"No. Guillaume's almost worse, because he's slicker. A monster hiding behind a polished, civilized mask. Most of his businesses are legitimate in the banking and real estate worlds, and he hides everything else. The most disturbing thing to me is that he has young daughters. All accounts say he reveres them and his wife, and yet he's fine with buying and selling women on the black market if they turn enough of a profit to make it worth his while."

"After the things I've seen overseas, it doesn't surprise me," he said in disgust.

"Me neither." Nothing would surprise her anymore.

Heath drove toward the lake, following Ty and Megan's rental car to the restaurant a few kilometers out of town. "This is it," he said as he parked out front of the Bavarian-style white plaster building decorated with brown wood. The wooden railings and shutters had little hearts cut out of them. Flower boxes bursting with fall colors of yellow, orange and crimson lined each window, giving the place a warm, charming feel.

"Great, I'm starving. Haven't had a good schnitzel in forever." She hopped out of the car and waited for Megan on the curb. Inside, the restaurant was dimly lit and full. She'd reserved a table for them earlier under a fake surname.

The hostess showed them to a table for four in the back. Chloe rounded the edge of it, intending to take one of the seats against the wall with Megan, but stopped when Heath went to do the same on the other side. After an awkward pause he grinned, pulled out the chair and offered it to her.

"Thanks," she murmured as she dropped into it. She always felt better with her back to the wall. They'd been trained to always be on the lookout for danger wherever they went. It was second nature for her to choose a position with some protection and the best sightlines wherever she went, but she supposed it was for Heath and Ty too.

She ordered a beer, and they spent the time waiting for their meals telling stories—Megan and her about funny things they'd encountered in training, nothing sensitive that would give them away if anyone overheard. Ty and Heath told funny stories about some of the jobs they'd worked together as security contractors.

Dinner was a golden brown, pan-fried chicken schnitzel smothered in hollandaise and topped with asparagus and crabmeat, served with roasted potatoes, veggies and braised red cabbage. Chloe wasted no time in digging in.

"This is the bomb," she moaned around a mouthful of schnitzel a minute later. Crispy on the outside and tender on the inside. Perfection.

"And you should know," Megan said with a laugh.

Chloe grinned around her mouthful. She hadn't enjoyed herself so much in months, since that time she'd coaxed Fleur out of her comfort zone and taken her to a racy male strip joint in Paris one night for the hell of it. She'd had to get Fleur drunk to make it happen, and the results had been highly entertaining—not to mention shocking for the shy social worker.

"We working more tonight?" Ty said as he scooped up a bite of bratwurst.

"No," Chloe said, looking at Heath. "There's nothing more we can do today." Besides, she wanted to let her hair down a little now that she was relatively safe and had backup if she needed it. It was rare that she got to be herself around anyone, and never with a man. She wanted to spend some time alone with Heath and see how things went, find out just how hot the spark between them could burn.

She had the feeling they would be hot as white phosphorus together.

They each had another drink, then Chloe ordered herself a slice of black forest cake, because it was criminal not to. Afterward, Heath insisted on paying the whole bill and refused to listen to anyone's arguments.

"Let me get it," Ty insisted. "I owe you big time for everything."

"Nah, forget it."

"You can't afford to buy dinner, I know what you get paid," Ty joked.

"You're on the hook next time then," Heath said, and pulled out his wallet.

Chloe was about to stop him, not wanting anyone to be able to trace them through his credit card transaction, but he pulled out some Swiss francs instead. Then she felt dumb for thinking it. Of course he would know to pay in cash and not by credit.

After paying he waited for her by the table as she stood, then followed the others to the front door. She liked the feeling of having him at her back, and his nearness heightened her awareness of him. "Feel like going for a walk?" she asked him.

He gave her a sidelong glance that heated her insides, the dark stubble on his face making him twice as rugged and contrasting with the incredible blue of his eyes. "Sure."

It was cool outside but mostly clear, and their jackets would be warm enough. "Let's head along the lake."

They said goodbye to the others, then crossed the street and started up the walkway along the lake. She breathed in the clean, fall air spiced with the scent of damp leaves. The mix of evergreens in the surrounding hills provided a stunning backdrop to the vivid bursts of yellow, orange and red turning leaves lit up by the ornamental lamp standards they passed.

"It's beautiful," she said, staring out over the lake and the thick forest on the other side that rose into the mountains.

"Yeah, and the view's not bad either."

Chloe couldn't help but smile. The line should have been cheesy, but from him, it wasn't. "Thank you. You're not hard on the eyes either, by the way." It felt good to flirt, and not have to hide who and what she was. She felt safe here for now, especially with him beside her. The novelty of it added to the magic between them.

One side of his mouth lifted as he gazed down the pathway before them. It was practically deserted, only a few people out walking their dogs. "Did you hear how Megan and Ty met?"

"Yeah, he was her temp SERE school instructor. She broke out of her holding cell at the camp and found Ty's campsite out in the woods a few miles away. Then he turned her back in."

"Crazy story."

"I know, right? I'm more scorched earth with stuff like that. I'd have kicked his ass if I ever crossed paths with him again, but Megan's more forgiving than me. And you know what? I think he suits her."

"I wasn't sure what to think at first, but now that I've spent some time with them and watched them together, I agree."

"I'm happy for her. But if your friend breaks her heart, he's gonna wind up on my hit list."

Heath chuckled, the low sound wrapping around her. "Ty won't hurt her. He's a good guy and he adores her."

"I hope it works out for them."

He shot her a curious look. "You've got your doubts already?"

"Well, yeah. Long-term, committed relationships aren't part of our skill set, if you catch my drift. But I really want it to work for them. Megan's awesome and she deserves to be happy." Maybe Megan could "break the cycle", so to speak, and have something resembling a normal life.

"I know Ty. I'm willing to bet they beat the odds."

Chloe cast him a shocked look. "Oh my God, you're a Boy Scout *and* a romantic?"

A wry smile tugged at his mouth, making her want to do some tugging of her own on it—with her teeth. "No one's ever accused me of being a romantic before. And I'm pretty sure you said yourself the other night that I might not be such a Boy Scout after all." He raised a dark eyebrow.

Oh, damn, he was sexy, for a Boy Scout. Or maybe because of it. And that little prelude he'd given her on the couch the other night suggested he probably liked control in bed. Arousal slid through her at the thought. She'd had to be in control her entire life. If she ever got into bed with him, she wanted to be able to let go completely just once, to see what it was like. Based on what she'd seen so far, she'd bet he could light her up like an incendiary cord.

"So I'm curious. Why explosives?" he asked as they continued walking. They'd passed the shops and restaurants now. From here the footpath continued along the edge of the lake, past homes and parkland.

"Because they're cool."

He huffed out a laugh. "To some people, I guess they are. Why to you?"

She thought about it a moment. "I dunno, there's something thrilling about controlling the chaos of it. Of knowing what materials to combine, and in what amounts, to get the exact result you want. Every target's its own challenge, whether it's bringing down a building, or blowing up a car...or something more precise. It's part science, part art."

"Did you pick that specialty?"

"No. I wanted to be a sniper, but my personality wasn't right for it, and there's no way I could've stayed still long enough anyhow. I'm a wild child, always will be, and my instructors saw that early on. Explosives and demolition aren't everyone's jam, but it suits me," she finished with a shrug.

"I've only ever been on the other side of them and seen the end result. IEDs, mostly. I was lucky I never got hit directly. The worst I had it was getting caught in the blast wave a couple times. Rung my bell and then some. A lot of other guys weren't as fortunate."

There was something underlying his words, something that made her think he'd lost people close to him that way, but she wasn't sure and wasn't going to ask. "It's been an ugly war. I don't use IEDs often, by the way. Too uncertain, too much risk of collateral damage. I prefer much more precise methods, to make sure no one gets hit but my target."

He looked over at her, his expression genuinely curious. "What did you use the other night?"

"Rigged his furnace with a charge that made it look like a gas leak. Of course they'll know it wasn't an accident, because the body was bound."

Heath shook his head. "I can't decide if I'm a little scared, or impressed."

"You can be both, I won't judge."

His chuckle warmed her from the inside out. "Okay, then I'm both."

They lapsed into quiet after that, and it was just as nice as the conversation had been. Most people felt the need to fill silence with talk. Heath knew who he was, and was totally comfortable with himself.

But she hadn't been kidding when she'd told him she was a wild child. Her entire life she'd had to work at suppressing that chaotic side of herself, although right now, she didn't have to.

She decided to shake him up a little and see how he handled it.

They walked for another fifteen minutes or so, until they came to a spot where the footpath split, one side continuing down the lake and the other heading back in a loop to town. She stayed on the lakeside path, and chose her spot a few hundred yards up. This area was deserted, and no longer lit by streetlamps. A quarter moon gave just enough light for her to make out his features as he walked beside her.

"Let's stop here," she said, leaving the path and heading for the edge of the lake. She crossed the grass and stopped on the pebbles, mere feet from water, taking in the way the moonlight shimmered on the surface. "Wonder how cold it is?"

"Cold."

"Hmm." She took off her jacket, toed off her boots.

"What are you doing?" he asked, shock in his voice.

"Seeing how cold it is."

"What? It's freezing."

Ignoring him, she reached for the hem of her sweater and pulled it over her head, then undid her jeans and shimmied out of them, immediately followed by her underwear.

"Holy shit…" He stepped toward her, glancing around them, as if afraid someone might see her.

Not worried in the least, she wound her hair into a knot at the top of her head, braced herself, then took the plunge. She yelped as she ran into the water up to her hips, then bent at the waist and dove the rest of the way in, keeping her head above water.

Laughing, she spun around to face him. "Yep, it's cold." She cocked her head. He was still standing at the edge, gaping at her like she'd lost her mind. "You coming in, or what?"

"No."

Chloe grinned and arched a taunting eyebrow. "What's the matter, you shy? You don't have anything I haven't seen before."

She'd been counting on his ego kicking in, and he didn't disappoint her.

With a grudging half-smile, he pulled off his boots and jacket, then yanked off his shirt, giving her a lovely view of his powerfully built chest, arms, and shoulders in the pale moonlight. Then it got even better when he stripped out of his jeans, leaving him in a pair of snug, black boxer briefs that hugged his muscled thighs.

He ran into the water, dove and a second later, surfaced right in front of her. "Jesus Christ, it's freezing," he gasped out, giving her an accusing glare.

Grinning, she wound her legs around his waist and slid her arms around his neck. "Don't worry, I'll help warm you up." She kissed him, swore she started to melt when he reached one hand around to cup her ass, the other holding the back of her head, a low sound rumbling up from his chest.

Most guys would have plundered now, taking as much as they could get. Heath didn't. Instead he seemed determined to drive her out of her skin with need. He took his time, kissing her like a man bent on giving her pleasure, stroking, caressing, not rushing her despite the cold temperature of the water.

A minute in, he lifted his head to gaze down at her, a sardonic smile playing around the edges of his mouth. "I think I'm numb from the neck down. You?"

"Uh oh, shrinkage?" She reached a hand between them to cup his groin, making him choke out a laugh. "Hmm, if this is you without any circulation, I'm looking forward to seeing you naked when you're warmer."

With that she darted away and dashed out of the water. His splashing footsteps gave her a few seconds' warning as she raced up the slight bank toward her clothes, then she was spun around and pinned to a tall, hard male body. This time his mouth came down on hers with single-minded intent. A man staking a claim.

Chloe sighed and allowed her body to relax into his, those strong, solid arms banded around her, chasing away the chill of the cold air on her wet skin.

On a low groan, Heath broke the kiss and gathered her to him, tucking her head into the curve of his shoulder. "If I wasn't so worried about your core temp and public indecency charges, I'd get on my knees right here and warm you up from the inside with my tongue," he muttered against the side of her neck.

Chloe shivered, and not just from the cold, totally on board with that plan. In spite of her chilled skin, her insides were raging hot. Arousal raced through her, settling in a relentless ache between her legs as she imagined his lips and tongue stroking her aroused flesh.

The shrill ringing of her phone pierced the quiet. Damn. Only three people had the number, so it must be important. And he was right, they needed to get dressed and warmed up. "Ah, hell. I'd better check that."

She pulled away and fished her phone from her jacket pocket as she began getting dressed. "It's Megan. Probably wondering what happened to us."

She hurriedly tugged on her clothes—no easy feat trying to drag denim up wet legs. When she turned to Heath, he was already dressed and reaching for his jacket. But she still remembered exactly what he'd looked like with all those muscles covered in brushstrokes of moonlight.

"Hey," she said when Megan answered, rubbing her free hand over her arm. "You calling to make sure we're both still alive?"

"No, I feel pretty confident you two could take care of yourselves if any assassins followed you from the quaint Bavarian restaurant," Megan answered with a laugh. "You coming back to the house soon?"

"Maybe." She looked back at Heath, who stood watching her, wishing they could have more time alone together. This had been fun and magical. She'd never forget it. "Why?"

"I've been in contact with Kiyomi back at base. Thanks to a few leads we've been following, I think we might have a possible location on your suspected Valkyrie. Her name's Eden. Can you come have a look at what we've got?"

Snapping back into operator mode, Chloe motioned

for Heath to follow her and started for the path. "We'll be there in twenty minutes."

Chapter Twelve

Back at Laidlaw Hall, Kiyomi stood next to Amber in an upstairs bedroom recently converted into an office. A bank of computers was spread out before them on the wide desk as they talked to Trinity via a highly secure video chat on the laptop in the center.

"Is Megan bringing Chloe back here?" Amber asked.

"Not yet," Trinity answered, only her head and shoulders visible. The former Valkyrie was back in the U.S. right now, working with "retired" NSA legend Alex Rycroft and the small team he'd put together there to help find the other Valkyries. Trinity was the eldest, and Kiyomi and the others looked up to her as the unofficial team leader. "Chloe won't come on board until she's rescued a shipment of women being trafficked out of North Africa into France."

Kiyomi's stomach clamped tight at the mention of the human trafficking, but Trinity continued.

"Megan's feeding us details as she can. She and Ty are staying with Chloe to assist, along with Ty's friend."

"The former PJ," Amber said.

"Yes. We've vetted him thoroughly. Everything checks out, so he's on board with us for the time being. Now," Trinity continued, her deep blue eyes focusing on Kiyomi through the screen. "You think Chloe may have had contact with one of our kind over the past few months?"

Kiyomi stepped a little to the right so the webcam could get a better angle on her, aware of the way Amber watched her with interest. "Yes. I think it's Eden." She was almost positive it was.

Trinity's expression never changed. "Why do you think that?"

"Gut feeling. The timeline and everything Chloe said lines up with it being Eden."

"Because?"

"Last I heard a few years ago, Eden was doing jobs in North Africa. Her appearance and fluent French would make her blend in perfectly there. If that's where Dubois is shipping these women from, then it's even more likely Eden knows about it and got involved with what Chloe's been doing."

"How do you know her?" Trinity asked.

"We were trained together in certain areas. CQB, self-defense, seduction techniques. The program cadre had already decided we were the right candidates for going after targets up close and personal. Soon after we finished that second training phase, she was moved into toxins, and I was moved into…more intimate things."

Trinity nodded, her deep blue eyes serious and full of understanding. "Ah."

Of all these new Valkyrie sisters they were gathering, Kiyomi had the closest bond with Trinity. As "intimate assassins" they were the rarest kind, and arguably the deadliest. None of the others knew the kind of life she'd led, except Trinity.

They also had the highest mortality rate. Most of their

kind didn't live more than a handful of years after graduating and being sent out into the field. It was a miracle that she and Trinity had both survived.

"You look exhausted," Trinity said to her gently. "Still not sleeping much?"

No one knew they talked privately a few times a week about things in Kiyomi's past, or that she was remotely seeing a therapist Trinity had hooked her up with. Her captivity had shifted something inside her. Rattled loose all the things she'd kept locked down before, and now she couldn't put them back. "Better than I was." This place and the people in it were allowing her to heal. She was finally surrounded by people who understood her, who cared about and wanted to support her. Especially Trinity.

"But not enough."

She opened her mouth to deny it, then decided there was no point. "No. Not enough." The bruises, lacerations and fractured ribs she'd suffered in Syria had healed within the first month she'd been here. Too bad her mind and soul hadn't recovered nearly as well.

Sleep was a double-edged sword now. On the one hand she craved it. On the other, she feared it. Because it didn't bring the welcome rest and oblivion it should have. It brought pain and terror.

Whenever she slipped into a deep enough sleep to allow for dreams, they turned into nightmares. Every. Single. Time. No matter how hard she pushed herself to exhaustion in the hopes that she wouldn't dream, it still happened. Every time, *he* appeared. Those dark, evil eyes filled with a fanatical gleam as he leaned over her helpless form.

You're mine now. I own you.

Fayez Rahman, the man who had done his best to break her and almost succeeded. It shamed her now to remember that there had been moments where she'd prayed for death to escape the suffering and degradation. His smile was even colder than his gaze, his oily chuckle enough to make her skin crawl.

She drew a slow breath, a slight twinge shooting through her ribs as she pushed the memories away. She had escaped that prison cell in Damascus because of Amber and Jesse. Against all odds, she had survived, though that experience had changed her forever. "I'm okay."

"You're going to be," Trinity said. "And we're glad to have you on this team."

That made her smile. She'd been too young to remember her mom or dad when she'd been put into foster care and then the Valkyrie Program as a child. She'd never had family, until now. "Are you coming back across the pond anytime soon?" Kiyomi liked Amber, but she had an incredibly special bond with Trinity.

"As soon as Megan brings Chloe there."

That couldn't happen soon enough for Kiyomi's liking. A low-grade hum started up, deep in her belly. The anxiety she now battled constantly and fought to hide. It embarrassed her. "See you soon, then."

"Absolutely. I'll update you both if I hear anything more on my end. Take care of each other."

"We will," Amber said, and ended the video chat. As soon as the laptop screen went dark, Amber turned to her.

Kiyomi stepped back and started to turn for the door, but Amber stopped her with a hand on her arm. Bracing herself, Kiyomi focused on her.

Clear, green eyes studied her for a long moment. "Remember what I promised you?"

"Yes." That Amber would help her find and end Rahman one day.

Amber nodded at her precious laptop. "Lady Ada and I are keeping our eyes and ears open for a lot of things, him included. I know where he is. When you're ready, come talk to me. We'll get him."

The words might have made a normal person laugh it

off or recoil in horror. But they weren't normal and never would be. And Amber's willingness to help her with this meant so much that Kiyomi had to swallow hard to push the lump from her suddenly tight throat. "Thank you."

Amber nodded once. "Anytime. And maybe the reminder will help you sleep better."

"Maybe." It surely couldn't get worse.

She left the room and started down the hall to her bedroom at the end. The aloof and mysterious master of the house had for some reason given her the most beautiful bedroom in the manor. The Blue Room was done in shades of blue and cream, a soft, soothing palate perfectly suited to the luxurious furnishings and a view that overlooked the formal garden and back lawn.

A few steps down the hall, she stopped. As much as she loved the privacy and tranquility her room offered her, she was all tangled up inside and the recent heavy rain had kept her cooped up in the house for the past two days. She needed air. Space.

Peace.

She craved it the way addicts craved their drug of choice. Solitude was something she needed to survive. Living here with people constantly coming and going was completely foreign after so many years spent alone, with only her handler to turn to.

The fresh, bright scent of lemon-oil greeted her as she descended the main staircase to the ground floor. This manor house was truly spectacular, but it wasn't her home and she'd kept to just her room and the shared living spaces out of respect for the owner's diminished privacy. Besides, the gym, gardens and sprawling grounds provided more than enough room for her to be on her own when she needed to be.

She strode straight for the gym, that horrible, out-of-control agitation growing with each step. She needed to release it, or explode.

A pair of boxing gloves sat on a bench inside the glass door. Unable to be bothered with worrying about her hands, she pulled her sweater over her head and stalked to the heavy bag hanging from a hook in the ceiling, and attacked it.

Punches. Kicks. Combos. Throwing her whole body weight behind each blow, using the painful impact of her knuckles to center herself. She vented her rage at the helplessness she'd been forced to endure. The degradation and shame she couldn't seem to escape or shut off. Not just from her captivity, although that's what had broken the dam inside her. *Everything* she'd been forced to do in the name of duty.

She didn't last long. Maybe twenty minutes at most.

Gasping, trembling with fatigue that told her she was far from recovered yet, she bent over, hands on her knees while she got her wind back and dripped sweat onto the floor. But the frantic, corrosive anxiety was quiet now. Vanquished by the violent exertion.

Outside the gym door, she stepped onto the aged flagstones that led to the crushed gravel path. It split into three at the door, going left and right along the house, the third straight ahead through the formal garden. She breathed in the crisp air, taking in the view as she cooled down. Fall had changed the landscape in the past few weeks, bringing the golden and amber tones to the trees that matched the honey-colored limestone of the house.

The roses were still in bloom as she walked over to the small gazebo set into the corner of the walled garden. A stone fountain mounted on the wall beside it sprayed water through a lion's open mouth, the quiet, rhythmic splash soothing as she sat on the garden bench overlooking the fish pond.

Breathe, she told herself, shutting down the residual chaotic thoughts that hammered against the mental barrier she put up. *Just breathe.*

Seconds later her eyes opened at the quiet thud of a cane and the trot of paws on the gravel path to her left.

Marcus paused beside his dog on the pathway when he saw her, his dark gaze meeting hers. An attractive man even with his facial scars. Somewhere in his forties, if she had to guess, with dark brown hair and a strong build that spoke of hard work. "Sorry to disturb," he said in his distinct Yorkshire accent, and started to turn around, aided by his cane.

"No, it's fine," she answered. It was his house, after all.

He stopped, and she continued, finding she was eager to talk with him. "Were you in town?" The old Cotswold market town of Stow-on-the-Wold was only a couple miles away up the hill. She hadn't been there yet, but wanted to go soon to explore it. Once she was up to being around strangers again.

"No, Karas and I were just out checking the fence in the far northwest pasture." He reached his free hand down to rub the piebald Anatolian Shepherd's head. The dog was like his shadow, following him everywhere. "We'll leave you in peace." He started to turn away again.

"No, please," she blurted, not wanting him to leave. He made her feel...safe. He'd watched over her from afar while she'd recovered, never said much. She wanted to thank him for all he'd done for her.

He paused to look back at her, his expression uncertain.

"I'd...like the company." He had a quiet, calm but watchful manner, and she was curious about him. At first, she'd been uncomfortable staying here in a house full of strangers without paying anything in return. Over the past few weeks, however, she'd begun to like it, and the strangers had become trusted friends. But as nice as the others here had been to her, she was lonely. She'd been lonely for most of her life, and that was doubly ironic given what sort of Valkyrie she was.

"You're sure?" His deep brown gaze measured hers.

"Yes."

He walked toward her with his uneven gait, his bearing proud and his loyal rescue dog at his side.

Though she saw him almost every day, Marcus Laidlaw remained an enigma. She'd been living in his house for weeks and yet barely knew anything about him, except that he'd served in the Royal Marines and then the SAS for most of his military career.

During a combat mission in Syria a few years ago he'd been seriously wounded and taken prisoner. Megan had helped him escape, but he still bore the marks of his ordeal. His left leg caused him a lot of pain, and the scars on the left side of his face and neck—and probably lower—were consistent with burns from an explosion. But whatever physical agony he'd endured, Kiyomi bet his mental wounds were even worse.

Invisible wounds were always the most painful.

Keeping the full length of the bench between them, he lowered himself onto the far end and stretched his left leg out while Karas sat facing them and accepted a pat on the head from Kiyomi. She was a friendly enough dog, but mostly aloof except with Marcus.

"Came out for a breath of air?" he asked, his clean, masculine scent reaching her. Dark and woodsy, like evergreens. It suited him and smelled fantastic.

She was glad he hadn't witnessed her frantic kickboxing session. "Yes. Feels good to be outside."

The scars near his left eye wrinkled with the hint of a smile. "Bit crowded in there, isn't it?" he said, nodding at the manor house.

She couldn't help but smile at his dry tone. "Yes. And I'll admit to feeling like a fifth wheel sometimes." All the Valkyries staying here were paired up with their boyfriends or husbands. While Kiyomi was happy that her new friends had found happiness, it also made her feel more alone and more of an outsider.

Seeing what they had only served as a reminder that she never would. Women like her didn't fall in love or find love in return, and she'd accepted that long ago. Men wanted her. Some had become obsessed with her. But none of them had ever loved her and no one ever would. She was…damaged by all the things she'd done. Tainted by what Rahman had done.

Then what about Trinity?

She couldn't ignore the whisper at the back of her mind. Trinity had been the same as Kiyomi was, gotten out, and now wore a beautiful engagement ring. Against all odds, she'd survived all her ops and had found a man who loved her enough to pledge himself to her for the rest of their lives. How had she done it? How had she overcome everything that had been programmed into her, and done the impossible?

"Aye, I know what you mean," Marcus said, interrupting her thoughts. He'd left as much space as possible between them, making sure he didn't invade her personal space.

An unwelcome twinge of embarrassment hit her. Marcus had been here to welcome them the day that Amber and Jesse had brought her to the manor. Kiyomi had been delirious from a combination of pain, fever and medication when they'd taken her upstairs and settled her onto the soft bed in the Blue Room.

But Marcus had seen what had been done to her, and had no doubt filled in enough details on his own to figure out the rest. He'd been standing at her bedside as Megan and Amber had checked the lacerations on her back, and while Kiyomi had hated an outsider seeing her that way, she couldn't deny that something about Marcus soothed her deep inside.

As an intimate operative, her observational skills were

honed to a razor's edge. She'd spent a lot of time watching Marcus these past weeks, trying to get a read on him. He was a creature of habit, and liked routine. He was also a loner, preferring to spend most of his time alone except for the company of his dog, Karas.

Intuitively she felt safe around him. Partly because he was quiet and respectful, and partly because he was friends with Megan, but it was more than that. He wasn't a creep who wanted anything from her or looked at her like an object. That was a welcome change.

"So, Megan says there's another development in the Valkyrie hunt," he mused, staring out at the garden and the tidy stable beyond the rear lawn.

"Yes. An acquaintance of mine, possibly."

He turned his head toward her, those dark, fathomless eyes locking with hers. "Is it, now. Is that a good thing?"

"If it's true, yes. Now we just have to find her to verify it."

"Ah. And from what I know about Valkyries, that won't be easy."

"No. But nothing worthwhile ever is."

His eyes warmed, the hint of a smile tugging at his lips. "Aye." He went back to staring out at the garden, the quiet settling around them.

"I wanted to thank you."

That dark gaze cut back to hers. "For what?"

"For opening up your home to all of us. I know that must be hard for you. And for…watching over me."

Something moved in his eyes, then he looked away. "It's been my pleasure."

He was uncomfortable with her gratitude. Kiyomi found that interesting. And they'd talked more in this past minute than they had her entire stay. "Can I ask you something?" she said after another minute. They had things in common that the others didn't. Dark, terrible things. He'd gone through his own version of hell. They'd both been captured and taken prisoner by the enemy.

He gave her his full attention. "Aye, of course."

"Do you sleep through the night since coming back from Syria?"

His face froze at her words.

Kiyomi flushed, wishing she'd never opened her mouth. He was quiet and private. She'd been trained to be polished, smooth as silk with her words, yet with him she just blurted out her innermost thoughts like an idiot. "I'm sorry, I shouldn't have—"

"No, it's all right." He shifted, fastened his eyes on the garden once more. "I don't sleep through often." After a pause, he glanced at her. "Nightmares?"

"Yes."

He nodded, his eyes full of understanding and a pain she wished she could wipe away. "They'll ease eventually. And dealing with everything in your head will get easier with time, I promise."

She half-smiled. "Okay. I'm going to hold you to that."

The back door of the house opened, drawing their attention. Amber stepped outside, the late afternoon sun glinting gold in her chocolate-brown hair. "There you are." She headed toward them at a brisk pace, a woman on a mission.

"Everything okay?" Kiyomi asked, tensing inside.

"Yeah, I just wanted to update you." She looked between them, then settled her gaze on Kiyomi. "I found something you should know."

"What?"

"I found out who Dubois is buying the shipment of women from." Her cold expression said it for her.

Rahman.

Kiyomi's stomach grabbed as she thought of the women. That would have been her fate if not for Amber and Jesse. Rahman had made a serious mistake in not killing her when he'd had the chance.

One day she would kill him for what he'd done.

No matter what it took, no matter the cost, her last act on this earth would be to kill him.

Chapter Thirteen

"**D**amn, I just don't feel right about this," Chloe said to the others around the safehouse kitchen table the next morning.

So much had happened since she'd left Paris. She suddenly had a team to help her, and she was trying to wrap her mind around that. Megan's sister Amber was monitoring various channels back in the UK, keeping them up to date on the latest dealings between Guillaume Dubois and the broker responsible for shipping the women to Marseille.

Unfortunately, their best plan for this op was now dead. A former Valkyrie working with Rycroft named Georgia was supposed to have flown in last night from the States to act as the rep, but intel at the last moment indicated her information might have fallen into Dubois' network's hands.

If true and they identified her, they would kill her on sight. The team had considered bringing Interpol in on this, but Rycroft no longer had contacts there he trusted implicitly. There was talk about a potential mole in the agency, possibly linked to Dubois.

That left them with only this backup plan of using Fleur, who had never been a real consideration before now.

Still, Chloe hedged. "I feel like I'm dangling a lamb out there when we know there are hungry wolves around."

"We're out of time and options. There's no other way to get someone on board that ship when it comes in," Megan pointed out.

Chloe made a frustrated sound and chewed her gum faster. The two of them had been over this for more than an hour now, going back and forth over various plans, and at this point Chloe had to agree that this one had the highest chance of working. Ty and Heath had joined them a little while ago to finalize everything before they drove to Marseille for her meeting with Fleur this afternoon. "I wish I could see another way."

Megan reached across the table to put a hand on hers, her hazel eyes sincere. "I know she's your friend. But with everyone else's cover blown, Dominic Dubois dead and various enemies out there on the hunt for us, she's our only shot if we're going to have someone there to meet the boat as usual."

Chloe expelled a breath, hating that she was right. Posing as the rep, "Gabrielle" had been involved with the business dealings between the broker and Dominic Dubois. That was all over now. The latest chatter confirmed the broker was still sending the women to Marseille tomorrow afternoon, but the only way to verify that was to have someone board that boat and find out.

Problem was, this was way out of Fleur's depth. "She's a civilian. She's got absolutely no training if something goes wrong, apart from some knife skills I showed her once." The op seemed low risk and simple enough on the surface, but Chloe had been trained to be ready for anything. The people they were dealing with were unpredictable, and dangerous.

"All she needs to do is get on board, verify the women are there, finish the transaction as usual, then disembark and leave the rest to us," Megan said.

Up until two nights ago, that had been Gabrielle's responsibility. Guillaume Dubois had immediately cut ties with anyone associated with Gabrielle once his brother was killed. Fleur had an existing cover as an accountant within Dominic's network, but it was flimsy at best. "Can Amber even build her a solid cover in such a short amount of time?"

"Yes. You'd be amazed at what my sister can do."

The pride and certainty in Megan's voice eased Chloe's worry a little, but not enough. She made a frustrated sound in the back of her throat. "Maybe with a good enough disguise I could do it myself."

"It's too risky," Ty said beside Megan, dismissing it. "Dubois has alerted too many people about you by now, and if he found you the other night it means he's got access to intelligence circles and facial recognition."

"I know," she said on a groan. "But even with the four of us posted nearby as backup, it doesn't feel good enough. I need to make sure Fleur's covered." Given Chloe's profession, making friends was next to impossible. For the past year, Fleur had been her only true friend.

"What did she say when you talked to her about it this morning?" Heath asked from the other end of the small rectangular table.

"I didn't want to tell her much over the phone, I just set up the meeting for this afternoon. But when I do tell her everything, she'll say yes, no matter what, because saving those women is her top priority." While Chloe admired her friend's determination and devotion to the cause, she wanted Fleur to understand exactly what she might face if her friend agreed to do this.

"Then we'll keep her safe," Heath said.

He'd said it to make her feel better, but he knew the potential dangers as well as she did. If something went sideways, none of them would be close enough to intervene in time to stop Fleur from getting hurt, save with a long-distance rifle shot from Ty, who would be acting as sniper, with Megan his spotter. "I'm going to lay everything out for her, face to face. She needs to know the whole story and all the risks before she decides."

"And if she's still in?" Megan asked.

"Then I'll explain the plan, get her set up and prepare her as much as I can."

"Okay," Megan said. "While you meet with her, Ty and I'll find us all a place for the night and start recon."

"I'll go with you to and from the meeting," Heath said to Chloe. "Make sure no one follows you there and back."

Her instinctive reaction was to refuse his offer. But she wasn't doing this on her own anymore, and having Heath there to watch her back would give her one less thing to worry about. "All right."

Ty glanced at his watch. "It's a seven-and-a-half-hour drive to Marseille. We'd better get going."

They packed up, sanitized the safehouse, then hit the road. "Want me to drive?" Heath asked her as they headed for their rental, while Megan and Ty took their own.

"Nope. Driving helps me think," Chloe answered. She was an unapologetic control freak. He would just have to deal.

"You could sleep for a couple hours. You didn't get much last night."

Try hardly any, because on top of everything else going on, she'd been all hot and bothered by their play at the lake. The interruption about Eden had put a damper on things. Maybe it was for the best. He tempted her to throw all caution aside and enjoy the fling while she could. She couldn't indulge in that until this op in Marseille was over.

Twenty minutes into the trip, however, her mind began to wander, distracted by the man beside her. He was impossible to ignore, especially with him so close and the unrelieved sexual tension simmering between them. She couldn't remember ever being this into a guy. He made her want him just by being close, and if she didn't have him soon, she might explode.

Her body remained at a constant simmer, making up her mind for her. Once they finished in Marseille, she intended to make the most of whatever time remained for them together, since he'd be leaving soon and she wasn't sure what would happen to her. Constantly living life on the edge made it tempting to go after what she wanted, and for once, she wanted to indulge.

She wanted Heath. On top of her. Inside her. Anything to stop this unrelieved, gnawing tension.

"Any new updates on the search for Eden?" he asked as they neared the French border.

With everything else going on, they hadn't talked about the other Valkyrie. "Not yet. Amber and the rest of the team are working on it." Chloe had been up half the night going over her previous interactions with the suspected Valkyrie with Amber and Megan. Another Valkyrie named Kiyomi was staying at the UK headquarters with Amber, and had been trained with Eden for a while. They needed to locate Eden and figure out if she was the same person Chloe had been dealing with off and on these past few months.

"Do you guys all know each other? Or know of each other?" Heath asked.

"No. The program was really strict, and apparently there were different phases. The people in charge were careful to keep us moving around, disrupting attachments and never knowing what the other trainees were doing. We were all trained to operate alone."

"So this team scenario is all new to you."

"I know *how* to work with a team. Just haven't done it before." So far, it wasn't as awful as she'd imagined. She trusted Megan, liked Ty, and was more attached to Heath than was wise.

She stopped to fill the car up about an hour out of Marseille. While Heath filled the tank, she went into the service station bathroom and changed into a disguise. Chin-length black wig, colored contacts, some simple stage makeup to change her features a little, and nondescript clothes that would help her blend in anywhere.

When she came back to the car Heath stopped in the act of hanging up the gas pump and stared at her.

"Done?" she asked, liking the way his gaze tracked over her body as she walked toward him with a little extra sway in her hips.

"Yeah." He didn't hide that he liked what he saw.

"Here, you drive this time," she said, tossing him the keys.

He caught them just before they hit his chest, a grin lighting his features, making him twice as hot and impossible to tear her eyes off him. "Hey, thanks."

"Sure." Allowing him to drive this last stretch gave her time to get ready for the coming meeting and memorize their surroundings as they entered town.

Once they were back on the highway, he glanced over at her as she checked something on her phone. "What's next for you after this? Will you go to the UK and help the others?"

"Not sure. Depends on what happens with Dubois." She had to take him out first before she even thought about what came next for her.

They arrived in Marseille right on schedule. She had Heath drive around a bit so she could get a visual of the main areas she was interested in.

Chloe made sure she was at the meeting point early, a small pub a few blocks from the waterfront. The briny scent of the salt air filled her nose, the cries of gulls swirl-ing in the air as she walked down the cobbled street to her destination with Heath somewhere behind her, close enough to keep watch but not so close it looked like they were together. It was strange but nice to know he was watching over her.

She chose a seat at the back of the pub in a spot that afforded her the best visual lines to the entrance and exit points, ordered a glass of wine, and waited.

"She's on her way in," Heath said through Chloe's ear-piece soon afterward. "No tail. You're clear."

Chloe didn't respond, watching the door. A minute be-fore the meeting was supposed to start, a woman in a trench coat and black hat walked in. Fleur, wearing a brown, shoulder-length wig to cover her bright auburn hair. She scanned the pub, an expression of relief crossing her face when Chloe waved at her.

Chloe stood and embraced her in a big hug, subtly watching the door. "It's so good to see you," she said in French, then put her mouth close to Fleur's ear and dropped her voice to a whisper. "Do you think anyone fol-lowed you?"

"Good to see you too," she responded, then whispered, "and no."

Chloe glanced around one more time before sitting. Three tables were occupied across the room, but no one was paying any attention to them except the server, and everyone was too far away to overhear them anyway.

Fleur ordered herself a pot of tea and some lunch. She frowned at Chloe when the waiter left. "You should have ordered something. I *know* you haven't eaten yet, and how many times do I have to tell you—energy drinks are *not* food."

"I'll have a few bites of yours." Making sure they still weren't being watched, Chloe got right to it. In a low voice she outlined everything she had gone over with Megan and the others, careful to keep her voice barely above a whisper when she talked about sensitive things.

Fleur listened in silence until she finished, taking it all in. What Fleur would need to do. Where Chloe and the others would be. And what the potential risks were.

Chloe studied her friend, looking for signs of worry or stress. "Do you understand? This could be a trap."

Fleur looked calm as ever. "My cover's safe, and solid. I can do this."

The steel in her friend's voice made Chloe's whole chest ache. Fleur was going to see this through, no matter what. It filled Chloe with a fierce pride—and a whisper of fear. "Are you sure?" She was only going to ask once. "You won't have comms with us. Even an earpiece is too risky if they scan you."

Fleur gave an emphatic nod. "I'm sure."

Okay then. "You go on board, meet the broker and verify the women are there. Then you go on deck to do the fund transfer. To signal that the deal's done, drop the stylus." As soon as Fleur gave that signal and left, Chloe and the others would take over, infiltrating the ship to neutralize the crew and free the women.

"Got it."

"But if something's off, if something doesn't feel right, you leave. Immediately," she stressed. She didn't want to scare Fleur. She just wanted her friend to be on guard.

"I will."

Chloe eyed her. "Promise?"

"Promise."

A reluctant grin tugged at Chloe's lips. "I ever tell you I adore you?"

Fleur lifted a shoulder. "Once or twice."

She sipped her wine, waited for Fleur to finish her meal, then paid the bill and stood. Dammit, she wanted more time. More time to spend with Fleur, to prepare her better. Chloe gave her a warm, genuine smile. "It was good to see you."

"You too, my friend." Fleur enveloped her in a floral-scented hug that made Chloe's throat tighten. "Think of the stories we can tell each other after this," she whispered. "And you're going to owe me several bottles of my favorite red wine, by the way."

"Deal," Chloe whispered back, squeezing her tight. "And take this, just in case." She slipped one of her blades into the pocket of Fleur's trench.

"Ugh, you and your knives," Fleur said with a mock shudder. Releasing Chloe, she stepped back and gave her a brave smile. "Guess I'll see you later, then."

Chloe nodded. "Yes, you will."

She stood there and watched her only true friend walk out of the pub in her disguise and disappear into the misty rain outside, while an ominous weight gathered in her chest.

Drawing in a deep breath to counteract the heaviness, she exited the pub a few seconds later and turned the opposite way up the sidewalk, resisting the instinctive urge to look back at Fleur one more time.

Chapter Fourteen

She was deep in her head.

Heath followed Chloe up the sidewalk, keeping a safe distance as she entered their hotel while he waited outside. He had only known her a couple of days now, but he could tell something was different. That edgy, high-energy vibe she always emitted was dimmed now. She seemed uncharacteristically somber, almost subdued when she stepped out of their small hotel a few minutes later wearing a different disguise.

She pasted on a smile as she walked toward him, her brown wig plaited into a long braid that draped over her shoulder. "Hi," she said in English and slipped her arm through his, posing as a couple of American tourists here on vacation.

"Hi." Heath glanced at her as they strode back down the cobblestone street together. The main tourist areas of the city were fairly safe, but there were pockets where you definitely had to have your wits about you. "Everything okay?"

"Yes, great," she said brightly.

He didn't push. She wouldn't tell him anything she didn't want him to know, and she was concerned about her friend. Hell, Heath hated putting Fleur in this position too, but they really didn't have a choice at this point if they wanted to save those women. "Ready to explore the waterfront a bit?" They needed to get a good read on the setup down there before they could finalize the plan for tomorrow's op.

"Sounds good." Already doing recon at the south end of the waterfront, Ty and Megan could hear everything they were saying via their earpieces. Heath and Chloe would check out the north side.

Wanting to reassure her, wanting the chance to hold her, he pulled his arm free of hers and curled it around her waist instead. She didn't stiffen or break stride, but she gave him a little quirk of her lips that made him grin in turn. He would take any excuse at this point to touch her, and posing as a couple gave him the perfect excuse.

He walked her down to the water's edge, pretending to point out various historical things as they surveyed the structure of the harbor. Boats and ships of various sizes were moored along the docks, cranes and other equipment busy loading and unloading the cargo. The ship they were targeting tomorrow was a smaller vessel, ironically called *La Liberté*.

But the only freedom the captive women aboard would find was dependent on this op going as planned.

Chloe was quiet but alert beside him as they continued their recon, and he could practically hear her brain humming as she processed everything. This was way different from anything he did on his security stints, but he wanted to do whatever he could to help.

After an hour or so they'd seen everything they needed, and headed back to the hotel. They were staying in adjoining rooms on the third floor, while Ty and Megan were booked in a different hotel a few blocks east.

Heath was just taking off his jacket in his room when a knock came at the adjoining door. He opened it, his heart giving a hard kick to see Chloe without the disguise. She'd washed her face so it was completely devoid of makeup, her thick, honey-blond hair falling in waves around her shoulders. She was effortlessly beautiful, and so sexy it was all he could do not to wrap his hands in her hair and kiss her until her knees gave out.

"Megan and Ty are on their way up," she said, all business as she moved past him with her computer when he stepped aside. She smelled like shampoo and the mint gum she always chewed.

"Everything go okay with Fleur, by the way?" he asked as she dragged a chair from the corner over to the desk where she placed her laptop. Even though he'd overheard everything, the women had spoken in rapid French, so he hadn't caught much.

"Yeah, why?" She continued setting up without looking at him.

Because it bothers both of us that we're putting an untrained civilian in this position. He crossed to the mini fridge and opened it. "I got you something." He handed her the can of energy drink.

The genuine pleasure and surprise in her eyes when she glanced up at him warmed his heart. "When did you get this?" she asked as she took it from him.

"Had room service bring it up while we were out."

She set it on the desk, looking a bit flustered. As if no one had ever done something nice for her before. Maybe they hadn't. "Thank you."

"You're welcome. Figured you could use a caffeine jolt right about now."

Any sign of discomfort vanished and a smile curved her mouth. "You figured right. Want some? I'll share."

"No, I'm good."

Still smiling, she cracked the can and took a long sip,

closing her eyes as she swallowed. "Mmmm, that's good."

"If you say so." What would be *really* good was seeing that same look on her face while he held her hips and buried his tongue between her legs. Or when he had her so close to the edge she could taste it, and hold her there as he buried himself inside her warmth. He wanted to watch her face at that exact moment, hear what sounds she made and drink in every moment of it the same way she was savoring that drink.

A brisk knock on the door pulled him from his fantasy. She opened it and Ty and Megan strode in.

"You ready to knock this out?" Megan asked as she headed for the desk where Chloe's computer was. She was high energy too, but in a quieter way than Chloe. More on the anxious side, whereas Chloe was flat out restless. Their nicknames made sense to him now: Itchy and Twitchy.

Over the next hour they reviewed what they'd seen down at the harbor, using a satellite map on Chloe's laptop. *La Liberté* was due to arrive in port around sixteen-hundred-hours tomorrow. Once the ship was located, he and Chloe would find a spot to hide and watch on the south side of it, while Ty and Megan took the north.

Fleur would board the ship without a wire or earpiece, determine whether the women were on board, then complete the transaction with the electronic fund transfer, signal them, then leave. From there, Chloe and Megan would take over, with him and Ty providing backup.

There was more at stake here than Fleur's and the captive women's safety. If anything went wrong and Heath had to fire his weapon on this unsanctioned op, his security clearance was up in smoke, possibly along with his career. But he was too invested to walk away now, and he would never turn his back when Ty, Chloe and the others might be in danger. He was going to do everything he could to keep them safe.

"Okay, so...we're good?" Megan asked as they wrapped up, looking at each of them gathered around the laptop.

Chloe was chewing away on her gum, still studying the map on screen.

"Chloe."

Her gaze shot to Megan, and she straightened. "We're good." But the lingering unease in her eyes proved she still had some major reservations about Fleur's role in this. Hell, they all did.

With a reassuring smile, Megan pulled her into a hug. "It's going to be fine. By this time tomorrow, all those women will be free and Fleur will be on her way home to Paris."

"Yeah, can't wait." Chloe squeezed her and let go. "See you guys in the morning."

Heath let them out and locked the door. When he turned around, Chloe was gone. Her laptop was still on the desk, but the door between their rooms was shut.

Annoyed at himself for being disappointed, he grabbed the sandwich from the bar fridge and wolfed it down. He'd just jammed the last bite into his mouth when the connecting door opened and Chloe walked through it wearing a tight pair of sleep shorts that barely covered her ass, and a T-shirt snug enough to show him she wasn't wearing a bra. It bore a logo mimicking AC/DC's, but read *AD/HD: Highway to—Squirrel*! instead.

Sweet Jesus.

He had to swallow twice to force the sandwich down his throat as she walked back to the desk and studied the map, not paying him any attention. "Something else on your mind?" he asked.

"Just...everything," she said with a frown, scanning the area where the ship was supposed to dock.

Then she straightened and wrapped her arms around

herself, framing her pert breasts. "It should be me on board that boat tomorrow. If something goes wrong, I could handle it. Fleur..." She shook her head.

Heath crossed to the table, turned a ladder-back chair around and straddled it, resting his forearms across the top. He was a protector and healer by nature, wanted to help ease her anxiety about this. "Want to go over everything again, see if we missed something?" He didn't think they had, but it might make her feel better.

She flashed him a half-smile and closed the laptop. "No. We've done everything we can for now." She straightened and stretched her arms over her head, making her breasts push against the material of her shirt for a second until she dropped her arms again. "It's late. Guess I'll turn in."

He couldn't tell if she'd done it to tempt him or not, and it was driving him crazy. If she was worried and still thinking about tomorrow, he would keep his hands to himself. "You can sleep after drinking that?" He nodded at the empty can.

"No, but you can. You have to be tired."

Not anymore, with her so close and wearing next to nothing. "I'm fine. But I could help *you* get to sleep."

She arched an eyebrow at his offer, amusement lurking in her gaze. "You think so?"

He lifted a shoulder. "I'm a PJ. I'm good with my hands."

"Hmm, I just bet you are." The heavy-lidded look she gave him made his blood pump hotter.

He wanted her under him. Naked. His tongue inside her.

He swung one leg across the chair seat and stood, watching her face as he advanced toward her. If she'd tensed or taken a step back, given any indication at all that she was hesitant or not into this, he'd have stopped.

But she didn't. She stood her ground, tracking him

with those big brown eyes, the mix of hunger and yearning on her face tugging at his heart.

He stopped directly in front of her, forcing her to tip her head back a little to look up at him. He reached out to tuck a lock of hair behind her ear, ran his fingers through its softness. "What do you say, firecracker? Wanna see if I can take the edge off for you?"

Molten desire filled her eyes. "Yes," she whispered, and reached for him.

Heath groaned as he covered her mouth with his, his fingers sliding deep into her hair to curve around her skull and hold her close. Chloe cupped his face in her hands and plastered her lithe body to his, her lips parting for the stroke of his tongue.

She leaned back against the edge of the table, hands moving to his hair as he lifted her shirt. Small, round breasts met his avid gaze, topped with tight pink nipples. Heath hummed his appreciation and leaned in, licking a path down the center of her chest to the inside curve of her left breast. He nuzzled her, rubbed his bristly cheek against her softness, then closed his mouth over the rigid peak.

Chloe gasped and pulled him closer, wrapping her arms around his head. "Heath..."

He didn't respond, busy sucking and licking, loving the sound of his name on her lips. He locked one arm around her hips and pulled her pelvis tight to his, rocking the ridge of his erection slow and gentle between her splayed thighs. He wanted her hot and wet for him when he finally touched her there.

She urged him to her other breast and he obliged, rubbing and rocking his erection right where she needed it. With a soft, needy sound she splayed her thighs wider. He palmed one side of her ass and squeezed it, eased his hand around between them to slide inside the leg of her shorts to find her hot center.

She was drenched against his fingers, her heat beckoning him. He lifted his head from her breasts to stare at her face while he grazed her swollen folds with his fingertips. She gasped and stared up at him through pleasure-blurred, heavy-lidded eyes, leaning back to give him more room.

Heath gently nipped at her lower lip, sucked it as he eased a finger inside her then withdrew, spreading her slickness up to circle the hard bud of her clit. Her breathless moan made his whole body tighten. "Can you get off like this?" he said against her parted lips.

"Yes. Don't stop," she whispered back, rocking against his hand.

He had no intention of stopping. Instead he shifted his hand, eased two fingers into her, curling them upward to rub her sweet spot while his thumb caressed the swollen knot of her clit.

"Ohh, yeah," she moaned, nipping his lower lip once before tugging his head downward.

Immediately he sucked her other nipple into his mouth, using his tongue in rhythm with his fingers between her legs. God, she was so soft, so hot. The way she moved, the unabashed way she sought and took her pleasure, was sexy as hell. Her thighs tightened around his hips, her muscles tensing, her breaths turning ragged as she reached the peak.

Heath raised his head and stopped moving his hand.

Those big brown eyes flew open, her lips parting in shock. She made a sound of protest but he cut it off with a deep kiss, twining his tongue with hers. It wasn't enough to just get her off. He wanted her to remember this, crave the tension and eventual release he could give her.

He kept kissing her, waited until the tension melted from her body before resuming his caresses between her legs. This time her moan was louder, unsteady. She locked her ankles at the small of his back, as if afraid he might try to walk away. Heath teased her now, touching his tongue to hers and then retreating. A sensual dance she responded to with utter abandon.

Rocking against his searching fingers, she released his head and reached down to shove at her shorts. Heath helped her, dragging the damp cotton down and off her long legs, dropping it on the floor as he sank to his knees before her and gripped the outsides of her thighs.

Chloe leaned back to rest her elbows on the desk, her tight pink nipples peeking out from the locks of hair tumbled over her breasts. Her eyes were dark and hazed with desire, her mouth pink and shiny from his kisses. And between her legs...

Heath gave a soft growl as he stroked his thumbs over the succulent flesh calling to him. Pink and slick, swollen with desire.

Firming his hold on her thighs, he leaned in and settled the flat of his tongue against her. Slow. Soft. Making her feel every single spot he touched as he licked up the length of her to settle his lips around her clit.

She seized his hair with one hand, her weight balanced on her other arm, the muscles in her thighs trembling slightly as she stared down at him. "Heath."

Yes.

He sucked ever so gently, stroking his tongue along the side of her clit. Chloe mewled in her throat and arched, her body forming a gorgeous, taut line of need.

He let go of one leg and slid two fingers inside her, pressing upward against that spot right behind her pubic bone with firm pressure as he enjoyed her.

Chloe whimpered and clamped her legs around his shoulders, her fingers tightening on his hair sending a sting across his scalp. He kept going, watching her face, paying attention to every little cue her body gave him. And this time when she got close, he didn't stop.

He slowed.

Her incoherent moan of need wrapped around him, his

senses filled with her scent and taste as he took her to heaven. She gave him everything, nothing held back as she came for him, her cries echoing in his ears while she arched against his mouth and clamped around his fingers.

Only when she went limp and pushed his face away did he stop, giving her intimate flesh one last, lingering kiss before easing back on his heels. He was hard as a steel rod in his jeans, aching to unzip his fly and find relief. But it was worth it.

She was worth it.

Chloe licked her lips and pushed up, her breathing still a little ragged as she pushed the tumbled blond strands back from her face. "Wow, I wasn't…expecting that," she finally managed.

Ignoring the ache in his dick, Heath pushed to his feet and wrapped his arms around her, pulling her close to bury his face in her hair. "Good?"

"Amazing." She nestled her cheek in the hollow between his chest and shoulder, her hands wandering over his back, down to his ass. Then around toward his pulsing erection.

Heath groaned and captured her curious hands. He wanted them on his aching flesh more than anything, but he would wait. He didn't know what the other guys she'd been with had been like, but he wanted to show her that he was an unselfish lover who didn't always expect her to reciprocate every time.

Still holding her hands, he eased back a little to look down at her. "Think you can get some sleep now?"

She studied him, as if unsure what to make of him stopping her. "Maybe."

"Maybe if I was wrapped around you?"

A hint of vulnerability flashed in her eyes at his offer, and a soft smile spread across those tempting lips. "Maybe. I think it's worth a shot."

He kissed her soft mouth. "I think so too."

Leaving her shorts on the floor, he scooped her up in his arms and carried her to her bed, where he planned on staying the whole night.

Chapter Fifteen

It had been a few months since she'd last had sex, but this was the first time Chloe had wanted to stay the entire night with a guy. Heath was on his side behind her, tucked up close to her body, one muscular arm wrapped around her waist.

After crawling in beside her he'd shut off the lamp, pulled the covers over them and cuddled into her. He had no idea what that did to her.

Lying here in the near darkness with him, listening to the sound of their quiet breathing, her body sated and warm. The quiet peace she so rarely got to experience. The rare chance to let her shields this far down around another person.

Except she wasn't the least bit tired after the release he'd given her—without expecting anything in return. And he was rock hard against her butt.

She pulled free of his arm and rolled to face him in the dimness, the tiny amount of light coming from the gap around the blinds on the window allowing her to see his face. The dark stubble on his face added to his rugged appeal, and even though she couldn't see the color, she could picture how vivid the blue of his eyes was this close up.

"Still can't sleep?" he murmured, stroking his fingers through her hair.

Ohhh, she liked that. She liked *him,* with his loyalty, rule following and gruff exterior. "No. And neither can you, like this." She slid a hand between them to cup the ridge of his erection through his jeans.

Her insides squeezed at the thought of him burying himself inside her. But not tonight—that was too intimate a step to take with him, because he'd already penetrated her defenses more deeply than anyone else had.

Maybe never, because after this op they would go their separate ways. He was different than the others. She wouldn't be able to walk away unscathed after him, and she needed to mitigate the damage.

He groaned softly and nuzzled her cheek. "You're making it worse."

"Am I? Maybe this will help." She flicked the button of his jeans open and tugged down the zipper so she could slide her hands inside his underwear.

Heath sucked in a breath when she curled her fingers around his warm, rigid flesh, sending a surge of feminine power through her. "You don't need to do this." His voice was sandpaper-rough in the quiet.

"I want to." She wanted to watch his face while she pleasured him, make him come undone while she was in control. And she wanted to escape worrying about Fleur for as long as she could.

Before he could say anything else, she leaned forward to capture his mouth, easing one hand up to cup the back of his head. Heath slid a hand into her hair and used his other arm to bring her closer as he rolled more to his back, giving her room.

Chloe paused to stare down at him in the dimness, aware of a little voice in her mind warning that she was edging into dangerous territory. Without the haze of lust and need clouding her senses, this threatened to be incredibly intimate. She didn't do intimacy. Intimacy made her vulnerable and she avoided that at all costs to protect herself.

You don't need to protect yourself from him.

She pushed that tempting voice from her head and kissed him again, determined to just enjoy the here and now. But damn, it was so incredibly hot to have this big, powerful man allowing her to take control this way. The tension in his body, the way his fingers flexed against her scalp and hip told her how much he loved what she was doing, yet he seemed content to let her take the lead, not asserting control or making demands.

Chloe took advantage of it, slowly easing her fist up and down him, varying pressure and speed while she used his groans and body language to figure out what he liked best. Then she used that knowledge to drive him out of his mind, teasing and drawing it out. His hips lifted, pushing his rigid flesh harder into her grip.

She broke the kiss to look down between them, the dark, swollen length of him trapped in her fist. Arousal and power swirled through her. She licked her lips, wanting to taste him. To take him in her mouth and make him insane.

The impulse surprised her. Oral was too intimate. But she needed to give Heath this.

Still stroking him, she leaned down to kiss a path down the side of his neck. He made a rumbling sound and tipped his head back, fingers kneading her scalp. She licked and kissed across his collarbone and down the center of his well-defined chest, gripping the base of his cock.

Heath tensed, his hand curling into her hair when her lips reached his abdomen. "Chloe," he warned.

The warning only made her want this more, driven by her own desire to make him lose control and the thick, hot anticipation pulsing between them. He smelled like soap and male musk, and he was hard to bursting in her hand.

At the first brush of her lips against the sensitive crown, he sucked in a sharp breath and clenched his fingers around her hair. Smiling to herself, Chloe rubbed her check along his length, adding slow, hot kisses on her way up to the tip.

He growled low in his throat when she flicked her tongue across the sensitive underside, his big body drawn taut. And suddenly she didn't want to tease anymore. She wanted to give this man the same level of pleasure he'd given her. Wanted him to always remember this moment—remember *her*—long after they parted ways. And they *had* to part ways. For both their sakes.

She parted her lips and took him into her mouth. Heath moaned and put both hands in her hair, his fingers moving restlessly. A startling, unfamiliar tenderness welled up inside her. She smoothed her free hand up his chest, laid it over his heart as she took him deeper, swirling her tongue around the swollen head of his cock.

His breathing changed almost immediately, the tension in his muscles building as she sucked. His belly and thighs tensed, his fingers gripping her hair, conveying his silent desperation and need. Need that she'd created.

She closed her eyes, focused on the feel of his hands in her hair, the tang of him against her tongue. She wanted to remember this stolen moment too. Wanted to give him so much pleasure, to share this unprecedented level of intimacy with him.

"You're gonna make me come, firecracker," he rasped out, the ragged edge to his voice only turning her on more.

The nickname was perfect, and the way he said it was like a caress over her senses. She took him deeper, tightened her grip on the base of him and sucked slower. A little harder.

Heath whispered her name, locked his hands in her hair and pushed his hips upward, his entire body strung taut. He seemed to stop breathing for a second, then he pulsed against her tongue, his guttural groan of release filling her ears.

She stayed with him, waited until he'd relaxed against the bed, all that gorgeous tension melting from his muscles before gently releasing him. She kissed his belly, the center of his chest, craving more of this magical connection between them. Wanting to stamp this memory into his heart forever.

"Come up here," he murmured, pulling her upward to gather her close. He cradled her cheek to his chest, his heavy arms wrapped around her shoulders, one big hand on the back of her head. He kissed her hair, ran his fingers through it in a slow, gentle rhythm that almost hypnotized her.

Chloe squeezed her eyes shut, fighting the strange new feelings bubbling up inside her. Him holding her felt good. Safe.

Right.

She shoved that scary thought aside, focused instead on the beat of his heart as it slowed to normal beneath her cheek. His scent and the warmth of his skin. The protective, almost cherishing way he cradled her.

Her heart hitched, a painful ache twisting beneath her ribs. Dammit, she shouldn't have done this. Shouldn't have allowed herself to feel so much. It only made her wish for things she couldn't have.

She started to pull away but he made a sound of protest in the back of his throat and tightened his hold. "Stay," he whispered against her hair.

In that moment, she, lethal assassin that she was, was helpless to fight the invisible pull he exerted on her.

Laying her cheek on his chest once more, she allowed

her body to relax fully while he held her. She listened to his heartbeat, the way his breathing deepened and slowed. He twitched slightly in his sleep, woke and gathered her even closer with a contented groan that made her whole chest ache.

She waited until he was deep under before slowly easing away, inch by inch so she didn't wake him. She even paused by the side of the bed to study him, drinking in the strong lines of his profile.

Soundlessly she gathered her bag and crept to the adjoining room to change into a different disguise. Making sure he was still asleep, she snuck out of the room and walked out into the brisk night air. A light drizzle fell, the city blanketed by a shroud of fog.

She zipped her jacket all the way to her chin and set off for the harbor once more. Crews were still operating the cranes and other machinery, loading and unloading the ships. She took everything in, staying vigilant to her surroundings and on alert for any threats.

When daylight broke, she had wandered to the far southern end of the city. Her phone buzzed. A message from Heath.

Where are you?

Again with that hitching sensation in her chest. Normally she would have ignored the message, but it didn't feel right after what they'd shared, and he was sticking around to help her and Fleur. *Getting the lay of the land.*

You okay? he asked a few moments later.

Yes. See you later, she typed, ending the conversation. It wasn't uncommon for her to go without sleep, or to do more recon in the middle of the night. But it had never happened because she needed space from a man she was developing feelings for, or because she wanted an excuse to avoid him for a while.

Somehow Heath was already under her skin, and he threatened to burrow even deeper the longer she was in his company.

She hadn't realized men like him existed in the real world, but she needed to get her emotional shields back in place before she saw him again. He tempted her like no one else ever had, made her want things that were impossible. She wasn't "normal" and never would be, and he was leaving soon anyway. Better to deal with that now so she could simply enjoy whatever time between them remained.

But she couldn't afford any more distractions until this op was over.

She stopped for something to eat, kept in contact with Megan and Amber via text on her encrypted phone. Amber had shored up Fleur's cover and was monitoring everything electronically from her end. Her boyfriend Jesse was helping Ty review and tighten security measures around the port in anticipation of the ship's arrival in a few hours.

All too soon, it was go time.

She met the others in Megan and Ty's hotel room. She'd steeled herself for the sight of Heath on the way over, but the moment those impossibly blue eyes locked with hers, that ache hit her beneath the ribs again.

Blocking all of that, she changed into her op clothes— her standard black cargo pants and a long-sleeved black T-shirt. The team reviewed the plan once more, including contingency plans.

When they were done, Megan gave Chloe a bright smile and slid her weapon into the holster in her waistband. "See you on the other side."

"You know it." She watched Megan leave, followed by Ty, who carried the backpack with the disassembled rifle and other gear in it.

Avoiding looking at Heath, she triple-checked her own bag. She stiffened when he came up behind her. Pressed her lips together when he put a caring hand on her shoulder.

"You okay?"

She moved away from his touch and stood. "Yeah. You ready to go?" More than anything she just wanted this over and done with, to have Fleur and the others safe.

He gave her an unreadable look. "What do you need from me?"

The question pierced her so deep she almost flinched. Her entire life as an operative, she'd never had teammates to rely on. People capable enough to hold their own on a mission, let alone ones she could trust. Someone to give a shit about her beyond her accomplishing the mission.

Yet here was this solid, caring man she barely knew, standing in front of her asking what she needed. And she got the feeling that he'd give her anything she asked for.

"I need you to do your job," she said curtly, hating herself for being so bitchy but not knowing how else to protect herself.

He gave a slow nod, those gorgeous eyes searching hers. "I will."

She knew he would. That almost made this worse.

She hitched her backpack onto one shoulder and adjusted her waistband holster to make sure her weapon was concealed beneath the bottom of her jacket. "That's it. I don't need you to watch over or protect me. I've been doing this shit for a long time."

His jaw tightened, annoyance burning in his gaze. "Maybe. But I'm going to watch over you anyway."

Because that's just who he was.

Hating the way he threw her off balance, and the sudden tightening in her throat, she sighed. "That's a sweet sentiment, but you need to know it irritates the shit out of me."

He stared at her. "You'll live."

That Others May Live. The Pararescue motto.

149

Chloe swallowed, the unspoken meaning reverberating between them. She couldn't afford to acknowledge her emotions right now, and he held the power to reveal every last one of them. She had to be strong. Hard as steel. Cold as ice. Fleur and the others were depending on her.

"Let's go," she said gruffly, and turned for the door.

He stayed on her like a shadow as they moved into position, hiding in an abandoned office within view of the docks. They split up, Chloe going inside while Heath moved around to the side to monitor the situation from there.

Alone, she was able to focus completely as she crouched beside a window and surreptitiously watched the ships through her binoculars.

"Package has arrived. Two o'clock," Heath's deep voice murmured in her earpiece.

La Liberté was being pushed toward the dock by a tugboat. "Copy," she answered. "You guys have a visual from your position?" she asked Megan and Ty.

"Negative. Moving to a better location now," Megan responded.

Chloe continued watching the boat as it drew near. Through the bridge window she could see the captain and other officers. A few other crewmembers were moving around the main deck. "No sign of our broker or the cargo," she told the others. Fleur should be arriving any moment now.

"Heads up," Heath said a minute later. "Our flower delivery's here."

Chloe scanned the dock and stopped on the woman approaching the vessel. Fleur was wearing the same disguise as in the picture she'd sent to Amber to beef up her cover ID—a light gray pencil skirt suit and black pumps, the deep brown wig wound into a tidy bun at the back of her head. She looked every inch the professional her cover claimed her to be.

Chloe watched her friend closely as Fleur reached the vessel and waited for admittance. Her friend was doing fantastic so far, no trace of nervousness in her posture or on her face. "I'm moving closer," she informed the others.

Quickly changing disguises once more, she made sure her weapon was out of sight before slipping out of the office and making her way to the dock. She was going to be as close as possible when this went down.

"She's going aboard," Heath said, and by the time Chloe rounded the corner to get a visual, Fleur was indeed aboard the ship. She hated that Fleur didn't have comms with her and the others, but at least Chloe was close now.

No one looked twice at Chloe as she strode down the dock, keeping her eyes on her friend.

A man appeared on deck with Fleur. Middle Eastern in appearance, middle-aged. "That our broker?" she murmured.

"Affirm," Megan replied.

Fleur and the man talked for a few moments. Then the man went to a hatch in the side of the vessel and she seemed to hesitate. She casually glanced around her, her gaze moving right past Chloe.

Then Fleur followed him out of view.

Chloe's heart rate picked up, her pulse thudding dully in her ears. *No. No, come back out.*

This wasn't the plan. They couldn't see what was happening. Had no visual, no way of knowing what was going on.

"Has she gone to check the cargo?" Heath asked tightly.

"I don't know," she murmured back, fighting back the alarm growing in the pit of her stomach.

"We've got a situation," Megan said.

Chloe stopped walking, dread making her guts clench at the tone her friend used. "Report."

"Dubois and his bodyguards are headed for the ship in

a speed boat. He'll be there in under thirty seconds."

A bolt of fear ripped through her. *No.* Dubois wasn't supposed to be here.

Chloe took off running for the ship, praying she would reach her friend in time.

Chapter Sixteen

Unease tightened Fleur's stomach as she followed the broker into a staircase and below deck to inspect the "cargo" she was supposedly buying for her boss. With each step she was more and more out of her depth.

This wasn't the plan. Wasn't supposed to happen. Now no one had a visual on her. But the broker had refused to bring any of the women on deck to speak to, insisting she go below with him to inspect the cargo. She hadn't seen a way to talk herself out of this without tipping her hand and blowing her cover. She could have just walked away. But saving these women was important enough to her that she'd stayed and accepted the risks.

The heels of her pumps tapped on the metal steps as they descended the well-lit stairwell. "Is it far down?" She wanted in and out of here as fast as possible. She would make sure the women were aboard and still alive, then immediately go back up on deck and signal Chloe and the rest of the team.

"Two more decks. Take off your shoes if they're bothering you," he said without looking back, his almost bored tone making it clear he didn't care one way or the other.

She wished she were like Chloe, able to kill this evil cockroach, then free the women herself. But she wasn't, and all she had was the knife Chloe had given her tucked into the sleeve of her suit jacket.

Her steps seemed to echo off the narrow walls, the broker a good twenty stairs ahead of her, nearly to the next deck hatch now. Her shoes were painful, but without them her feet would be completely unprotected. If she had to run for it, she wasn't sure which was worse, being barefoot, or trying to escape in these torture contraptions.

Metal groaned as the man opened the hatch and stood waiting for her with an annoyed expression. "In here. Hurry up."

Fleur hurried, her heart thudding hard against her ribs as she followed him through the hatch into the dim interior. As soon as she did, she smelled it.

Sweat, unwashed bodies and human waste.

She swallowed a gag, barely kept from covering her nose as she followed him down a narrow corridor. It was quiet. Way too quiet, and she didn't see any other crewmembers on this level.

The broker stopped beside a panel and hit a switch. Blinding white light lit up the space. Fleur squinted and held up a hand to shield her eyes, her unfocused gaze landing on a sight before her that made her stomach twist.

A large shipping container with a hole cut into the side, metal bars acting like a jail cell window.

"In there," the man said, and tossed something at her.

Fleur reflexively caught the flashlight to her stomach. Swallowing, doing her best to cover her revulsion and fear, she switched it on and aimed it at the metal bars.

She saw nothing but darkness inside. She stepped closer, keeping the beam of light at eye level. A few paces from the container, she stopped. Eyes gleamed in the residual light that penetrated the bottom of the container. She couldn't see them well enough to make out their faces, but she could tell all the people trapped in there were staring back at her.

A wave of rage swept through Fleur.

She couldn't tell them she was there to help. That they were close to freedom.

"Satisfied?" the man asked in a bored tone.

"How many are there?"

"Twenty-seven."

She turned to face the monster who had facilitated this evil transaction. "One is missing."

He shrugged. "Died on the way here."

"What did you do with the body?"

"Shark food, by now."

It took everything Fleur had not to react outwardly to that hideously callous statement. The prisoner had died of God only knew what, and they'd dumped her overboard like a dead fish.

For an instant she fantasized about slitting his throat with her knife. Catching him off guard and leaving him down here to bleed out all over the floor. "That will change the price."

"No, it won't."

She put on her stoniest expression, pretended that her heart wasn't beating ten times too fast, aching for these women and filled with hatred toward him and the men who had done this. "It will. My employer won't pay for something he doesn't get."

"We'll see about that." He turned and started for the stairs. "Let's finish the transaction topside. An important guest is arriving shortly."

She faltered. "Oh? Who's that?" She forced herself to follow him. She would finish this in plain sight where

Chloe and the others would see her, finish her part in making this rescue possible. And she hoped the team found an excuse to kill this evil monster in the process.

He shot her a cold smile over his shoulder before disappearing through the hatch. "The seller."

Fleur stopped dead, her heart rocketing into her throat. It wasn't possible. Guillaume Dubois? Here?

Blood pulsed in her ears as she climbed the stairs back to the main deck, thinking fast. What should she do? Dubois wouldn't recognize her, he'd never seen her before. He had taken over this transaction now that his brother was dead. Was he here just to oversee it, or was he hoping Chloe showed up? Fleur was good at lying, but was she good enough to convince him she was who her ID claimed she was?

Her palms were damp, her fingers cold by the time they reached the main deck. She needed to handle the "payment" now, then get out of here before Dubois got aboard. She pulled the tablet from inside her suit jacket. She walked past the broker, moving to stand near the bow where she was supposed to, so the team could see her clearly.

Oh, God, Chloe, please be out there.

She dropped the stylus, signaling to the others that the women were aboard. Then she crouched to pick it up, steeling herself for what came next. "Let's take care of the payment before—"

"Ah, here we are." He smirked as a group of men exited the bridge to her right.

The blood drained from her face.

Guillaume Dubois, flanked by two bodyguards. Big men in tailored suits that no doubt hid weapons.

The way Dubois' cold blue eyes fastened on her made her insides curdle. She struggled to keep her expression calm while her heart threatened to implode, her fingers curling reflexively around the tablet.

Chloe's close. She won't let anything happen to you.

Her protector was watching her. Fleur prayed her friend would be able to keep her safe.

GUILLAUME EYED THE pale woman holding the tablet. Supposedly an accountant from his brother's organization. Here to take the place of the beautiful and treacherous "Gabrielle" at the last moment, no doubt.

After what had happened, he was suspicious enough to come here in person and ensure everything was legitimate.

"Camille, is it?" he asked as he walked toward her.

"Yes." Her face was stiff. The set of her shoulders too, and her pupils were dilated slightly. He made a lot of people nervous, but this woman was genuinely afraid. And there was no reason for her to be that way unless she'd done something wrong.

"Check her ID," he said to Jean-Pierre. His head of security had already checked before leaving Paris. Everything looked okay on the surface, but that wasn't good enough for Guillaume.

The woman paled even more, reluctantly reached into her jacket to produce a thin wallet. She handed it to Jean-Pierre, who glanced at the contents and walked back to give it to Guillaume.

The ID matched her. But that didn't mean shit.

Guillaume stopped a half-dozen paces from her and waved Jean-Pierre and his other bodyguard off. This woman was no threat to him and he was more than capable of defending himself.

Her gaze followed his men as they retreated back into the bridge with the broker.

"I'm told you inspected the cargo. Was everything in order?"

Her gaze snapped back to him. "N-no. One girl was missing. The broker said she died during transport. They threw her overboard."

There was a distinct tremor in her voice. "Really." He nodded at the tablet. "You're going to authorize the transfer?"

"Yes."

"You don't mind if I witness it?" He wasn't asking.

She hesitated a second too long. "Of course not." She focused on the tablet, her throat moving as she swallowed.

He stepped closer, watching her, not the tablet she had turned on. She darted a sidelong look at him, her right hand on the screen as she pulled up the banking information.

He stopped next to her, close enough to smell the sweet scent of her perfume and see the pulse throbbing too fast in her throat. And when she pulled up the banking information, she betrayed herself.

"That's not my brother's business account, Camille," he murmured.

She went rigid, her eyes still on the screen. Caught in the act of trying to steal his money. "Oh. It's not? My mistake." Her fingers trembled slightly as she pulled up a different account. Still not the right one.

Guillaume seized her arm, banded his fingers tight enough around her right wrist to leave marks. "Who are you working for?" he demanded through clenched teeth.

She wheeled to the side, her left arm flashing out. He hissed in pain as something sharp sliced through his forearm and immediately let go.

Camille turned and raced for the gangway. Guillaume cursed, ignored Jean-Pierre as his head of security burst out of the bridge, and reached inside his jacket to draw his own weapon.

Taking aim at Camille's back, he fired.

She crumpled to the ground feet from the gangway, blood blooming on the back of her suit jacket. Guillaume was on her in an instant. He grabbed her by the hair, and wound up with a fist full of wig.

Enraged, he seized her real hair and wrenched her head back. She was choking, blood dripping down her lips and chin, her eyes filled with shock and agony.

He leaned down to snarl in her face. "Who do you work for, bitch? Where's Gabrielle?"

She struggled weakly, fighting to breathe.

He shook her, ready to strangle the life out of her rather than let her choke on her own blood. "Where is she? *Tell me!*"

She thrashed in his hold, her mouth opening and closing. Beyond the ability to think. She wasn't going to tell him anything, and he was out of patience—and control. This bitch knew who had killed his brother. He was certain of it.

"I don't have time for this shit," he growled, then grabbed her by the back of her collar, dragged her to the edge of the deck and tossed her over.

Her body hit the water with a splash and Guillaume turned to Jean-Pierre. She was a plant. There would be others watching nearby. Someone would have heard the shots, and might have seen what he'd done. He had to escape. "Let's get out of here."

"What about the cargo?"

"It's being handled."

Chapter Seventeen

No! Chloe watched in horror as Fleur hit the water and went under. She was too far away to help. A scream of denial locked in her throat as she raced down the dock.

"She's surfaced," Heath said in her earpiece, his voice uneven, as if he was running.

"Copy. We're heading after Dubois," Megan said.

Chloe didn't respond, her feet thudding on the wooden dock as she scanned the water for Fleur. She caught sight of her friend's head bobbing above the waterline, one arm flailing.

Reaching the edge of the dock, she vaulted off it, hitting the water in a clean, shallow dive. The shock of the cold water took her breath away for a moment.

She knifed through it, staying beneath the surface, heading for the last place she'd seen Fleur. Only when her lungs threatened to burst did she come up for a breath, pushing her arms and legs to move faster, harder. She was vaguely aware of the roar of a boat motor somewhere nearby, her sole focus on saving her friend.

The cold was already numbing her legs and arms. She wasn't going fast enough. Fleur was getting weaker by the second. "Fleur! I'm coming. Just keep your head above water," she shouted. Oh, dammit, she was still too far away. She'd never reach her in time—

A dark head surfaced a few yards from where Fleur had just been.

Heath. Somehow, he'd gotten there.

He shook the water from his face and turned in a circle, searching for Fleur. Before Chloe could call out, he dived under the murky surface, coming up a few seconds later with Fleur, one hand on her forehead, her head resting on his shoulder as he swam to the gangway. Chloe choked back a sob and swam toward them, pushing herself as hard as she could go.

Heath reached the gangway of the nearest ship. Two crewmembers were there to help pull Fleur from the water. Heath vaulted up and straddled her, immediately checking her vitals.

When Chloe got there twenty seconds later, someone grabbed her hands and pulled her up. Cold water sluiced off her as she pushed everyone aside to kneel beside Fleur. Her friend's face was eerily pale, blood soaking the front of her clothing and the gangway beneath her.

"No pulse and she's not breathing." Heath immediately started chest compressions. "Get me the ship's portable defibrillator."

Chloe jumped to her feet and raced up the gangway. One of the crewmembers was already on his way down carrying a bright red emergency medical kit. She grabbed it from him and tore back to Heath, walling off the terror rising inside her. Heath had dried Fleur's chest as best he could.

Dropping to her knees, she ripped the kit open and pulled out the defibrillator, then reached around Heath's hands to put the paddles in place. She hit the charge button, waited until the light came on to signal the machine was ready. "Clear."

Heath lifted his hands and she hit the button.

Fleur's chest jerked with the force of the electrical current.

Chloe held her breath, fighting the urge to shove Heath aside and take over as he checked for a pulse, keeping one hand on the dressing he'd pressed to Fleur's wound. He was a pro. She needed to let him work without interference, much as it killed her.

Fingers on Fleur's carotid pulse, he nodded. "Got a rhythm."

Battling tears, Chloe leaned over Fleur's head, cupping her friend's face in her hands. "Fleur, can you hear me? You're going to be okay. I'm here." She'd lost so much blood.

Hazy blue eyes opened a crack.

"That's right, look at me," Chloe continued, holding Fleur's gaze while Heath set about stopping the bleeding from the gunshot wound in her friend's chest. "I'm right here."

Fleur gasped, choked as blood streamed from her mouth and nose. Chloe bit down hard on the inside of her cheek and held Fleur's face while Heath sealed the pressure dressing. The position of the wound told her Fleur had been shot through the lung, and the bullet might have nicked her heart or a major blood vessel as well.

"Keep talking to her," Heath urged as he worked, prepping a large bore IV.

Chloe blurted out something, then just kept talking. She wasn't even sure what she said, but she needed to focus Fleur and distract her from the terror and pain. She was dimly aware of the crowd gathered around them on the gangway, and another on the dock. In the background, the eerie wail of sirens echoed on the air. Hopefully coming to help Fleur, and to go after Dubois.

Chloe and Heath looked at each other. Shit. She couldn't be here when the cops or first responders arrived, but how the hell could she leave Fleur like this?

Heath's intense blue eyes held hers. "Go," he said. "I've got her. *Go*," he ordered when Chloe hesitated.

Heart being ripped in two, she bent to kiss Fleur's forehead. "Hang on, my friend. I'll see you soon." *I'm sorry. I'm so, so sorry.* She forced herself to her feet, refused to look back as she ran down the gangway to the dock, searching for an escape route.

Just before she darted up an alleyway, she glanced back. Heath was still bent over Fleur on the gangway while a crowd of people gathered around, still doing everything he could to stabilize her.

Chloe hurried away, a haze of tears blinding her. She'd lost her earpiece in the water and her phone was shot, so she had no way to contact the rest of the team, who would have scattered or tried to follow Dubois. It was too soon to go to the RV point they'd established as a team prior to the op, and doubling back to the hotel to find the others was risky with Dubois possibly still in the area.

She waited almost another hour before she couldn't take the uncertainty anymore, and headed for the hospital. She grabbed some scrubs from the laundry in the basement, changed into them and tucked her hair up inside a surgical cap before entering the emergency department. Fleur wasn't there. She'd been rushed to surgery as soon as the ambulance crew had brought her in.

Chloe's heart thudded as she found her way to the operating rooms. She pushed through a doorway, was about to stop at the nurse's station to ask about Fleur when Heath stood up from a chair down the hall. He stared at her for a long moment, salt stains marking his still-damp clothes.

She hurried toward him, and he held a door across the hall open for her. The room was thankfully empty. "When did you get here?" she asked as soon as it closed.

"Came with the ambulance."

"She's still in surgery?"

"No." His eyes were somber, full of empathy. "Chloe…"

She shook her head, took a step back. "Don't say it."

He was quiet a moment. "I'm sorry. We revived her twice on the way here, but her heart gave out on the table. She's gone."

Grief sank its talons deep into her chest, piercing her heart and lungs. For a moment she couldn't breathe. Everything burned.

"When I finally met up with the others, I told them I'd wait here in case you came by."

Her throat was so tight she had to swallow twice to clear it. "What about Dubois?" she whispered. *Please tell me that bastard hadn't gotten away at least.*

Rather than answer, he stepped forward and gently took her by the upper arm. "Let's go back to the hotel. We'll talk to the others there."

She ripped her arm free, anger punching through the pain. "What. Happened?"

He released a hard exhalation. "Dubois is in the wind. Amber's trying to track him, but so far, nothing."

The news hit her like a blow. But there was something else. Something he was holding back because he didn't want to tell her. "And? Just say it," she snapped when he didn't answer immediately.

"Megan and Ty searched the hold of the ship. They found male migrant workers being smuggled here. The women weren't on board."

Chloe stared at him while that horrific final blow sank in. The women hadn't even been aboard. So Fleur had died for nothing.

"Come on," he said softly, and took her hand this time.

Numbness threatened to swallow her. Her core temp was still low from being in the water and then staying in her wet clothes for so long, but the shock and horror were the most dangerous. It took everything she had to compartmentalize all of it as she walked with Heath out to the parking lot.

You can't fall apart. You can't.

They took a taxi to a restaurant a few blocks from their hotel, paid in cash, then walked the rest of the way.

"My phone's trashed from being in the water," she said to Heath when they entered their room. It was untouched, her normal anti-trespassing measures still in place. "I need to make a secure call."

"Here." He handed her his—another burner phone Megan or Ty must have given him. "The others are waiting for us. When you're ready, we'll call them."

She nodded woodenly. "We'll need to talk about our next move. But first we need intel on those women, and Dubois." She sat on the foot of her bed and called Trinity. The other Valkyrie already knew about the failed op and what had happened, so Chloe didn't have to rehash anything.

"Are you all right?" Trinity asked her.

"Yes." But no, not really. How could she be? "I need you to make arrangements to have Fleur's body transported back to Paris for burial. Her parents are gone, but she has a half-sister who should be contacted." Chloe would have handled it herself if she could have.

"Of course. Give me her name and I'll handle everything."

It felt wrong. So wrong to hand over something like this to someone else. Fleur had been *her* friend. Her responsibility. Not only had Chloe failed to protect her friend, she couldn't even see to her burial. But under the circumstances she didn't have a choice, and she had to trust that Trinity would handle everything.

"Thank you," she murmured, aware of Heath watching her from the doorway between their rooms. A strong, steady presence to anchor her in the midst of this emotional hurricane.

"Amber's been trying to track Dubois. All evidence indicates he's still in the area, possibly even staying in Marseille."

Chloe tightened her jaw. Would the bastard do that? It made no sense, was too stupid a risk after what he'd done, even if he thought he was above the law here. "Keep me informed."

"I will."

Ending the call, she lowered the phone to her lap and stared at the carpet. Heath was still there, his wide shoulders all but filling the doorway. She couldn't summon the nerve to look into his face. "It should have been me. I should have met with the broker." Things might have ended differently. And if not, at least it would be her dead instead of Fleur.

Quiet footfalls on the carpet made her stiffen. Her muscles were rigid as blocks of concrete as Heath sat beside her and tried to ease her into his arms.

She pushed away and stood, avoiding looking at him. She didn't deserve comfort. This was her fault. Fleur was dead because of her, and there was no escaping that hard truth.

"It wasn't your fault," he said quietly.

"Yes, it was." She turned away, unable to bear his concern. Then she stopped. "Thank you, for everything you did for her. I owe you." Oh, shit, her voice was shredding, the wall holding her grief back bowing under the weight of the guilt and pain. And she had nothing to go on at the moment as to the whereabouts of the missing women or Dubois.

"Like hell. Chloe—"

"I'm gonna have a shower." She hurried to the bathroom, locking the door behind her for good measure. It wouldn't keep him out if he wanted in bad enough, but it helped give the illusion of more privacy.

Was Dubois really still in Marseille?

His brother had stayed here many times during business meetings. And Guillaume's ego was just as big as Dominic's had been. They'd both thought they were untouchable. That their money and influence could protect them from any threat.

Not this time.

The hair on her arms and the back of her neck rose as an iron determination formed in her gut.

She glanced at the small window on the far wall, the pressure of her weapon a reassuring weight against the small of her back. There was a fire escape below it that led to the alley beside the hotel. The others would want to wait until they had a solid lead, then come up with a plan before acting.

Chloe was done with that. She'd been trained to be a lone wolf. And she was a damn good one.

Reaching into the tub, she turned on the shower, then pulled the curtain shut and started for the window. If Dubois was still in the city, she had a fair idea of where she'd find him.

And once she did, he was a dead man.

****

Alone in the adjoining bedroom, Heath sank onto his bed and pushed out a deep breath as he ran his hands over his face. They smelled of the harsh disinfectant soap he'd used to clean up at the hospital earlier.

Fuck, what a mess.

He'd done everything he could to keep Fleur alive, even on the way to the hospital, trying to buy her enough time for the surgical team to repair the internal damage from the bullet wound. But it hadn't been enough, and now Chloe blamed herself, shutting herself away in the bathroom when all he wanted was to hold her tight and comfort her in any way he could.

The anguish in her eyes when he'd told her Fleur was gone would stay with him forever. But that haunted, devastated look when she'd found out her friend had died for nothing was even worse.

He flopped back onto the pillow, staring up at the ceiling. He was exhausted, but Chloe had to be worse and he didn't know what the hell to do for her. Megan had offered to come stay with her, but he'd turned the offer down because he wanted to be the one to help Chloe.

He'd already been seriously into her last night, but now, after watching the way she'd instantly raced to save Fleur… She'd risked everything to help her friend. Hadn't hesitated, had placed herself in serious jeopardy without a second thought.

Heath had no defense against that kind of loyalty and bravery in a woman. People showed their true character when tested in times of danger and severe stress. What he'd seen from Chloe today had shifted something deep inside him. There was no way he could just walk away and move on when this was over. He would never find anyone as amazing as her.

He waited a while, then glanced at his watch. Frowned. She'd been in there for almost half an hour now. More than enough time to grieve in private in the shower. The thought of her crying alone in there damn near shredded his heart.

He got up and walked through the connecting door, heading for her bathroom. The door was still shut, the shower still running. She had to be out of hot water by now.

Pausing for a second, he knocked twice. "Chloe? You

okay in there?"

Silence.

He waited a beat, trying to think of something comforting to say, and came up blank. "Chloe." He knocked again. "Just answer me and I'll leave you alone."

Nothing.

Dread gathered inside him. He tried the door, but it was locked. Muttering a curse, he took a metal coat hanger from the closet, straightened the hook, and managed to jimmy the lock free.

Pulse tripping, he pushed the door open. "Chloe?"

The shower curtain concealed the tub. He gripped the edge and pulled it aside, cursed even as his gut clenched.

Empty.

Whipping out his phone, he dialed Megan. "She's gone. Must have climbed out through the bathroom window."

"Shit. She's going after Dubois."

Oh, Jesus, no. He spun around and raced for his room to grab his weapon. "How do we find her?" Going after Dubois alone right now was tantamount to suicide.

Megan's worried sigh filled him with foreboding. "We can't."

Chapter Eighteen

It took Chloe less than thirty minutes to find some disguises to suit her purpose. She broke into a closed drycleaner shop and found a couple of outfits to use, changed into the skirt suit and packed the rest in a satchel she'd snagged from an unsuspecting patron outside a bakery. Not nearly as seamless as what Megan could do, but it did the job.

Although if Megan knew what Chloe was up to, she would try to stop her. And Amber was no doubt hot on Dubois' electronic trail, if she hadn't found him already.

Chloe didn't care what the others were doing. She was handling this herself *now*.

Her plan was simple: find Dubois and kill him. He would die for what he'd done to Fleur, and that was the end of it. She would worry about locating the missing shipment of women later—if she survived this hit.

The odds were against her. Dubois had his personal security detail with him at all times, and he had countless dirty resources in his pocket. There was a good chance she would either be captured or killed, but that was a risk she was prepared to take. All she had to do was think of Fleur, of everything her friend had selflessly done to help protect others, and the memory of her body being thrown over the side of the ship.

A fresh burst of rage exploded through Chloe, burning away the searing grief and the heavy weight of exhaustion trying to dull her mind. She hadn't slept in too long. Soon she would hit a wall. It was looming ahead of her, just out of sight.

No. Stay sharp. You have to stay sharp.

She had to do this now, or she might not get another chance. Amber's technological wizardry gave her a huge advantage. But Chloe was here on the ground, and determined to find Dubois first.

Thankfully, her list of potential places to hunt for him was blessedly short. A man with his ego and wealth only stayed at the best places money could afford. Enquiring at the front desk of the InterContinental Marseille, she hit pay dirt.

"May I help you?" the man at the front desk asked her with a smile.

Chloe adjusted the non-prescription reading glasses she'd found in the satchel. "Yes, I'm checking to see if a guest might still be here," she replied in flawless French. "We had a business meeting earlier and he forgot some important legal documents. If he hasn't checked out yet, may I leave them here for him?"

"Of course. The name?"

"Guillaume Dubois."

The man checked the system and gave her a smile. "I'll have them delivered to his room first thing in the morning."

Hiding her reaction, she smiled back and handed over a legal envelope with blank paper in it. "Thank you so much."

She exited the hotel, paused in an alley a half block

over to change once more, this time into a police uniform she'd taken from the drycleaner. It was a few sizes too big, and too long in the legs and sleeves, but it would do, and she didn't have to worry about hiding her weapon. After plaiting her hair into a braid at the back of her head, she doubled back and chose a different entrance into the hotel.

The lobby was practically deserted as she passed by it and walked down the hallway to a service staircase. Security rooms were usually located in the basement of these places, and she found it easily enough. One man and one woman looked up as she entered the room. She introduced herself and asked if there had been any disturbances on the top two floors where the most expensive suites were located.

Both of them looked surprised and told her nothing had been reported.

"We got a call from Mr. Dubois' head of security that someone had been lurking around in the hallway outside his suite just over an hour ago, unauthorized. Can you check the surveillance footage?"

"No one alerted us, and I didn't see anything." Frowning in concern, the man pulled up the requested footage.

"Start it at ninety minutes ago," she told him.

Chloe watched over his shoulder as he rewound the video. Her heart rate picked up when she spotted Dubois' head of security on camera. He and another man walked to the end of the hall and entered two adjoining rooms, checking to make sure they were safe. The head of security exited the room and headed back down the hall for the elevator.

The security guard fast-forwarded the video, stopping when someone else appeared on screen. Dubois and his head of security. Dubois went first, his bodyguard letting him in the suite at the far end.

Gotcha, you son of a bitch.

No one else came or went during the rest of the video. "There's no one else," the guard said. "Want me to go back earlier?"

"No need. Just another rich asshole being paranoid. Thanks for your time."

She left the security room, stopped by the hotel laundry to grab a change of clothes, and headed back to where she'd stashed her satchel. The weight of her weapon pressed against the holster in her waistband, the urge to act beating at her. She might know where Dubois was, but going after him now was too dangerous. She could call in a bomb threat to evacuate the building and force him out that way, but with so much chaos and that many people in the way, it would be harder to isolate him.

She'd have to wait, try to catch him and his security off guard.

A light drizzle began to fall just after midnight. Chloe huddled in a doorway off a deserted side street and allowed herself to doze off and on. By the time dawn broke she was half-frozen and stiff from the cold. She changed into the hotel uniform she'd taken from the laundry, wound her hair up in a bun at the back of her head, then walked back to the hotel and entered a door in the back with other staff arriving for their morning shift.

She positioned herself by the front lobby doors, moving from place to place, doing various tasks to appear occupied, finally ending up outside where the valet crew was busy bringing up patrons' cars.

Her chance came far more quickly than she'd anticipated.

Chloe dropped the cloth she was using to wipe the windows down when she spotted Dubois' head of security striding through the lobby for the front doors. She ducked out of sight, chose her position with care as the man came out. He scanned around him, his gaze pausing on her only for a moment before sliding past, and spoke to the valet attendant. He stayed put until a black Mercedes pulled up to the curb minutes later, then pulled out his phone and called someone, presumably Dubois.

Her pulse pounded dully in her ears as she waited, standing beside a tall topiary that gave her concealment. Watching through the slim gap between it and the window, she spotted Dubois the moment he appeared in the lobby. He was dressed casually in khakis and a button-down shirt, freshly shaved, striding across the marble floor with the air of a man who thought he owned everything and everyone. A wealthy businessman who looked anything but the cold-blooded murderer who had shot Fleur down yesterday.

He exited through the front doors, heading for his car where the head of security held the back door open for him.

Now.

Everything slowed around her, her exhausted body automatically going into op mode.

She stepped out from behind the topiary. Dubois was fifty feet away, his back to her.

Chloe's breathing was slightly uneven as she reached into her hotel blazer for her pistol. Her fingers curled around the grip, her gaze locked on her target as she started to draw her weapon—

A flash of pink appeared in her peripheral vision. She glanced toward it just as a little girl burst out of the lobby doors, pulling a pink suitcase. "Told you I'm fast, Papa!"

Chloe froze on the sidewalk as Dubois reached out an arm and curled it around the girl. "I can't believe how fast. Much faster than your sister and mother," he said, smiling down at her as he reached for her suitcase.

No. Her hand was locked around the pistol, disillusionment ripping through her. *His daughter.*

Dubois turned to usher the girl into the backseat. His

gaze caught on Chloe. Held for an instant, his face freezing.

Releasing her weapon, Chloe forced herself to calmly turn away, pretending to wipe at the glass beside her on her way up the sidewalk.

A car door slammed shut, then the quiet purr of an expensive engine followed as the Mercedes pulled away.

Hands trembling slightly, Chloe darted a look over her shoulder, expecting Dubois' head of security to be coming after her. But he was inside the car as it drove away at a sedate pace. Taking Dubois out of range.

Chloe stared after it, choking back tears of rage and bitterness. She might have just lost her only chance at killing him. And she wasn't sure how she was going to live with that.

****

Heath waited until he was out of the cab before calling Ty. "No luck at the InterContinental. I'm coming back to the hotel."

"We'll meet you up at your room," his friend replied. "Amber said the trail on Dubois went cold after he left the InterContinental, but she's hunting for a new lead."

"I'm three blocks away." He tugged his hood up as the rain fell in a cold, gray sheet. "See you soon." Between the three of them they'd tried eight different hotels, searching for any sign that Chloe might have been there. Goddammit, he never should have left her alone. Should have known she would go after Dubois.

Valkyries didn't get close to many people. Chloe had loved Fleur. As tough and badass as she was, this loss had rocked her to her core, and now they'd lost her.

A sick feeling roiled in the pit of his stomach as he trudged along the deserted sidewalk through the rain. Chloe had exploded into his life like a shooting star. The thought of never seeing her again, of something bad happening to her, was impossible to accept.

She could be anywhere right now. Had she found Dubois? They hadn't heard anything on the news, and neither had Amber with all her electronic surveillance, so maybe Chloe was still okay. He had to hope she was, and that she contacted them soon.

He did a double take as he passed by an alcove in an old building, then stopped short. His heart surged, then clenched when he spotted Chloe huddled on the step. She was dressed in an InterContinental hotel uniform, the jacket soaked with rain, her hair slipping from her bun to lay around her shoulders in wet tangles.

"Chloe," he breathed, rushing over to crouch in front of her, grasping her hand and cupping the side of her face. Jesus, she was soaked through, her skin freezing and she didn't seem to notice or care. He did a visual sweep, looking for blood and any other sign of injury. "Are you hurt?"

She didn't answer him right away, the haunted look in her eyes making alarm bells clang in his head. "I let him get away," she murmured in a leaden tone, staring at his chest. Dark circles marked the skin beneath her eyes. She looked so exhausted and defeated his heart twisted. "He was fifty feet from me. I had my hand on my weapon, ready to draw it and fire. One shot, that's all it would have taken."

"What happened?" he asked, gently rubbing his thumb across her cheek. Damn, she was freezing, a blue tinge to her lips.

"Couldn't do it, because his daughter was there. I couldn't let her see him die." The self-loathing and exhaustion in her voice worried him. "So I watched him get into the car. I stood there and let him drive away. I only got a partial plate."

Heath didn't give a shit about Dubois at the moment. "Hey, look at me."

She hesitated, then slowly lifted her eyes to his.

The pain there twisted his insides. "Are you hurt any-where?"

She dropped her gaze. "No."

Satisfied that she was physically okay, he wrapped his arms around her waist. "Up you come." He lifted her to her feet.

She pushed at his chest. "I failed her."

Fleur. "You didn't fail anyone. And if Fleur cared about you half as much as you did her, you winding up dead or in prison for the rest of your life isn't what she would have wanted."

When she protested the tug on her hand his patience came to an abrupt end. He bent to scoop her up in his arms, ignoring her protests. "You're soaked and freezing. We're getting you warmed up and in dry clothes, then the others are coming to meet us." And this time he wouldn't be leaving her alone in the bathroom.

Rather than argue, she seemed to sag in his hold and dropped her head against his shoulder. It twisted his in-sides, seeing this strong, fearless woman spent to the point that she'd lower her guard and lean on him.

Thankfully, there was no one else on the sidewalk on the way to the hotel. The lady at the front desk gasped in alarm when she saw him carrying Chloe. Chloe shifted in his arms and said something in flawless French to the woman, giving her a smile. The woman returned it, though she still seemed a bit worried.

"What did you say to her?" Heath asked as he carried her into the elevator.

"That I twisted my ankle and you were being my hero by carrying me to our room." She pushed gently at his shoulder when the elevator doors slid shut. "You can put me down now."

He didn't want to. "Maybe I like carrying you."

Those deep brown eyes lifted, and he found himself

wanting to do whatever it took to erase the painful shadows in them. If she'd been injured, he could have fixed it. This...

Though it went against every instinct that wanted to comfort and protect, the logical side of him knew she would resent him if he didn't let go, so he set her on her feet. He stayed right behind her as they walked down the hall to her room, then followed her in and locked the door before grabbing her hand and leading her into the bathroom.

Without a word he started the shower then turned to face her. She took a step back, frowning. "I can manage."

"I want to make sure you're not hurt."

"I'm not."

"I want to see for myself."

She heaved an irritated sigh and rolled her eyes, then started taking off her sodden uniform. He helped her, tugging the wet material down her arms and legs. She had scrapes on her knees, elbows and the heels of her hands, but otherwise appeared unhurt. When she was naked, he urged her into the shower, stripped and stepped in behind her.

She looked at him over her shoulder. The exhaustion that had dulled her eyes was gone, replaced by suspicion. "I'm fine."

Physically, yeah. The rest, not even close, no matter what she said. "Pass the shampoo."

She stared at him for a long moment, then relented and handed the tiny bottle to him. The invigorating scent of mint and lime filled the shower as he spread it between his hands and began lathering her hair.

Chloe was stiff at first, but as the hot water beat down on her shoulders and his hands massaged her scalp, she began to melt. Soon she let out a groan and let her head drop forward, her eyes closing as he worked the lather into her hair.

After rinsing her hair thoroughly, he used the shower gel to gently wash the salt from her skin, making sure to keep his hands away from her breasts and between her legs. When he was done, he shut off the water, wrapped her in a big towel and lifted her from the tub. She put on a hotel robe while he got dressed again. He came out of the bathroom to find her sitting on the end of her bed, plaiting her damp hair into a long braid over her shoulder.

Heath sat down beside her, unsure what to say. He'd never been in a situation like this, and talking about painful things had never been his strong suit. Still, for Chloe he was willing to try. "You want to talk about it?"

She shook her head. "There's nothing else to say."

Okay. "I'm sorry about Fleur. I know it hurts."

She looked at him, studied his eyes. "Yeah, I guess you do know."

He damn sure did. He'd lost his mom, and friends in the line of duty. Had been unable to save them, or avenge them later. Lifting a hand, he ran it over the crown of her head, pausing to curl his fingers around her nape. "Dubois will pay for what he did."

She searched his eyes, then nodded. "Yes. He will." She stood and walked around to the head of the bed. "I'm tired. Think I'll crash for a bit."

Heath was relieved to hear it, though he would rather she ask him to climb in next to her. "Sure." She'd gone without sleep for too long, and after the emotional toll she'd just withstood, she needed rest.

Still, he couldn't help pausing to admire the sight of her naked body as she let the robe drop to the floor before sliding between the sheets. Tucking them around her, he placed his hands on either side of her head and bent to kiss her temple. "Sleep tight. I'll be right through that door if you need anything."

Leaving the connecting door between their rooms open so he could keep eyes on her this time, he pulled out his phone to text Ty.

Chapter Nineteen

"How's she doing?" Ty whispered when Heath let him into his room a few minutes later.

"Sleeping." Finally. "Where's Megan?"

"She's at our hotel talking with Amber. They're following up a possible new lead on Dubois."

Heath groaned. If they found something and Chloe heard about it, she'd go right back to the hunt.

"Problem?" Ty asked.

"Yeah." He nodded at the connecting door. "I don't want her to go through any more."

Ty nodded and dropped into an easy chair. "I get it. But that's not how it works with these women."

Annoyed, off-balance, Heath sat on the foot of his bed to regard his best friend. "You should have seen her when I found her. She's done, man."

Ty watched him steadily. "You're awfully protective of her."

Heath shot him a hard look. "Hell yeah, I'm protective of her. Not that I can do anything to protect her from what happened," he muttered under his breath.

"I feel you, man, I really do. Especially since I know how you're wired."

And why. Ty knew all about Heath's past and why he was the way he was. "It makes me fucking insane that I can't protect her," he admitted finally.

"That she won't *let* you protect her, you mean."

"*Yes*." That was exactly it. "Jesus."

Ty nodded. "I know. It was the same for Megan and me."

"Was? Meaning it doesn't bother you now, what they do and that she's still in danger?"

Ty's expression was wry. "Let's just say it's a work in progress."

Heath shook his head at himself, bewildered about what he was feeling, how it had happened in such a short time. After seeing what his mother had gone through, he'd made the conscious decision long ago to protect himself, and that meant probably never letting a woman into his heart. And yet after yesterday Chloe was deep in there, whether he liked it or not. What the hell did he do about that?

"I didn't even know her a few days ago. Now I want to either lock her up to keep her safe, or stand between her and anything or anyone that poses a potential threat to her," Heath said.

"Feels awesome, doesn't it?"

He glared at Ty for the dry attempt at lightening the mood.

Ty sobered. "Sorry. No, I know it sucks."

"I barely know her." Didn't seem to matter, though. She'd blown past all his walls without even trying. Watching her dive off that dock yesterday to get to Fleur had irrevocably changed him. It was like being halfway up a rock face, but with no harness and ropes. Foreign. Terrifying. Yet he couldn't stop it.

"So?"

"So this…doesn't make any sense."

"It never does." Ty stretched his legs out and crossed his ankles. "These women…" He shook his head. "They're incredible and impossible to resist. If that makes you feel any better."

That was supposed to make him feel better?

"Just remember that she's not like anyone else you've ever been with."

He snorted. "Like I didn't notice?"

"No, I mean she's got a screwed-up history and tons of baggage she probably hasn't ever dealt with. She probably feels as lost as you do in all of this."

Heath frowned. "What do you mean, a screwed-up history? Aside from being an assassin," he added.

"They're all orphans." When Heath just stared at him, he continued. "All of them lost their parents young, were put into foster care and then fed into the Valkyrie Program if they showed the right scores on their aptitude tests."

Wait. "You're saying it was an involuntary program?"

"Yeah."

"Jesus Christ," he muttered, sickened and horrified. He imagined Chloe as a frightened young orphan, being subjected to that kind of treatment, and a giant wave of protectiveness rose inside him.

"They were taken in when they were alone, young and impressionable, then essentially brainwashed. They're trained to kill their targets no matter what gets in the way, to never get attached to anyone. Look at Megan and Amber, they were split up as kids and led to believe the other one was dead or a figment of their imagination. And the training is fucking brutal. In some ways, tougher than what you and I went through. And if they manage to make it through all that, the prize was being sent out alone to hunt dangerous targets for the government."

It was hard to accept that the government would do that to innocent girls. But it also explained why Chloe was as strong as she was. And why Fleur's death was hitting her so hard. Chloe had let Fleur in. She'd let him in as well, though in a different way.

"Have you seen her mark yet?" Ty asked.

"What mark?"

"I'll take that as a no." His buddy regarded him somberly. "She'll have a brand on her left hip."

"A *brand*?" A growl built in his throat. "Who fucking branded her?" And how had he missed it?

"Her head trainer. They did it on graduation. It's a Valkyrie design."

Jesus Christ. The thought of someone putting a branding iron to her skin made him want to put his fist through something. "That's goddamn barbaric."

"Yup, but to them it's a rite of passage and a mark of pride. I just want you to know what you're up against," Ty said. "I got lucky with Megan, but these women have emotional shields like you wouldn't believe. They have to, to survive."

Heath nodded, processing all of that. But if his friend was trying to warn him off getting emotionally attached, it was way too late for that. "I'll be leaving soon anyway, so it doesn't matter." Not that it would stop him from constantly wondering about Chloe and whether she was okay.

She made him want things he'd never considered himself ready for. Could see himself trying a real relationship, even if it had to be a long-distance one for a while, and wasn't that a kick in the ass for a guy who'd sworn never to go there? Not that he was even sure she would be up for that.

Bottom line, he didn't want to lose her. He also didn't want to spook her, and he'd seen enough friends' long-distance relationships implode after a few months apart.

"Just so you know, the offer I made still stands. Once you've finished your contract, I'd love to make you a permanent member of the team," Ty said.

Heath gave him a tight smile. He couldn't do that if Chloe was still in the picture and they weren't together. Seeing her and not being able to have her would be like a dull knife being repeatedly plunged between his ribs. "Thanks, I'll think about it."

"I hope you do. There's no one else I'd rather have on board."

Heath sat up straighter and changed the subject. "So. If you get a lead on Dubois, you'll be going after him?" The mission had been to free the captive women, but that had all changed now.

"Yes."

Heath appreciated that his buddy didn't bullshit him.

"You gonna stick around for that?" Ty asked him.

He didn't want to be part of a hit squad, but he also didn't want to leave them without backup against such a dangerous enemy, and couldn't stand the thought of not being here to watch Chloe's back. "I'll stay until the last minute before I have to leave for Syria."

He'd already contacted his boss there, saying he was dealing with a personal situation. But he didn't feel right pulling out of his upcoming contract this late, and the guys there were depending on him. He'd made a commitment to them. He couldn't leave them hanging and shorthanded when they were in harm's way every time they left their secure compound.

Ty nodded once. "That's all I needed to hear." He stood. "Text me when Chloe's up and we'll grab something to eat. If there's any update on Dubois, I'll let you know."

Heath let Ty out, torn about whether he wanted the team to get a lead on Dubois or not. He didn't want Chloe and the others in danger any more. But while Dubois was alive, Chloe would always be a target.

Silently cracking the connecting door open, he checked on her. She was asleep in the bed, curled on her side facing him, her chest rising and falling in an even rhythm.

The sight of her like that, so vulnerable despite her formidable internal strength, turned his heart over.

His feet carried him across the room before he even realized he was moving. He eased onto the bed and tucked his body around hers, carefully wrapping an arm around her to hold her close as she slept, unsure if he'd ever get the chance again.

****

Chloe was warm and cozy as she began to climb through the heavy layers of sleep toward consciousness. Normally she snapped awake in an instant, but this time her body was heavy and lethargic. Something was lying across her middle.

An arm. And there was an equally hard body against her back.

Her eyes opened. *Heath.*

He was wrapped around her, his breathing deep and even in sleep. Gray daylight filtered through the window on the other side of the room, the steady patter of rain against the glass soothing.

Then everything rushed back and the pain hit. Fleur lying dead in a refrigerated morgue drawer right now. Fleur being shot in the back because she'd taken Chloe's place on that boat. Having Dubois in her sights, and letting him get away.

She closed her eyes, pulled in a steadying breath as she fought the onrush of grief and guilt.

Don't feel. Don't feel.

It was so much easier when she could keep everything compartmentalized. She'd been trained to do it automatically, to never get attached or let emotions rule her.

She'd failed on every one of those counts on this mission, including when it came to the man holding her right now.

Heath's breathing changed and his arm tightened around her. "You awake?"

His deep murmur against the back of her head helped ground her. She focused on the feel of him, so solid and warm around her. It wasn't weak to allow herself to soak up this bit of comfort, was it? As long as she was aware that this was only temporary and she didn't show how much her heart was breaking? "Yes. What time is it?"

He shifted to look at his watch. "Not even noon yet. You hungry?"

"No."

"You only slept a couple hours. Go back to sleep." He cuddled her closer.

Can't. Her mind was too busy jabbing at her with sharp knives.

Fleur's dead because of you. It should be you in that morgue. You're a failure and an embarrassment, not worthy to call yourself a Valkyrie.

Her heart surged faster, a spurt of something close to panic bursting inside her. She didn't want to humiliate herself further by losing it in front of Heath, but if she didn't do something to take her mind off everything, she would.

Frantic to escape her thoughts, she rolled to face him. He was still dressed, lying on top of the covers. She stared into his eyes, that bright, piercing blue gaze that saw things inside her she wanted to hide, grabbed the back of his head and kissed him.

He stiffened, caught off guard for a second, but a heartbeat later one big hand slid into the back of her hair and his mouth slanted across hers.

Relief slammed into her. *Yes. Make me stop hurting.*

Chloe grabbed his shoulder with her free hand, threw

the covers off and started to roll on top of him. Heath caught her by the hip and turned her to her back, his big body coming down on hers. She gasped at the heat and weight of him, staring into his eyes.

"You sure?" he murmured.

God, don't be a Boy Scout right now. She needed the opposite. She needed hot, fast and furious, the chance to be transported away from reality for a little while.

Lifting her head, she nipped his lower lip. "Yes."

Heath's eyes darkened, his pupils expanding. Then his mouth came down on hers, the pressure and weight of his body increasing. She undulated beneath him, her hands wandering over his broad back to grab his shirt and wrench it upward. He peeled it over his head, flinging it aside as his mouth covered hers once more.

She sank into it, letting herself drown in him. He took over, that talented mouth moving down her body, making her quake and shudder as it moved from her breasts to her belly and between her thighs. So soft. His tongue was so soft as it flicked and teased, shooting pleasure through her veins, his strong hands gripping her hips to hold her still.

She whispered his name, getting close, needing him to fill her, for him to chase away this horrible emptiness and make her burn.

He kissed her inner thigh. "Turn over." He turned her onto her stomach, seized her hips to bring her up on her hands and knees.

Chloe tossed her braid over her shoulder to look back at him, her whole body pulsing with unrelieved need as he rolled a condom down the length of his cock and positioned himself behind her. But then he stopped, his gaze riveted to her Valkyrie mark.

He bent, smoothing his lips over the brand on her left hip. The branding process had killed the nerve endings there, but she felt the caress deep in her heart.

Then he straightened, his eyes so intent the breath

backed up in her lungs. Her heart thundered in her ears, that first slow thrust inside her dragging a cry from her throat.

She gripped the sheet beneath her, forgot how to breathe when he reached around to cup her mound, two big fingers gliding over her clit while he pushed deeper. Stretching her, filling her completely.

"I need you." Her voice cracked. She bit down on the inside of her cheek to keep from blurting out anything else, her emotions raw and volatile.

"I'm right here. *Feel* me," he urged in that delicious, deep voice. "Feel me inside you."

She didn't have a choice. He was hard and thick and hot, stroking her in time with his fingers. Release hovered at the edge of her consciousness, explosive and terrifying. But there was no going back now, her body had taken over, rocking with him as ragged moans poured from her throat.

"Let me make you come," he whispered, his mouth at the side of her neck, his tongue caressing another sensitive spot. "I want to feel you clench around my cock."

The pleasure intensified, rising and rising with his smooth, controlled rhythm. Chloe writhed in his hold, helpless as the rush took her. She bucked when it hit, her cries loud in the room.

"Ahh, Chloe." Heath's voice dropped to a ragged groan at her ear. He went rigid against her back and shuddered, buried deep inside her as he came. His forehead dropped to her shoulder, their ragged breaths mingling in the silence.

She lowered herself to her stomach, trying to catch her breath. But as soon as the physical release faded, the emotions she'd locked inside began to bubble up. They beat at the lid of the box she'd shoved them into with increasing force, threatening to burst free. And it only got worse when Heath curved his heavy arms under her and turned them so she was tucked into the cradle of his body.

She squeezed her eyes shut and swallowed hard. *No. Not like this.*

It hurt. Hurt to know what her failure had cost, and hurt worse to be emotionally attached to a man she couldn't have.

The pain ripped through her with sharp talons. Guilt. Grief. Impending loss. Of knowing she would wind up alone again soon.

A bubble of panic rose in her chest. She shoved upward, trying to twist away, a split second away from the dam bursting and not wanting him to witness that final humiliation.

"Don't," he said softly, pulling her to his chest this time. "You don't need to hide it."

She shook her head, shoving at his shoulders, frantic to prevent him from seeing her fall apart. "Let me go," she managed between gritted teeth. Tears were already burning her eyes, scalding the back of her throat and filling her chest with fire.

He didn't. His arms tightened and he cupped the back of her head in one hand, pulling her firmly into him.

Nooo...

Chloe's shoulders jerked on a dry sob she struggled to contain. Damn him, he wouldn't let go, and she didn't have the heart to hurt him to get free. So she did the only thing she could, shoving her face into his chest as she crumpled beneath the pain.

She couldn't remember the last time she'd cried, but this level of agony was what she remembered feeling when her mom died. There was no controlling it. No compartmentalizing it.

Hard, painful sobs ripped through her. She choked on them, her throat and chest on fire.

Through it all Heath said nothing, just held her tight.

So tight, his whole body curving around her, his arms surrounding her with fierce pressure. As though he wanted to absorb her pain, take it himself to lessen her suffering. Offering her shelter and comfort. Understanding.

It broke her heart, shattering the shields she'd spent a lifetime reinforcing. And when the storm finally passed, she sagged in his arms, lying limp as her upper body jerked with the aftershocks of her tears.

She lay there, wrecked as a new clarity took hold, sweeping away the fog in her mind. Fleur was gone, and soon she would lose Heath forever as well.

Chapter Twenty

*H*ell.

        Heath lay wide awake, his arms around Chloe. She was quiet, her little sniffles pulling on his aching heartstrings.

He'd never seen anyone cry like that. As if she'd been waging an epic battle between pain and pride, using all her strength to hold it in—until she couldn't and she just...broke. It wrenched something deep in his chest to see someone so strong suffering like that.

What a shit-show this whole thing had been. The only good part was meeting Chloe. He hadn't thought so at first. Now...

It was like he'd been sleepwalking, and she'd snapped him wide awake. She wasn't his usual type, definitely not the kind of woman he had ever envisioned bringing home to meet his family one day, yet now he couldn't imagine letting her go, because any woman after her would seem bland and lifeless by comparison.

But how the hell could it ever work between them? She

wasn't the settling down type, and he was due at his next job in nine days. He'd be gone for months, and she'd disappear long before he was done, off on another deadly hunt.

She gave a shuddering sigh and tried to roll away again, wiping at her eyes.

"No, it's okay," he protested, urging her to lie down again. "You stay put." He went to the bathroom and brought her a warm washcloth.

She wiped her face, her shoulders still shuddering, and avoided his gaze. Her face was blotchy, her nose and eyes red. He wanted to kiss every mark away, make the pain stop. But this wasn't a bullet or shrapnel wound he could treat. All he could do was be here for her.

He set the cloth on the nightstand next to him and tucked a lock of hair behind her ear while she pulled the sheet up to cover herself. "You can talk to me."

She shook her head. "You know everything already."

He could tell it bothered her to have him watch her right now. It made her feel too vulnerable, and embarrassed. She had nothing to be embarrassed about, but he understood so he gathered her close and tucked her head beneath his chin. "Can I do anything?"

"No, but...this is nice."

Yeah, it was. He stroked a hand over her hair, down the length of her spine. "Want to go back to sleep now?"

"Can't." She snuggled closer, making his chest constrict, and gave an exhausted sigh. "I don't think I've cried since my mom died," she murmured almost absently.

His hand stilled on her back. Was she serious? "How old were you?"

"Six."

Whoa. That couldn't be healthy. "What happened?"

"Bone cancer. I was too young to remember much, but I know it was awful. She was in terrible pain at the end. She would cry because the medicine couldn't take it away."

God, that must have been hell to watch. Even worse than what his own mother had gone through. "And you didn't have any family to take you in?"

"No. She was a single mom. Got pregnant in eleventh grade and her mom kicked her out. My dad took off, denied any responsibility, and my mom was too proud to fight him. So we moved to a different town."

So they'd both grown up without a father.

She was quiet a moment. "I'm glad she left all that behind and raised me on her own. I wouldn't have wanted to be part of a family like that anyway."

He didn't blame her. "Ty said you went into foster care. Did they take good care of you?"

"Yes. But I was hurting about my mom. My foster parents were good people and they tried to make me feel safe and cared about. It just wasn't going to work. I was put into another foster home, and that's when I landed on someone's radar involved with the Valkyrie Program."

It was still hard to wrap his mind around the whole thing. "But you didn't have a choice."

"No. I was proud, though. Less than thirty-percent of us made it through the selection process. Of course, we didn't know what the program was called until the final training phase, after we'd been put into our specialties."

"What happened to the ones who washed out?"

She shrugged. "They were funneled into other programs. Intelligence work, investigative work. At least, that's what we were told. None of us know for sure what happened to them."

It boggled the mind. What other top-secret programs was the U.S. government hiding from the world?

"So how long's your contract in Syria?"

"Three months." Too damn long. "I can't pull out now. The guys there need me. I can't let them down."

"I get it." Then her expression turned pensive.

"Hmmm."

"Hmmm? What's that mean?"

"Nothing. Just thinking ahead."

As in, she was contemplating them being together after his contract was up? "To what?"

"Wondering if you'll still remember me then."

He snorted. "You gotta be kidding. Like I'd ever forget you, firecracker."

She was silent a moment. "What will you do after the contract's done?"

He'd planned to go home and spend some much-needed time with his family, then join a couple PJ buddies for a rock-climbing trip. But he'd planned all that before he'd met Chloe. Now everything was different, and the idea of going home or rock climbing wasn't half as tempting anymore. "Ty wants me to join the team permanently."

"You're considering it?"

"Yeah." He resumed running his fingertips along her spine, wondering how in hell it would ever work between them. Even if she was willing to try a relationship, could they make it work long-distance? "What about you?"

"I'm going to finish what I started."

"And then?"

"If I make it that far, I'll worry about it after. But I'd like to help Megan and the others."

It chilled him to hear her say she didn't expect to survive going after Dubois. "Don't talk like that."

"Like I might die?" She gave a humorless laugh. "Chances are, I will. Just how it is."

God dammit. He crushed her to him. "No. I couldn't take that."

She pushed against his chest gently and tipped her head back to look into his face. "You can't save me, Heath. But it's so incredibly sweet that you want to." She laid her palm against his cheek, her expression turning serious. "I never expected to meet anyone like you. I've spent most of my life staying distant and detached. But a few days with you, and look at me—I'm a wreck."

"It's okay to fall apart every now and again." He stroked her hair. "Just like a taco."

She blinked at him. "Huh?"

"Tacos. You like them?"

"Yeah, of course. Everyone does."

"There you go. They fall apart all the time, and yet you still love them. And so do I." He kissed the tip of her nose.

She let out a startled laugh, then groaned and closed her eyes. "Oh, man. And now you decide to show me you've got a sense of humor, too."

He hugged her tighter, unable to keep his feelings buried a moment longer. "What if I wanted to see you after this is over?"

She grunted. "How would that work? You're going to Syria, and my life is…uncertain at best. I'm not exactly relationship material."

"Yeah you are." If she wanted to be.

Now her smile was tender and sweet, piercing him. "You're a dangerous man, Heath. You make me want to stay when I should be running in the opposite direction, for both our sakes. You make me wish for…"

"For what?"

"Things that can never happen," she whispered back.

It was far from the *no* he'd been fearing. "They can if we both want them bad enough."

She laid her fingertips on his lips to stop him from speaking, her eyes haunted by doubts and fears she wouldn't voice aloud. "Being with you is an unexpected gift. Let's not complicate things any more than they already are. Let's just enjoy each other while we can, and let that be enough."

Frustration pulsed through him, an instant denial forming on his tongue. But he sensed if he pushed her right now, she'd shut down and turn away. That was the last thing he wanted. "I'll be there for you if you ever need me," he finally said. "I want you to know that."

She groaned and leaned forward to rest her forehead on his chin. "You're killing me, Heath."

He kissed the top of her head. "I wanted you to know."

"I do know it." She wound her arms around him and hugged him. "I've never met anyone like you."

"A rock-climbing former PJ?"

She huffed out a laugh. "Well, okay, yeah. But I meant someone with your level of character. Like the way you tried to save Fleur yesterday. You dived into the water without hesitation and put yourself at risk by staying even when the cops were on the way."

So had she. "I was just—"

"Being you. I know. And I appreciate it more than you'll ever know." She swallowed. "I'm glad you were with her until she lost consciousness."

Him too. "When did you two meet?"

"About a year ago. But when we were in contact working the shipments together, I felt like she understood me better than anyone. She was the most authentic person I ever knew—until I met you. And that's why I'm going to rescue those women and get Dubois, to honor her."

Heath didn't like it. At all. But he understood it. "I know," he said on a grudging sigh.

"Thank you." She lifted her head to brush a soft, tender kiss across his lips. It eased him to see the shadows mostly gone from her eyes. And if he wasn't mistaken, that was a distinctly mischievous glint in them now. "Can I see your butt tat?"

He let out a startled laugh. "What?"

"Your green feet. Come on, you said you have 'em." She reached down to smack his ass. "Lemme see."

Chuckling, he eased away and rolled onto his stomach. "Have at 'er."

"Oh, I will." She sat up, pushing her long, thick braid out of the way as she settled on her knees beside him, giving him a gorgeous view of her body. Her hands smoothed down his back, over his hip, and paused on his right ass cheek. "Hmmm, nice," she murmured, bending to nip at the tat of the two green feet. "*Very* nice."

Yeah, there was no way they were leaving this bed to go have dinner with the others.

Chapter Twenty-One

"Still nothing on the women. Sorry. I'm as frustrated as you," Amber said to Chloe on the phone late that evening.

After spending most of the night wrapped up in Heath's arms, first sleeping and then losing herself to more pleasurable things, Chloe had been hungry for something else—justice. She still hurt inside, but not nearly as much as she had been, and actively working on this with the others helped lessen the burden. She didn't feel so alone anymore.

"It's not your fault," she told Amber. Dubois had moved the women when he suspected Chloe might come for them. "You'll keep us updated if you find anything?" Amber was working on various things simultaneously. Locating the women—Dubois could have sold them already—finding Dubois, and looking for any possible signs of the missing Valkyries.

"Of course."

Chloe had learned from Megan, and in her few dealings with Amber over the past few days, that Amber was the quieter, more serious of the sisters. Harder, more remote. "Thanks. Here's Megan."

Megan took the phone, talked for another minute, then ended the call. "Okay, so all dead ends so far. What's the plan now?" She grabbed a piece of cheese from the platter on the table between them and popped it into her mouth.

"We need to find Dubois," Heath said, nursing a beer in one of the easy chairs pulled up to the small coffee table in the center of their group.

Her chest hitched just looking at him, remembering what they'd shared together, the things he'd said to her. It was going to hurt like hell when he left, but she would never regret their time together. "Exactly." She searched the platter of cheese, crackers, fruit and veggies for something that might tempt her. It was all so…healthy, and the only caffeine was the carafe of hot coffee. Making a face, she picked a cracker, put a piece of pickle on it and put it in her mouth.

"Way better than Pop Tarts, am I right?" Heath said with a knowing gleam in his eyes.

"Nope, not even a little. So. Dubois." She would hunt him down and kill him. But with the trafficked women still unaccounted for, the focus of Chloe's mission had changed. She wasn't willing to kill him at the cost of losing those defenseless women. It would make Fleur's death twice as meaningless.

No. Chloe would locate him, capture and interrogate him to find out what she needed to know. As soon as he'd given her what she needed, he would die.

Megan's phone beeped. She checked it, smiled. "She's here."

A minute later, Chloe was face to face with the legendary Trinity Durant. The former Valkyrie was maybe five or six years older than Chloe, and gorgeous. Straight, shiny black hair cut into a sleek, chin-length bob, elegant makeup that emphasized her deep blue eyes, and clothes that hugged her curvy, knockout figure.

"Chloe," Trinity said after hugging Megan. "So nice to finally meet you."

"Same." She offered her hand, got a firm shake in reply. The woman oozed sex appeal and confidence. And a lethal vibe Chloe recognized instantly.

"All right, what's the latest on Dubois?" She headed straight for the table and helped herself to the food.

"Best we can guess right now is that he might be at his country estate not far from the Normandy landing beaches," Chloe said.

Trinity nodded and sank into the chair Heath had vacated for her—what else would you expect from a Boy Scout, after all? "Do you know it?"

"Yes. I've been there. I know the layout, have a basic idea of what kind of security he has. That was a few months ago, though. Given everything that's happened since, he might have upgraded everything."

"Oh, God, I hope so," Megan said, with a grin. "And Amber can't wait to hack into everything and disable his system."

Chloe glanced at Heath. One shoulder braced against the wall, he watched her with such admiration and desire that she wished things could be different, that she could have the chance at something normal with him. Which made no sense. On paper they were a disaster. But together in person, they worked. In a mere matter of days, Heath had ruined her for anyone else.

Time and fate were working against them, however, and trying to continue a relationship after this was done wouldn't be safe, for either of them. Even if she killed Dubois, she would still have a target on her back. She didn't want to put Heath in constant danger. He deserved better.

"Show us," Trinity said, sliding Chloe's tablet across the table to her.

She found pictures of the house online. "All right, here we go. Guillaume Dubois' stupid extravagant country estate." Eighteen of the most gorgeous acres money could buy, with a stone, chateau-style mansion set in the front third.

She pointed out all the features on the property, and the layout of both floors. "His office is on the lower floor, looking out over the gardens."

"Looks a bit like the one at Laidlaw Hall," Megan said, leaning closer. "I feel right at home already."

It felt so damn good to go over intel and plan an op with such a qualified team. Such a relief that it wasn't all on just her shoulders.

"We'll need a staging area. Far away from the target in case things don't go smoothly," Trinity murmured, her eyes on the map.

"Where's Dubois going to send the ship?" Ty asked, scooting closer to study it.

"Somewhere on the northern coast," Chloe said. "Opposite of where we are, and close enough to England to smuggle the cargo across the Channel. Fleur said something about this next shipment of women possibly being destined for Britain, and I heard rumors about that too."

"Calais?" Ty said.

"Too obvious," Chloe answered. Guillaume never went with the obvious, but he'd want a port close to the UK.

"A smaller port, maybe?" Heath asked.

She shook her head and went with her gut. "A major one. He's going to try and slip the women in somewhere busy enough that they go unnoticed." No easy feat, with the security available now, but Dubois' money greased a lot of wheels and made things a lot easier for him. The team couldn't rely on any help from the port authorities or cops.

She weighed her options, looking at the coastline

available. Not Paris. That was too risky, even for him. Her gaze tracked southwest down the coastline, mentally marking the location of his country estate. "I'm betting the Normandy coast, but away from Calais," she said, her gut confirming it.

Everyone looked at her. "You sure?" Trinity asked.

"As sure as I can be. It's near the English Coast, and from there he can funnel the women either to Paris or across the Channel and get top dollar in Britain." It made her angry and ill.

Trinity nodded. "It's as good a place as any to start with."

It was. Energized and resolved, Chloe shoved to her feet. "Okay, so we're off to the Normandy Coast then," she said, hopeful for the first time since Fleur had died. She couldn't bring her friend back, but she could see this mission through, then deal with Dubois. That was all she would allow herself to focus on right now, and it would have to be enough.

As the others started chatting, Megan grabbed her arm and towed her through the connecting door into the other room. Shutting it, she faced Chloe and widened her eyes. "Well?"

"Well, what?"

Her friend groaned. "Come on. You and Heath. What happened?"

For about two seconds Chloe considered lying to cover it up. But why should she? She had nothing to hide and wasn't ashamed of her actions. "Everything," she admitted.

Megan squealed and clapped her hands, bouncing up and down. "I knew it! I called it, too. Told Ty there was something brewing between you guys."

"I can see why he's Ty's best friend." She shook her head, her happiness fading beneath the heavy ache forming in her chest. "He's...an amazing guy."

Megan's eyebrows rose. "Amazing? Wow."

"I know." There was no other way to describe him. Of course he'd have his flaws, everyone did. So far, everything that mattered was evident in his actions, and to her they spoke a million times louder than words.

Her friend frowned. "But? I feel like there's a but."

"But it's just temporary. And you know why."

Megan's hazel eyes were thoughtful. "A few months ago, I might have agreed with that. But not now, because I've learned that sometimes things have a way of working out."

Chloe shook her head and pushed out an exhalation. "Hoping for any of that right now is just too much."

"I understand. But how about I'll keep hoping for you, then?"

Chloe smiled through the ache. "Thanks, Itch."

"Anytime, Twitch."

God, it was good to have Megan back in her life. She closed the distance between them in two strides and pulled her friend into a hard hug. "I *missed* you, dammit. Thought about you all the time." She understood why the Valkyrie instructors had taken such pains to sever bonds of friendship and make them into autonomous operatives. Still, it had been a long, lonely life of solitary service to her country.

Megan seemed startled for a moment, then returned the embrace just as fiercely. "Me too."

****

Heath closed his hotel room door behind Megan and Ty a few minutes later and turned to face Chloe.

She was watching Heath from the adjoining doorway, and arched an eyebrow. "Up for another road trip?" She held up the keys. "I'll even let you drive."

Rather than answer, he crossed to her, hungry for another taste of her. "You like it when I drive," he reminded her, making her grin as he took the keys and kissed her.

The long drive to the coast gave them a much-needed breather. Chloe slept for most of it, waking a few minutes before they arrived at their rental unit in a village fifteen minutes from the water. Everyone else was staying in the near vicinity, but spaced far enough apart to avoid possible detection. "We've got just over two-and-a-half hours until we meet again to go over the final plan for the Dubois op tonight," he told her.

"Yeah."

Now that she was awake, he could practically feel the pent-up energy pulsing off her. She needed to blow off steam and get a change of scenery. He had an idea, though he'd gone back and forth on the way here about bringing it up. "Wanna get out of here for a while?"

"Maybe. What'd you have in mind?"

"Ever seen the landing beaches?"

"No." She eyed him. "Why, you want to go?"

"Yeah." It was like a date, but he considered that a good thing. Everything between them had been rushed and intense so far. They had a few hours to themselves before the meeting; he wanted to slow things down and spend quality time outside the bedroom with her. Let her see part of him he would have kept hidden before. He wanted her to know him, baggage and ghosts and all.

After watching him a moment, she nodded and settled back in her seat. "Okay, then let's go."

Her eager acceptance made him smile. He'd originally wanted to visit the landing beaches during his leave, and now he could. He'd just never imagined doing so under these circumstances...or with this incredible woman by his side.

Twenty minutes later she stood next to him, gazing out at the massive shell craters pitting the infamous battlefield of Pointe Du Hoc. The sharp point was the highest spot between the American sector's Omaha and Utah landing beaches, and had been heavily defended by German forces.

"Man, can you imagine what this must have looked like on D-Day? I don't know how the hell they made it up that cliff under that kind of fire," she said with a shake of her head.

"I know. Those Rangers were badass motherfuckers." The cliff was a hundred feet tall, and the troops had faced withering fire long before their landing crafts had even hit the beaches in the distance.

She nodded, gazing at the scarred landscape before them, and the waves of the Atlantic rolling onto the beach below in the distance. "Ever wonder what you'd have done, if you'd been there?"

"What do you mean?"

She lifted a shoulder. "I like to think I'm pretty brave in the face of danger. But that…" She nodded at the point and the beach beyond it. "I honestly wonder if I'd have had the guts to step out of the landing craft that morning."

He stepped up behind her and wrapped his arms around her waist. She leaned into him, fitting snug and warm against the front of his body.

He loved holding her. Loved that this strong, inde- pendent woman had let him in as far as she had. But he wanted even deeper. He wanted all the way in, until she couldn't stand being without him.

"You don't make a charge like that because you're brave," he told her. "You do it because of the people be- side and behind you."

"I don't know what that feels like." She tilted her head back to look at him. "Is that what it was like for you?"

"Yes." She'd never had teammates beside her and at her back when she'd gone into harm's way, except for yesterday. "There were plenty of times when I was afraid on the battlefield, but you do what you have to do." When fear had intruded through all his mental shields during a mission, seeping through all the professionalism and training. "Your focus is on getting the mission done, and making sure everyone on your team gets to go home alive."

Her brown eyes shone with admiration as she gazed up at him. "That was romantic and sexily alpha at the same time, fyi."

He gave a quiet laugh. "Didn't feel like it at the time, I promise you." He squeezed her tighter, enjoying the feel of her and glad he was able to share this moment with her in this hallowed place. "And, *fyi*, you'll never have to go into harm's way alone ever again."

Her little smile turned his heart over. "That's a pretty mind-blowing concept for me."

"You'll get used to it." He tucked her back into his hold and rested his chin on the top of her head, taking in the panoramic view and thinking of the sacrifices made on that terrible day.

Next they drove to the Normandy American Cemetery and Memorial.

They were both silent as they entered the cemetery. Almost two-hundred acres of beautifully manicured grounds containing more than nine-thousand burials. Even though Heath had known what to expect, the sight of all those white marble crosses still hit him hard.

The visual impact of all those crosses laid out would affect even the hardest heart, but the American flag flying above them was too much.

An instant lump formed in Heath's throat, the backs of his eyes stabbed by a thousand pinpricks. Before him lay a testament to the cost of war. Every one of these graves marked someone's son, husband, father, brother, friend. It made him think of the friends he'd lost in service to their country. Made him wonder for the millionth time if their sacrifice had been worth it.

He had to believe it was. He couldn't handle the alternative.

Something brushed his hand, then slender fingers twined through his. "You okay?" Chloe asked.

He nodded, not trusting himself to speak as he took it all in and remembered his dead buddies. During his tours he'd seen a lot of death. But losing a friend never got any easier, and his mother's violent death would always haunt him too.

He was thankful he hadn't seen it, but he would never stop feeling that he should have been there to protect her. That he should have forced her to leave that abusive asshole before it was too late. Maybe then she would still be alive.

Chloe squeezed. "You lost friends overseas."

She was so perceptive. Even after just a few days together, she saw the deepest parts of him. No one had ever done that before. Not even his family, and he loved them to death. "Four."

"And your mother. You blame yourself for not being there to save her."

God. He finally found the courage to look at her, unashamed that his eyes were wet. "Yes."

A nod. Then she turned her gaze back to the crosses in front of them, allowing him some privacy while still giving him the comfort of her support. "We'll honor them all today in this sacred place. Together."

Her quiet words almost did him in. If she'd made a big deal out of it or tried to fawn all over him, he would have been embarrassed and probably annoyed. The way she'd handled it was just so damn perfect. "And Fleur," he managed past the restriction in his throat. He hadn't known her, but he wished he had. To earn Chloe's love and loyalty, she must have been an amazing person.

Chloe flashed him a poignant smile that pierced his

heart. "Yes. And Fleur too."

They stayed where they were for another ten minutes or so, standing side by side in silence as he privately grieved for his lost friends. When he tugged on her hand, she didn't say a word, just walked beside him down the path. Driving away from the cemetery later, he felt more at peace than he had in a long time.

As soon as they were inside their rental condo, he picked her up and carried her to the bedroom, where he laid her down on the bed and took his sweet time making her come with his mouth before sliding deep inside her. She was right there with him, urging him on with sweet gasps and whispers, holding him close.

In the aftermath he rolled them so she was on top, her cheek nestled into the hollow of his shoulder. A level of peace he'd never experienced before flowed over him.

Chloe's phone rang. On a groan she reached across him to grab it from the nightstand. "Hey, Itch. Everything good?" She listened for a minute. "Copy that. I'll tell him."

"Something up?" he asked when she ended the call.

"Amber got a location on Dubois," she said, lying back down on him. "He's in Belgium and staying overnight at a hotel, so the country property's clear except for some minimal security."

"So the op there's a go?"

"Yep. We're meeting at the primary RV point at 22:00 hours." She snuggled closer, gave a soft, contented sigh, and her not jumping up after knowing Dubois' location told Heath he'd stolen just as much of her heart as she had his. "Which means we don't have to leave for another couple hours."

He slid his arms around her, savoring the warmth of her body and the silken softness of her skin. "Perfect." Because he selfishly wanted her all to himself like this for as long as he could.

She was quiet for a few minutes before speaking. "Why hasn't some smart woman locked you down yet?" She sounded baffled.

"The honest answer is, I've never been into long-term before."

"No? How come?"

The truth forced him to confront his demons and dig up things from his past he'd rather forget. But he'd tell Chloe. "I've always had a hard time trusting when it comes to romantic relationships. I guess it's from watching what happened to my mom over and over growing up. The guys she brought home were all great at first. But eventually the shine would wear off and they'd start showing their true colors. They'd stop being nice at some point, stop faking what they were, and they all turned out to be abusive assholes." And their true colors had nearly always manifested in the form of bruises on his mother. "It just turned me off the whole long-term commitment thing, I think."

Until now. Because of Chloe, everything had changed. She'd shown him the strength of her loyalty, had demonstrated the true depth of her character. He'd seen the true essence of her, didn't have to worry that she might be hiding behind a fake veneer—and that was the basis for his fear of commitment all these years. Chloe was *real*, and it opened up a part of him he'd kept closed off his whole life.

"I can understand that," she said. "Although you've already seen me at my worst, and you're still here."

"That's because you're different." He hugged her closer to kiss her forehead.

"Bet your ass I am," she said proudly.

Heath grinned and lay there soaking up the contentment of being with her. So strange, to be this at peace with someone who brought such chaos. But hell, he couldn't imagine losing Chloe now.

He was free climbing now, halfway up the rock face with nothing below to break his fall. But it was another kind of fall he faced now.

For the first time in his life, he wanted a real relationship with a woman.

Chapter Twenty-Two

In the back of the van, Chloe checked her weapon one more time, holstered it, then glanced around at the others in the dim interior. "You got comms ready for us?" she asked Trinity

"Yep." She handed everyone an earpiece that they slipped in and activated. While Chloe was acting team leader for this op, Trinity was overseeing the whole thing and reporting anything pertinent back to Alex Rycroft. "Comm check."

Everyone checked in.

"Okay, time to get this party started," Megan murmured, tugging the black ski mask over her face.

"Guys, you good to go?" Chloe asked Heath and Ty, who were seated across the van from her.

"Yep," Heath said, giving her a little smile that made her heart kick hard against her ribs.

It was now after midnight and they were a few klicks from Dubois' country manor. Amber and Jesse were in a different van parked on the other side of the estate, having flown in that afternoon to assist in the op to infiltrate the house and search for intel about the missing shipment of women.

Everyone knew the plan inside and out, but Megan had been antsy all afternoon. Chloe snapped her fingers twice to get her friend's attention and held out a hand. "Hands."

In the act of pulling out her gloves, Megan paused. "What?"

She wiggled her fingers impatiently. "Hands."

Megan made a huffing sound and grudgingly held out her hands.

In the dim lighting Chloe tutted as she examined the raw, bloody mess all around Megan's nails where she'd picked the skin away. Both hands. That meant her anxiety level had to be bad. "You still do that before an op, huh?"

"Man, does she know you or what," Ty said with a chuckle. Then to Chloe, "I've tried everything to get her to stop."

Megan snatched her hands back and pulled on her gloves, ignoring them. Anxiety had been her constant companion her whole life, something she'd had to figure out how to manage. Picking at her fingers was a habit—coping mechanism, really—she'd developed that she'd never broken. "I'm way better than I used to be. I'd give you some of the credit for that, but now I don't want to."

Grinning, Ty grabbed her and pulled her in for a kiss. "You love me."

"I do."

That much was obvious. Ty was a solid, stabilizing force in Megan's life and Chloe was seriously impressed. And if her friend's anxiety about the future started to get the better of her, all she had to do was look at the promise ring on her finger. Ty loved her and would stand by her through anything.

Chloe bet Heath would be like that in a relationship too, and it made the yearning inside her so sharp it hurt. This afternoon at the landing beaches he'd allowed her to see the most private part of him, and it had touched her deeply. She'd never felt so close to anyone in her life, and while it scared her a little, it also filled her with a joy she'd never experienced before.

But she couldn't think about any of that right now. They had to infiltrate Dubois' manor house and get all the intel they could if they were going to have any chance of rescuing the missing women.

"Amber, how are things looking on your end?" Trinity asked.

"All systems go. All your tracking beacons are operational." Amber was handling security systems and overwatch using all her electronic wizardry from her makeshift mobile command center. "I'll start the security system hack when the entry team's in position."

"Perfect. Let's rock," Chloe said.

On the way out of the van Heath squeezed her shoulder before pulling on his own mask. "Ready?" he asked.

"Yep." Chloe would act as tour guide and lead them into position inside the house. Heath was going in as her backup, and there was no one she trusted more to protect her while she and Megan searched for secret files.

For someone who had always operated alone until recently, it was an incredible feeling.

"Jesse, you all set?" Amber said.

"Locked and loaded," her boyfriend responded, already providing overwatch and protection for them on an incline at the north side of the property. He would report any movement or comings and goings on the front grounds and give them security updates.

"This is so high tech compared to what I'm used to," Chloe said as she checked her weapon one last time. Whenever she took out a security system, it was with wire cutters and duct tape or bullets. This was so much slicker. "Imagine the things I could have accomplished with all this tech and firepower behind me."

"I'd say you had plenty of firepower behind you already," Heath said dryly, holstering his pistol.

He was so cute. "Touché."

"All right, anything else you want to go over before we do this?" Trinity asked.

Chloe looked at the others, then shook her head. "Nope. Let's do this." She held her hand out, palm down. "Everyone in. Valkyries on three."

Megan grinned and put her hand on top of Chloe's. Heath and Ty followed suit, then Trinity placed hers on top.

"Okay." Chloe's whole body was charged, excitement and anticipation stirring in her gut. "One. Two."

"*Valkyries*," everyone said, throwing their hands up.

"I'm so pumped," Chloe said under her breath as she tugged her mask down over her face. "Amber?"

"Roger. Initiating hack of the perimeter security now. Stand by."

Heath stood behind Chloe. Megan moved in behind him, Ty at her back.

Facing the direction of the manor house, Chloe locked her focus in. When they found what they were looking for, she was going to use it to nail Guillaume Dubois' ass to the wall. "Okay, team. Follow me."

AS SOON AS they started moving, Megan's anxiety level dropped to almost zero. It was always that way when she was in op mode.

She followed close behind Chloe, with Ty and Heath bringing up the rear. In the lead, Chloe moved swift and sure up the grassy incline that led to the field adjoining Dubois' estate.

It wasn't easy for her old friend to let others help with something like this. Megan was glad to see Chloe opening up and accepting the others on the team as part of this mission.

Their involvement wasn't completely altruistic, however. Megan and Trinity wanted Chloe to come on board as a permanent member of their team, and they were prepared to do whatever it took to make that happen. Starting with rescuing these women and taking down Dubois.

"You still read me?" Trinity asked via comms.

"Loud and clear," Chloe murmured back.

The more time Megan spent with Trinity, the more she appreciated the older Valkyrie's ability to calmly take charge and organize things. When Trinity was at Laidlaw Hall, she spent a lot of time with Kiyomi. Megan wanted to hang out with them more once this was taken care of and she brought Chloe back with her. Chloe was easily the most social and outgoing Valkyrie Megan had ever met. It must have been extra hard on her to be alone all these years.

"Perimeter cameras going down in three, two, one... Out." Amber announced.

Chloe stayed in front as they jumped a ditch and ran across the expanse of grass toward the eight-foot-tall stone wall surrounding the manor.

"You're clear," Jesse told them.

Music to Megan's ears.

"Interior yard is clear too," Amber reported, now watching the hacked security feeds on her computer. "I've got everything on a loop so it won't raise suspicion."

Heath boosted Chloe up to scale the wall. She straddled the top, checked, then dropped down on the other side. "Go," she told them.

Heath jumped up to grab the top of the wall and hoisted himself to the top, then reached down for Megan's hands while Ty boosted her up. They dropped down on the other side, followed by Ty a second later, and took up a diamond formation as they moved toward the house.

It was an impressive chateau, but not as nice as Laidlaw Hall she thought with a mental sniff. Dubois had bought this place with dirty money. Whereas Marcus had inherited his ancestral home, and worked damn hard to maintain it with the money he carefully managed.

They headed straight for the side entrance where the hired help came and went, as it had the best entry point for their purposes. Megan stepped up to the door and used her little electronic gadget to unscramble the key code, then punched it in.

Click.

"We're in," she whispered and eased the door open an inch, pistol up and ready, Chloe and the guys stacked up behind her. The mudroom was empty, the house quiet.

"Two heat signatures, but they're faint. One downstairs near the kitchen, the other upstairs near the master suite," Amber reported.

So Dubois might still be in Belgium. Perfect. "Copy. Moving in now." This was a simple get in, steal what they needed, and get out mission. To maintain the air of secrecy they had to avoid all contact with the guards, or it would tip Dubois off that he was no longer safe here and the women would likely be lost forever.

She led the way through to the lower hallway, then stopped to let Chloe take point. They'd gone over the floor plan until Megan had it memorized, but Chloe was the expert here.

They snuck down the hall, moving toward Dubois' office. According to Chloe the man had backups of his backups at all his places, so if they were going to find what they needed, it would be in there.

"I got movement," Amber said. "Guy on upper floor's headed downstairs."

Chloe gestured behind her and the team ducked out of sight into the butler's pantry. Megan waited at the door, curbing her impatience. She wanted to get this done and get out of here without any hiccups.

It felt like half an hour before Amber spoke again.

"He's still in the kitchen. Midnight snack time, I guess."

Megan stifled a groan and waited with the others until Amber gave them the all clear, then crept out of the pantry. This time Chloe made a beeline for the office. Megan stayed hot on her heels, lock pick kit in hand.

While the others kept watch she picked the lock on Dubois' office door and snuck inside with Chloe, while Ty and Heath remained outside to guard them. "How's our window looking now?" Megan asked Amber. That idiot security guard had just deleted a serious chunk of their time.

"You're gonna have to work fast. You've got T-minus eleven minutes."

Well, crap.

She and Chloe spread out and began their search. While Amber walked Chloe through hacking Dubois' password on his desktop computer, Megan looked around for more enticing things. The custom-built cabinets held financial files they might find useful later. She kept going, searching for a thumb drive or something like that hidden away where no one was likely to look.

The massive antique desk had no false bottom on the underside or in any of its drawers. She checked the art next, pushing aside the corner of each painting on the wall. "Bingo." A safe.

She removed the painting, propping it against the wall to get a closer look at what she was dealing with. Electronic keypad. Fingerprint biometric scanner. She sighed in disappointment and disapproval. All this money, and this was the level of security Dubois used to keep his private stuff safe?

Well, bonus for her. "Let's see how thorough his cleaning service is," she murmured, taking out a few items from her pocket. She sprayed a fine layer of dust onto the tiny screen, then put a piece of tape over it to preserve any print there. Shining her penlight on it, she smiled. "Not that thorough."

With the print intact, she used her electronic scrambler to get the code to the keypad, then pressed her thumb over the print. "*Et voilà*," she whispered as the door opened.

"Anything good inside?" Chloe whispered, still at Dubois' computer. Amber was remotely copying the files on it now, and would then use Lady Ada to scan them for relevant information.

"Yep. Jewels, cash, and a couple of these little gems." She pulled out the two flash drives, then swept the interior to make sure she hadn't missed anything. "Sending you the files now," she told Amber, and plugged the flash drives into a transmitter her evil genius sister had given her earlier.

As soon as she was done, she carefully checked the rest of the room while Chloe finished at the computer, making sure they'd found everything of use in here. "How are we doing on time?"

"Three minutes. Shut everything down and start exfil."

Hell. Megan replaced the painting, checked the alignment, then headed for the door. Chloe finished shutting down the computer and joined her. "Coming out," Chloe whispered, then quietly opened the door where the guys waited.

"Guys, you're cutting it close," Amber warned. "You've got forty-two seconds to get over that wall before the system is up and you set it off. Haul ass."

Megan followed close behind Chloe as they rushed back to the side entrance, their rubber-soled boots quiet on the rug lining the hallway.

"Guard number two is headed downstairs," Amber said.

"First guard's outside on the east lawn," Jesse added. "Better make it quick."

The door squeaked when Chloe opened it. Everyone froze, checking behind them, then they stepped out, shut the door and raced for the wall.

"Seven. Six. Five," Amber counted down.

Megan ran for the wall and jumped, catching the top of it. Strong hands boosted her up. She hopped off and landed in a crouch on the other side, drawing her weapon to scan while the others landed behind her. "Clear?" she murmured.

"Negative. Hold your positions," Jesse answered.

Megan immediately shifted back into the shadows cast by the wall. "Sitrep."

"Car approaching the south end of the driveway," Jesse said.

Beside her, Chloe went completely rigid. "Is it Dubois?"

Hell. Megan automatically reached out to grab Chloe's upper arm. "Stand down, Twitch."

Chloe shook her hand off and eased forward a step, the predatory energy coming from her palpable. "Is. It. Dubois."

"Stand by," Jesse answered.

Heath intervened, grabbing her shoulder. "Chloe. No," he said in a hard whisper.

Chloe didn't move, her gaze trained on the driveway, every muscle drawn taut as she waited for word from Jesse.

Megan's insides pulled tight. Shit. Despite the cadre's attempts to curb it, Chloe was still impulsive. If it was Dubois and Chloe went after him, their plan was shot to hell. The entire team would be exposed, with Dubois' security team hot on their trail.

Megan watched her friend closely as the tense seconds ticked past. If Chloe tried to pull this, it was up to Megan and the others to stop her. Her stomach muscles tightened, that familiar, hot burn starting up in the pit of her belly. She didn't want to hurt Chloe, but if it came down to hurting her versus risking the safety of the entire team, Megan wouldn't hesitate. She couldn't.

"It's Dubois' wife," Jesse reported finally. "Daughters in back, and a security guy driving."

Chloe made a frustrated sound as Megan breathed a sigh of relief and relaxed. Crisis averted. "Let us know when it's safe to move," she told Jesse.

They watched the vehicle come up the driveway, the beam of its headlights cutting through the night. "Wonder why they're arriving here at this time of night?" Megan murmured.

"Because Dubois' got dirty work to do tomorrow, and he doesn't want his precious family around to find out what he's been hiding," Chloe muttered, buried rage in her voice.

The car passed by, plunging them once again into darkness.

"You're clear," Jesse said.

They hurried back to the van, which Trinity had moved to a predetermined location. Everyone hopped in the back and Ty slammed the door shut behind them as Trinity started the engine. "Think you got what we need?" she asked.

"Let's hope," Megan replied, tugging off her mask.

Chloe peeled hers off and tossed it aside, the dimly lit interior allowing Megan to see her friend's face. Chloe's was not happy. "Hey." Megan nudged Chloe with her knee. "We'll get him. But not without planning everything first. There's too much at stake to risk everything with a knee-jerk, emotional reaction."

Chloe shot her a dark look, but Megan shrugged. "You know I'm right." Chloe went back to staring straight ahead, and Megan shared a look with Heath. She hoped Chloe cooled off by the time they got back to their hotels because they needed to regroup and start planning for to-morrow if Amber found anything useful in the files they'd sent.

Chloe stewed for a while on the drive back to the coast, but things improved a little when Heath got up and crossed to the other side to sling an arm around Chloe's shoulders. Her friend shot him a quelling look but didn't push him away, then leaned into him.

Thank you, Heath. The last thing they needed was for Chloe to go off reservation again in her vendetta to get Dubois.

About twenty minutes from their destination, Amber called. "Hey, you find anything?" Megan asked.

"Did I ever. I'll fill you all in when you get here."

"Looking forward to it," Megan said with a smile.

Trinity parked behind the hotel Amber and Jesse were staying at and everyone got out.

"I hope she got something good," Chloe muttered as they trekked inside the building, Heath holding her hand. Megan suspected to keep tabs on her as much as to be affectionate.

Amber met them at the door with a big smile. "You're just in time. Step into my office." She nodded behind her where she had Lady Ada and a few other computers set up on a table.

"What did you get?" Chloe asked, chomping on her gum as she impatiently scanned the various screens.

"All kinds of financial records, cash withdrawals and payments I'm guessing he didn't want on the books. In addition to various dates, locations and ship names listed in a ledger."

Chloe's face brightened. "How recent?"

"Tomorrow recent enough for you?"

Chloe sucked in a breath, her gaze darting between the screens. "Show me."

"Here." She pointed to a line she'd isolated. "It references a shipment of jewels coming into Le Havre tomorrow aboard a boat called *Le Dauphin* at seventeen-hundred hours tomorrow."

"It's the women," Chloe said in triumph. "Dominic used to call them his jewels." She straightened, glanced around at everyone. "Anyone want an energy drink before we start? Because we're gonna have a long night ahead of us."

Chapter Twenty-Three

"How are you feeling?" Heath asked Chloe, passing her a coffee he'd just picked up in town. They were alone in their room, having wrapped up yet another meeting with the team a few minutes ago.

They'd been up until four that morning laying out the basic plan and logistics for how they were going to rescue the women, then had gone to bed and crashed for a few hours. Amber was keeping an eye on things on her end to update them with any important new intel. If nothing major changed, they'd be heading for the port soon in preparation to meet *Le Dauphin* when it came in.

"Better now, thanks." She took a sip, her eyes half-closing in bliss. "Oh, yeah, that's what I'm talkin' about. Sweet caffeine."

Seeing that look on her face, Heath smiled. He'd put that same look on her face several times in the past few days, and not because of caffeine. He was addicted. To her wild, vibrant energy so opposite to his own. To the startling glimpses of vulnerability she'd given him.

To her intensity. Chloe didn't do anything half-heartedly. Whether it was planning or executing an op, or coming undone beneath him, she gave everything her all.

She was the most complex woman he'd ever met, and the strongest. He respected her goals and drive, if not always her methods. Things might have gone to shit last night if it had been Dubois in that car instead of his wife and kids. Chloe had been ready to charge headlong at him for the chance to put a bullet in his skull, heedless of the danger she'd be placing herself and the rest of them in.

She could be wild and crazy and impulsive, but she was also fun with an adventurous side that was addictive. She made everything so vivid. His life was going to be even duller when he left for Syria soon.

After everything he'd discovered about her, and all they'd been through in such a short time, he couldn't imagine walking away without the promise of a future with her. She was part of him now, and he wanted more than he'd ever let himself want before.

They were just finishing their sandwiches and veggies when Amber called. "Jesse and Trinity are down at the port," she told them. "They said there's heightened security around the area the ship is due to dock at. I'm monitoring the satellite feed of the area now."

"Sounds good," Chloe said.

"Has Rycroft verified everything on his end?" Heath asked. Rycroft had pulled some big strings for them from back in the States. Since Dubois might have local law enforcement on his payroll or blackmail list, Rycroft had secured a clean team from out of the area to secure the ship once it moored. From there, Heath and the rest of the team would handle getting the women out and to safety.

"Yep, Trinity just got off a call with him. Everything's a go, so saddle up."

"Copy. We'll contact you from the port," Chloe said, then ended the call and went to change and gather her gear while Heath did the same. When she emerged from the bathroom a few minutes later dressed in tight black cargo pants and a fitted long-sleeve shirt, her hair tucked up beneath her knit cap, he couldn't help but give her a once-over.

"Ready?" She grabbed her bag and started for the door. As she passed by him, Heath caught her arm and spun her around. Her eyebrows crashed together in an irritated frown. "What?"

He didn't care if she was annoyed by his timing, he had to say this. He cupped her face in his hands, that little flash of vulnerability in her eyes tugging at him. "Promise me you'll stick to the plan out there."

She narrowed her eyes. "Don't scold me like I'm a misbehaving puppy."

That's not what this was. Not even close. He leaned in closer. "Chloe." Her expression smoothed out, replaced by one of curiosity as he stared into her eyes. "I need to hear you say you won't put yourself at unnecessary risk, no matter what happens tonight. Or the team."

Her jaw tightened. "You're not my keeper, Barrett."

"No, but I'm going to be your guardian angel, watching over you to make sure nothing goes wrong."

"That's romantic, but unnecessary."

"It's completely necessary." One, because she wanted Dubois enough to act impulsively, and two, because if anything happened to her, he couldn't take it.

Her lips curved in a knowing smile. "Not falling for me and my charms already, are you?" she murmured.

"And if I was?"

All traces of humor vanished as she stared up at him with those big brown eyes. "Then I'd feel compelled to warn you against it."

Not dissuaded in the least, he stroked his thumbs over her cheekbones. "Why's that?"

"Because life expectancy for people like me isn't that

great."

Everything protective in him flared to sudden, sharp life. "It is when you have a guardian angel to watch over you."

She wrapped her fingers around his wrists and lowered her gaze. "You're getting me all tangled up inside when I need to be getting into op mode," she complained, but there was no sting in her voice.

"Promise me. I need to hear you say the words."

Her gaze lifted to his. "Fine. I promise not to do anything stupid."

"Thank you."

Her expression softened. With a half-smile she wrapped her arms around his neck for a slow, soft kiss, then pulled back just as his body started to thrum. "Hold that thought until later. We've got work to do."

They took their own vehicle to the port at Le Havre, Ty and Megan going a different route. The entire harbor was a mass of activity, with container, tanker and cruise ships coming and going, along with other commercial vessels. They used the special IDs Amber had made them to enter. There was no sign of Dubois, and Heath was relieved. Extracting a promise from Chloe was one thing. Trusting her to stick to it when the man she wanted dead was right in front of her was another, and Heath intended to be ready for anything, just in case.

Everyone arrived on time and took up their positions around the dock, then checked in on comms. "Head's up. *Le Dauphin's* being pushed into the dock now," Amber announced.

"What? It's over three hours early," Chloe said with a worried frown, peering through her binos through the window overlooking the water. Then she gasped and blurted, "Watch that bus."

Heath kept his eyes on the luxury tour coach pulling up close to *Le Dauphin*. This far away from all the cruise ships, there was no reason for a tour bus to park there. *Shit*. "They're going to offload the women onto it."

"Not happening," Chloe snapped, setting down her binos and reaching for her weapon. "We can't wait for the cops to show. We've gotta handle this ourselves." Unfortunately, right out in the open for anyone to see.

Heath was right behind her as they rushed to the door. "How many crew members do you see?" he asked the team.

"Five," Amber answered. "Three on the bridge and two on deck. Not sure how many below."

Christ. The last thing they needed was to engage in a firefight in broad daylight in such a busy place, but the alternative was following the bus and hoping they could intercept it in a quieter location.

"I'm alerting our police contact," Trinity said. "But Chloe's right—we're on our own for now."

Chloe immediately took charge. "Heath, you're with me. Meg and Ty, back us up from the north side. Jesse, you back us up from the south. We'll come in from the west and make sure that bus can't move. Go."

They waited behind a stack of shipping containers on the dock as the crew deployed the gangway. Moments later, the first of the women appeared through a hatch on deck, blinking and shielding their eyes with their hands, armed guards overseeing the unloading.

Heath stole a glance at Chloe. Her jaw was set, her mouth a bloodless line as she stared at them with laser-like focus. A powder keg about to blow.

A sharp cry made him whip his head around. One of the guards had struck a woman. She was on her knees, holding the side of her face and cowering as he stood over her. He drew his weapon and pointed it at her head.

Shiiiiit.

"Motherfucker," Chloe snarled, and burst to her feet, firing two shots before Heath could stop her. The guard dropped, a stunned look on his face as he clutched at his chest.

Goddammit. Heath pulled in a hard breath and surged to his feet to follow her.

Chaos erupted. Men shouted, swarming the women, who screamed and ran back toward the hatch they'd come out of. "Take out the guards," Chloe said over the noise, and Heath had no choice but to cover her ass as she popped out from behind cover to fire at another one. "We have to get the women out before they start killing them."

More shots came from the other direction, dropping two more guards. Ty and Megan, or maybe Jesse.

There were three more guards on deck, all armed with rifles, now returning fire. Heath fired his own weapon as they rushed for the end of the gangway, dropping a guy at the top of it. Chloe surged past him, racing up it toward the deck. Another guard appeared, the barrel of his rifle pointed right at Chloe.

Heath's heart stopped. He aimed to fire but Chloe let loose with two shots, nailing the bastard in the chest.

Right behind her as they reached the deck, they swiveled around, searching for more shooters. "We clear, Jesse?" he asked, his heart rate elevated.

"For now, but I had eyes on three more before they disappeared through the hatch."

Chloe stalked toward it, pistol up. "Going below to secure the women."

She darted to the side, angled her body just as the hatch flew open. She hit the guard with a solid roundhouse to the diaphragm, doubling him over as he pulled the trigger. Shots ripped past Heath, making him dive to the deck. Another man burst through the opening. Heath raised his rifle and fired just as the first man sprayed another hail of bullets in a wide semi-circle.

Chloe jerked partway around, a grimace of pain flitting across her face as she grabbed her left hip and fell.

Chloe! Heath fired at a man who popped around the far corner, and raced for her.

PAIN SEARED THROUGH Chloe's left hip and upper arm as she rolled, narrowly avoiding more bullets as they slammed into the deck where she'd just been.

Gritting her teeth, she jackknifed upright to fire. She hit the shooter in the chest with both shots. He went down even as she rolled onto her right side and got to her feet. Damage wasn't too bad because she could still move her arm and leg.

Heath was racing toward her. Another guard darted out behind him. She wheeled to the side and fired past Heath, striking the man center mass.

"I've got you covered at the bow," Jesse said in Chloe's earpiece. "Get down the gangway."

"Negative. I'm not leaving without the women," Chloe responded. She waved Heath off but he kept coming. "I'm fine," she insisted, keeping her weight off her left foot as she swiveled to scan for more threats. "Anybody got a view of the crew in the bridge?"

"Got all three in cuffs," Megan replied. "They're saying two more men are down in the hold."

"Roger that. Heading there now." Heath gave her an are-you-shitting-me look she completely ignored, and started for the door that would lead them below deck, confident that he'd follow.

"Chloe."

"I'm fine. Let's just do this," she snapped, focused on the door, weapon in her right hand because she didn't trust her left at the moment.

Heath blocked her, running a cursory gaze over her before sending her a hard look. "I'm taking point."

His set expression warned her not to argue, and she wasn't a hundred percent right now. The pain was getting worse, and an edge of shock had taken hold, her hands trembling slightly and her breathing uneven. She fought both, focusing on the mission: the women below. "Fine."

She stayed on him like a shadow as he opened the door and swept the stairwell. "Clear," he whispered, then started forward.

The crew had shut off the power, leaving the stairwell in darkness. She and Heath descended the stairs, the tac lights on their weapons lighting the way. Chloe clenched her jaw as she followed him, fire shooting through her hip with each step, her progress marked by a fine trail of blood spatters on the metal stairs. She slowed her breathing, forcing her body to counteract the lash of adrenaline flooding her system.

Heath paused at the bottom of the stairs near the closed hatch. She moved in to his left, keeping her weight on her right foot, grimaced as she raised her left hand to grip his shoulder. *Go.*

He went through the hatch, clearing the space as she came through after him. She barely caught a flash of movement out of the corner of her eyes, then Heath fired. A grunt sounded, then the clatter of a weapon falling. Heath advanced toward the suspect while Chloe spun around, bit back a curse as her left leg threatened to give out, watching their other side.

"*Ne tire pas,*" a voice called out beyond Heath. *Don't shoot.*

"*Sortir,*" Chloe ordered, still watching their backs. "*Les mains en l'air.*" *Come out. Hands in the air.*

"Got him," Heath said. "Twenty yards ahead."

"Clear behind us," she answered, moving with him.

"Tell him to get on the ground and put his hands behind his head."

"*Monte sur le sol, et mets tes mains derrière la tête,*" she snapped. Then to Heath, "Any sign of the women?"

"Not yet." He quickly moved in on the prisoner, zip tying the man's hands behind his back and checking him for weapons before straightening and pulling out a flashlight, giving them a decent amount of illumination. "Ask him if there's anyone else down here."

She asked him that, and where the women were. "Just him and the other guy. He says the women are on the other side of this bulkhead." She nodded to their right.

"Watch him. I'll check it out."

Chloe divided her attention between the man on the floor and Heath as he checked the door for any sign of booby traps, then drew his weapon and entered the hatch.

A blast of hot, muggy air escaped, carrying the stench of human waste. Chloe held her breath, heart beating fast.

"They're here," Heath said.

Chloe limped over to peer inside the open doorway. Twenty-seven faces looked back at her, and the sight of them huddled on the floor in terror broke her heart. They sat frozen, too afraid to move, staring at her and Heath with wide eyes.

Forcing aside her anger, Chloe lowered her weapon and gave them a reassuring smile. "*C'est bon. Vous êtes en sécurité maintenant.*" *It's all right. You're safe now.*

She tapped her earpiece. "Hold secured, cargo accounted for."

"Copy," Megan replied. "We're clear up here, and our cavalry's just arrived on shore."

About ten minutes too late, and now there was gonna be a lot of red tape and paperwork to deal with because their team wasn't supposed to have been solely involved with taking down the ship. "Are they Rycroft's?"

"Yes."

"I'm not leaving until I know these women are safe," Chloe replied.

"That's what I told her you'd say. So she said to head to the RV point as soon as you can, while she and Rycroft deal with the aftermath."

Perfect.

Bless him, Heath was already moving around the room, checking on the women. They cowered when he got close, until Chloe explained he was checking them for injuries. "See anything?" Chloe asked, scanning the women. Christ, some of them couldn't be more than four-teen.

"No visible serious injuries, but they all need fluids. It's gotta be a hundred-and-ten in here, and that's with the door open." Anger vibrated in his voice and she decided she more than liked and admired him. She might even be falling for him.

The cops finally arrived. The head of the unit came down with Trinity to take over.

Heath walked over and stood in front of Chloe, those impossibly blue eyes burning with too many emotions to decipher. "You're leaving now, whether willingly or over my shoulder. Which is it gonna be?"

She loved this take control side of him, and she was hurting enough to let the order slide. "How about option three, with my arm around your shoulders?"

He immediately stepped close, wrapped an arm around her waist while she reached up to lock hers across his broad shoulders. The pain and stiffness in her hip and arm were way worse now. A groan escaped her gritted teeth as they hit the stairs.

Without a word, Heath bent and scooped her up into his arms. She winced but didn't fight. "I think it was just a ricochet," she managed as he climbed toward the top deck.

"They still leave holes," he growled.

Yes, they did. And they hurt more than she'd thought they would.

Megan and Ty were there with Jesse when they got topside. Megan's gaze immediately zeroed in on the blood dripping from Chloe. She whipped around, waving for a cop near the bridge. "We need an ambulance."

"No," Chloe protested. "No hospital." She looked up at the man who'd done the impossible by stealing her heart. "Heath's got me."

He nodded, eyes on hers, an unbreakable bond solidifying between them. "Yeah. I've got you."

Chapter Twenty-Four

“**D**efinitely a ricochet,” Heath said as he checked the wound in Chloe's hip and upper arm at the hotel minutes later, tamping down his anger. Because he was pissed. Pissed that she'd up and initiated the attack without prior knowledge and agreement by the team. Pissed that she'd been hit.

“They ruined my Valkyrie mark,” she complained, frowning down at the brand on her left hip. The bullet had gouged a path through the fleshy part of her hip, taking part of the mark with it. He still couldn't believe someone had taken a fucking brand to her.

“Hold still,” he told her, pinching the edges of the wound shut so he could suture it. She'd refused to go to the hospital. He wasn't a plastic surgeon, but his stitches were neat enough that it shouldn't leave too bad a scar when it healed. The round had missed bone and nerve, though it had hit her glute minimus. “Can you still wiggle your fingers?”

She wiggled them. “Yeah.” Sighing, she laid back

down on her side on the bed where he'd put towels beneath her to catch the drips.

She'd been lucky. A direct hit would have shattered her hip joint or pelvis and done internal damage. Then she would have had no choice but to go to the hospital—and she'd have been sidelined for months, maybe forever. "You're gonna be sore for a while. And stiff. You won't be able to operate like this."

"I know." She scowled at the far wall as he stitched.

And suddenly he couldn't hold back any longer. "You could have gotten everyone on board that boat killed today. Including us and the women. You realize that, right?"

The scowl turned into a pout. "Can you save the lecture for later?"

Stubborn, impulsive, frustrating woman… He drew a breath, struggled for patience. "No. You need to acknowledge what you did, apologize for it, and swear you'll never pull that shit again. And don't just apologize to me. You owe it to the others, too."

She turned her head to nail him with a look equal parts hurt and annoyed. "All *right*. I'm sorry. For everything you just said. I shouldn't have gone off half-cocked like that, but I…" She sighed, winced as he hit a particularly painful spot. "I told you I'm not used to the whole team dynamic thing. And when that asshole pointed his weapon at the woman…" She laid her cheek on top of her folded hands. "But I'm sorry, and I'm glad you weren't hurt. And I'll tell the others that too."

He raised an eyebrow. "And?"

Another sullen look. "And I won't do it again."

His anger faded. "Thank you."

She eyed him hopefully. "So I'm forgiven?"

"Mostly." It was hard to stay mad when she was lying there bleeding and looking sorry for herself. He kept stitching. "Now I'm mostly mad that you got hit."

"At least the women are safe. And this'll give me time to find Dubois and figure out the best way to get him."

Heath was increasingly worried by her obsession with that, afraid she would get herself killed. "He'll know you were involved today. You'll be at even greater risk."

"Not as much risk as he is," she muttered darkly.

He shook his head. The woman made him crazy. "I want to hug and shake you at the same time."

She looked up at him, giving him puppy dog eyes. "I could use a hug."

He gave a grudging chuckle. "Hug after I stitch you up. Shake once you're healing up."

"Deal." She went back to staring at the wall. "Wonder how it's going with Trinity right now?"

"We left her one hell of a mess to clean up."

"Megan said Rycroft will handle everything. I'm looking forward to meeting him one day."

He put in the last two stitches, bandaged it, then checked the one on her arm. It was seeping, the back of the bandage nearly clean. "I'm going to put you in a sling to keep you from moving it."

She made a face. "I don't need a sling."

He caught her chin and brought her eyes to his. "I know you're tough. I know you're badass and pretend not to feel pain like the rest of us mortals. But right now, I need you to do as you're told and let me take care of you."

Her eyes softened. "I am letting you."

"Well, let me do more of it."

She flopped down on the pillow with something between a sigh and a growl. "You're spoiling me. If I was on my own, I'd have to just suck it up and deal."

The image that conjured was too awful to contemplate. "Well, you're not on your own now. And if anyone deserves some spoiling, it's you."

She looked up at him in surprise. "Yeah?"

KAYLEA CROSS

"Yeah." Planting a hand beside her head, he leaned down and fit his lips to hers in a soft, slow kiss.

She'd scared the shit out of him today. When he'd seen her get hit, he'd wanted to bellow in denial, his only thought to get to her. Protect her. Save her. Throw himself on top of her to shield her if necessary.

Her lips were soft and pliant under his, her restless energy subdued now. He stroked her hair and straightened. "You squeamish about needles?"

She stared at him a moment, thrown by the abrupt shift in topic, then snorted. "Please."

Yeah, that's what he'd thought.

He gave her a shot of antibiotics in her uninjured hip, then secured her left arm across her chest with a sling and kissed her once more. "No moving that until I say," he warned.

"So bossy," she said with a huff. He could tell the pain and fatigue were getting to her now. She was still and quiet, two things she rarely was.

"Damn right. And you're going to take all three of these too." He handed her the tablets and a bottle of water.

She looked up at him. "Can I have a—"

"No energy drinks. Just water."

Pouting like a sulky child, she took the tablets and swallowed them with a sip of water. Then her phone beeped. "It's Megan. She's on her way up."

Heath let her in a minute later. "How's our patient?" she asked.

"Being as difficult as you'd imagine."

"Hey," Chloe protested with a frown. "I'm lying here being good, not moving my arm." Then to Megan. "They ruined my Valkyrie mark."

Megan stepped to the side of the bed and peeled the edge of the bandage back. "Bastards, they did too." She tutted and covered it back up. "I'll rebrand you later if you want."

"Over my dead body," Heath growled, horrified.

Both women looked over at him with startled expressions. "She was *joking*," Chloe said.

"Joking," Megan confirmed, clearly fighting a grin. "Her mark's way more badass this way. More badass than mine. I'm kinda jealous."

All these women were insane.

"Anything from Trinity?" Chloe asked.

"Oh yeah. She's up to her eyeballs in bureaucratic tape and bullshit, but she's handling it. Rycroft's working on securing all video that might have captured us there. Basically, they're in full damage control mode. They're the best. By the time they're done sanitizing everything, it'll be like we were never there."

"And the women?" Chloe asked.

"Were all checked out before being taken to temporary housing. Trinity supervised it personally, and two of Fleur's colleagues were there to take over. They're going to be fine." She reached into her pocket. "Brought you something. I got it at the—"

Heath swiped the energy drink from her before she could hand it to Chloe. "Nuh-uh. That's contraband."

"Ugh, he's just no fun at all," Chloe complained, gazing at the can like a child denied a piece of cake at their own birthday party.

"Nope," he agreed, not bothered in the least. "And now you're gonna sleep until I wake you up."

"I'm not tired," she argued, but her lids were already drooping.

"Yes you are, and you're gonna get more and more tired over the next five minutes."

She narrowed her eyes. "What did you give me?"

"Something to take the pain away and make you sleep."

Megan chuckled and came over to set her arm around his back. "Oh, I like this guy."

239

Chloe sent him an annoyed look. "I like him too, dammit. But when I wake up, I want a meeting about Dubois." Her voice was slightly slurred already, the meds kicking in. Couple more minutes, and she'd be out cold, not feeling any pain. "I'm ready to end this once and for all."

Megan nodded. "All of us are. And we're going to get him."

Heath was never more aware of the deadline looming before him as he was right then. What if he wasn't there when they went after Dubois? He wanted to be there. Needed to make sure he had Chloe's back while she put herself in harm's way again.

She may have operated alone in the past, but not anymore. Now she had him and the others to watch over her.

****

Chloe squinted as she looked down at the pictures Amber had taken an hour earlier. "Do I look dead to you?" she asked Heath.

"Yes, and put them away, because I don't like looking at them," Heath ordered.

Though Rycroft and Trinity had done a damn good job at sanitizing the scene on board the ship and dealing with the local authorities on their behalf, it wasn't perfect. People had seen what had happened. Word would have circulated by now about a small team taking the ship and freeing the women. Dubois' eyes and ears would have reported to him immediately.

The only way to protect Chloe now was to prove to Dubois' network that she was dead. The blood on scene would help, and Trinity had worked something out with the head pathologist at the local hospital. They had a fake death certificate in Gabrielle's name, and now these shots of Chloe lying on a metal autopsy table, looking dead. She and Megan had done an awesome job with the makeup.

"Think Dubois will buy it?" she asked.

"Let's hope so," Megan replied, uploading the last of the images to send to Rycroft.

She hoped so too. Once Dubois was gone, she would be safe. Faking her death would make her as safe as she could get until then.

She didn't want to jinx herself, but she wanted to end this and then go to England to help the team find the remaining Valkyries. Especially Eden.

And she wanted Dubois gone fast, because she wanted more time with Heath before he left for Syria. He'd taken such good care of her over the past two days, barely letting her lift a finger. She'd been annoyed and grumpy about it at first, but she had to admit, it was damn nice to have him there seeing to her needs. He'd brought her food, washed her hair and helped her shower, helped her dress and made her stay off her feet.

She wanted a relationship with him. But she wasn't ready to say it, because none of what she wanted was possible until Dubois was gone, so she was trying not to think about it.

Megan picked up her phone when it rang. "It's Amber. Hey," she answered. She listened, her expression hardening. "You're sure?" A pause. "All right. Hang on, I'm putting you on speaker so the patient can hear you." She hit the button.

"What've you got?" Chloe asked.

"A possible hit on Dubois."

Chloe caught her breath. "A location?"

"Maybe. There's a series of high-level meetings in Milan with someone known to be tied to the Italian mob. Dubois was seen at the hotel this morning. The meetings are supposed to wrap up tomorrow. If he's there, he'll likely be headed back in a day or two."

"He'll go back to Paris," Chloe said, adrenaline

pumping through her. "He'll want to see his family after being gone." This bastard's days were numbered. When he came back to France, they would be ready.

"I've planted the pictures of you," Amber continued. "Only a matter of time before he sees them. You got a plan in mind? With you on the DL, we're not taking the added risk of going after him yet."

"We'll wait for him to go home, where he's most comfortable."

Where he wouldn't see her coming until it was too late.

Chapter Twenty-Five

6 6 **J**ust received this from our source inside the coroner's office," Jean-Pierre said over the noise of the jet's engines, holding out his tablet for Guillaume to see.

The images on screen showed a dead blond woman lying on an autopsy table, with a bullet hole in her upper chest. Her face was slightly gray from blood loss, purple showing around the eyes, nose and mouth. But even in that state he recognized her, and his pulse kicked up a notch.

Gabrielle.

"When was she brought in?" he asked, unable to stop staring at the images.

"Just before six o'clock last night, after the shipment was intercepted."

"And the cargo?"

"Being held at a detention facility while the investigation is carried out."

Guillaume studied the photos. It gave him tremendous satisfaction to know she'd been shot by one of his men. "What's her real name?"

"They don't know yet. She had no ID or other iden-
tifying items on her. They're searching their databases
now but so far no one's reported her missing."

"If she's a Valkyrie, she won't have any. And there
would be a mark of some sort. A tattoo, maybe." He'd
heard whisperings about it through his sources.

"I'll check into it."

No matter. Finally, a bright spot had punched
through the canopy of black cloud that had been hovering
over him ever since the night Dom had been killed. Burying his little brother would haunt him always. The pain
still raked him with sharp claws upon waking and whenever his mind wasn't occupied with other things. But at
least this bitch was dead. With her gone, Guillaume and
his family were safe.

Now it was time to get back to running his empire.

He handed the tablet back to Jean-Pierre, satisfied
with what he'd seen. "Have them contact me immediately
once they know her real identity. Offer whatever incentive
you have to." He wanted to know the name of his
brother's killer. Find out who she really was.

"Of course."

He leaned back in the plush seat, exhaustion weighing on him. "What about the latest offer?" With Dom
gone, it was up to him to handle this less-savory part of
the business. Guillaume didn't relish it, but he was first
and foremost a businessman, so he would be stupid to give
up such a profitable revenue stream.

"Here." Jean-Pierre tapped the tablet and brought up
another screen. "I just received these this afternoon."

Guillaume took the tablet back and began scrolling
through the images. "They're older than the last batch."

"Yes. But a better price, and considering the loss we
just took, I thought this was the best option."

These women were in their twenties and thirties, by

the looks of them. And not all of them were pretty. Guillaume frowned, trying to imagine them cleaned up. "They won't get the same prices the last ones would have." Gabrielle alone would have netted him a small fortune. He would have preferred to capture her and make her suffer the pain she'd deserved, but at least she was gone.

"They were the best I could get on such short notice."

Their buyers would be impatient. The seizure in Le Havre had cost Guillaume's bottom line, but more importantly, it had also left a black mark on his reputation in the business. Already there were rumblings that he had been exposed, that he posed too great a risk to do business with anymore. Several people had pulled him aside to ask him about it personally at the meetings.

He'd been humiliated, but the sidelong looks and the way people had stopped talking when he'd come close told him he needed to address this immediately. He and his network were busy doing damage control before it got even worse. Once rumors like that spread, they were impossible to stop. "All right, make the call."

Recouping some of his loss was better than nothing.

Guillaume folded his hands across his middle and closed his eyes to get some rest, but his cell phone woke him several minutes later. His eldest daughter.

He smiled. "Hello, my angel. How are you?"

"Good. Papa, when are you coming home?"

"Tonight. I'm on the plane now."

"Yay! Then you can come to my piano recital tomorrow."

"Sweetheart, I wouldn't miss it for the world."

Jean-Pierre drove him home from the airport. It was past the girls' bedtime, but his wife would be up. Guillaume couldn't wait to see her. She treated him like a king, worshipped him, and always stood by his side. He loved her impossibly hard for that.

He carried the flowers he'd purchased into the house.

The kitchen light was on, but his wife wasn't there. "Vienne?" he called as he strode toward the living room.

Quiet treads on the carpeted staircase behind him made him turn around. The welcoming smile on his face froze at the cold expression on hers. "What's wrong?" he asked.

Vienne stood on the third tread from the bottom wearing her favorite satin dressing gown, one elegantly manicured hand resting on the handrail. She swallowed, something like horror in her liquid brown eyes as she stared at him. "I had a disturbing telephone call a few minutes ago." Her voice was a soft rasp. As if she didn't dare to speak any louder.

He took a step toward her, concern for her safety punching through him. "Who was it? Did they threaten you?"

Vienne shrank back, clutching the halves of her gown together at the throat. As if the thought of him touching her revolted her. "*Stop*."

He halted, taken aback by her reaction. "Vienne, what—"

"Is it true you've been buying and selling women as part of your business?"

Shock blasted through him. The blood drained from his face, leaving him dizzy, a cold sweat popping out on his skin as his heart began to hammer. No. No, this couldn't be. "Don't be ridiculous. Who told you that? Who did you talk to?" Guillaume would hunt them down and kill them for this.

She swallowed, a sheen of tears making her eyes glisten. "Don't you dare lie to me." Her voice was so quiet. So cold the words iced the air between them. Guillaume could feel their chill from where he stood.

He stared at her, struggling to come up with a plausible lie. She'd caught him so off guard that she must see the truth in his face. "I…"

A sob escaped her. She clamped her lips shut and shook her head, looking at him like he was a monster conjured up from the bowels of Hell. "Get out."

"What?" he gasped, stricken. She and the girls were the best part of his life. He'd loved her since he'd met her at that party when he was twenty. There was no one else for him and never would be. Only Vienne.

Her spine straightened, steel entering her expression. "Get out and never come back here."

"Vienne," he croaked, reaching a hand toward her. "Don't. I don't know what you were told, but it's not—"

She turned and rushed up the stairs, leaving his heart to hit the floor and shatter into a million bloody pieces.

The master bedroom door slammed upstairs moments later. And she absolutely would have locked it against him. Because the mere sight of him now disgusted her.

Reeling, Guillaume dragged in a ragged breath. The pain in his chest was awful. Like someone was crushing his heart in a vise.

He doubled over, forced air in and out of his lungs as his stunned brain scrambled to find a solution. Who the fuck had told her about the women? And why hadn't he denied it faster? He was so damn angry with himself for not coming up with a lie in time.

Under the shock and grief, rage began to grow. He would find whoever had told her and kill them in a horrible way. In the meantime, he had to figure out how to win his wife back. He'd make her stay with him if it came to it, or take their girls. Because the thought of living without her or the girls was unbearable.

Feeling half-dead inside, he stumbled back through the kitchen. Jean-Pierre shot off the stool at the island, his brows crashing together in alarm. "Sir—"

"I'm going to the chateau," he mumbled, and walked to the door. "Stay here with them. I'll call you tomorrow."

He walked out into the cold October rain, terrified that the life he'd built had just been irrevocably shattered.

****

"I'll be damned, you were right. He came alone," Heath murmured to Chloe.

It was almost midnight and Dubois' vehicle had just arrived at his country estate near the Normandy coast. They lay prone side by side on a small hill that allowed them to see over the wall surrounding the estate. The rest of the team was scattered elsewhere, ready to act when Chloe gave the signal.

"Told you. By all reports, Vienne Dubois is a genuinely good person. No idea how she went this long without knowing what he was really up to, and not sure I believe that anyway. Either she's clueless, or he was just that good at duping her."

"Based on what you've told me, I'm guessing he was."

"Probably. People lie to their spouses all the time."

They'd taken a big gamble by coming here. Chloe was still recovering and couldn't walk or move her left arm without pain. If it had been up to him, they would still be holed up someplace to allow her more healing time, but she'd refused to listen to reason, adamant that she was coming for Dubois and that she had a plan. Since he had half of France in his pocket, no cop or legal organization was going to take him down anytime soon.

But throwing him in jail wasn't enough for Chloe. She wanted blood vengeance and wouldn't stop until she had it.

Heath wasn't entirely comfortable with it, but his choices were either to go with her, or have her do it without him. There was no way he would allow her to do something so dangerous on her own, so here he was.

Hours ago, Chloe had leaked the truth about the trafficked women to Vienne via an anonymous call from a source within the organization Fleur had worked for. The woman had told Vienne everything they knew about Guillaume's involvement with past shipments, including the one they'd stopped in Le Havre, and sent pictures along with irrefutable evidence lifted from the thumb drives they'd stolen from Dubois' safe. That meant Interpol would take him down.

Chloe wasn't going to give them the chance. She needed to do this herself.

She reached her right hand up to tap her earpiece. Her left arm was still bound in the sling across her chest, her entire upper arm various shades of blue and purple and green. "He's here. Alone," she informed the rest of the team, waiting nearby. Then to Heath, "I had to make sure he was alone."

She didn't want the wife or kids to see him die. Because she was an orphan who had seen her mother die, tough as she was, she refused to traumatize Dubois' kids that way.

It made Heath fall for her even more. "You sure this'll work?"

"Yes, because he feels safe here. He thinks I'm dead, and he's more worried about saving his marriage right now than anything else."

He shook his head in grudging admiration. "You drive me crazy, but I love that you're such a badass."

A slow smile spread across her face. "Me too." She kept watching the house through the binos.

They waited there in silence until the master bedroom light on the second floor went off. "Ten more minutes, then we get to work," she said quietly. Then softer, almost to herself. "Hope he knows Wagner."

Chapter Twenty-Six

Guillaume dragged a hand down his face and set the empty tumbler aside on his desk. He'd been in his estate's office all night, had only dozed a couple of times in his chair. He was fucking heartsick over Vienne and the girls. She wouldn't return any of his calls or messages. How could he fix this? She wouldn't go to the media with it, would she?

No, of course she wouldn't. He was just panicking. Vienne was the epitome of class, and a protective mother. She wouldn't want this to hurt their girls. He'd always said she was too good for him. Now she knew it was true.

He looked away from the nearly empty bottle of scotch on his desk, the liquor rolling sour and acidic in his stomach. He knew his wife. There was no coming back from this. Her rebuff last night had been final. She would be speaking to her lawyer first thing this morning, if she hadn't already.

No matter what he did, it was over. He could beg and grovel and apologize. But in the end, it wouldn't do any good. Now that Vienne knew what he'd done, she would never let him near her again. The only thing left to decide was whether he was going to force her to stay, and how far he was willing to go to make it happen.

Bile rushed up his throat. He surged from his chair, gulping, struggling to breathe as agony crashed over him in a dark tidal wave. A terrible sound clawed out of his throat, like something a wounded animal would make. Panting, he spun around and grabbed the edge of a table, throwing it with all his might. It crashed into the wall, scattering papers and other items.

A glint of light caught his eye on the edge of the carpet. Bending, he picked up the ceramic paperweight his daughters had made him for his birthday last year.

Love you forever!

The words gutted him. He imagined the looks of pain and confusion on their precious faces when their mother told them they were getting a divorce. Or, God forbid, the day they found out what he'd done.

He sank to his knees on the floor with an anguished cry, tears streaking his face. This was too great a loss to bear. He'd already lost his brother. Now his whole family?

He barely heard the knock on the door, hurriedly scrubbed at his face. "Come in," he choked out.

Jean-Pierre stopped in the doorway, his eyes widening in shock. "I'll come back." He turned to leave.

"No." He pushed to his feet, wiping at his eyes. "Stay."

Jean-Pierre reluctantly came in and shut the door. "I take it she still won't talk to you?"

He shook his head. "What's happening?" Jean-Pierre had been at the other house all night. Guarding Vienne and the girls, but also to keep watch for him.

"She's been on the phone most of the morning."

To her lawyer. "How is she?"

Jean-Pierre hesitated. "She's…"

"What?"

"Not well," he finally said. "Her eyes are swollen. She hasn't slept either, has been crying most of the time."

Oh, God, he couldn't bear to know he'd caused her so much pain. The horror, disappointment and betrayal in her eyes last night would haunt him forever.

He dropped into the chair behind his desk, feeling empty. "Did you find out who told her?"

"Someone linked to the organization the woman you shot in Marseille was involved with. The one that took in the women from the shipment in Le Havre."

Guillaume stared at him. "So she's haunting me from the grave." He gave a humorless laugh, thinking of Gabrielle lying ice cold in the morgue, getting the final laugh. "They both are."

Jean-Pierre shifted his feet, looking uncomfortable. "I'll just let you—"

"I'm going to have a shower and then head into the city to see my lawyer. Alone." He needed time to think, come up with a plan for how he was going to throw himself on Vienne's mercy. He couldn't give her up without a fight, even if it was futile.

Jean-Pierre and two other security team members were waiting for him by the back door when he came downstairs half an hour later. He felt like dog shit and didn't look much better, but he had things to take care of and he needed to at least see his girls. However much Vienne loathed him now, he prayed she wouldn't try to keep the girls from him. If she did, he would fight her with every last Euro he had.

"You sure about going alone?" Jean-Pierre asked him.

It was his job to worry about Guillaume. Still, today it annoyed him. "I'm sure. Call me if there are any updates. I'll be in touch once I know what my plans are."

Outside, the weather perfectly matched his mood.

Leaden gray clouds as far as the eye could see, the ground damp and a cold wind gusting through the almost naked trees.

His Audi was parked at the side of the house. He headed for it, his mind churning around something he'd thought of in the shower and couldn't let go. Had Gabrielle leaked his activities to someone before dying? He couldn't shake the feeling this had to do with her.

His fist tightened around the keys. Goddamn her, ruining his life from beyond the grave. He'd had her killed too late.

A few paces from the Audi, he stopped. Maybe it was the lack of sleep, or his emotional state, or just plain paranoia. But something in his gut told him not to get into that car.

Gabrielle had worked in explosives. Car bombs were an efficient way to kill targets.

He scanned the surrounding property, seeing nothing suspicious. Was he crazy? He had a good security system and two men had been here with him all night.

But he still wasn't getting into that vehicle without being certain.

Guillaume pivoted and shouted for Jean-Pierre, who came running out of the house. "Have one of the men send up a drone to check the property."

"Why, is something—"

"Just do it. And come check this thing for me to make sure it's okay, then start it." He held out the keys.

Jean-Pierre didn't move for a moment, then came and took the keys. They studied each other in stony silence for a few seconds. Guillaume paid the man well to watch over him and his family, enough to take a bullet— or a car bomb. It was part of the job as head bodyguard, whether Jean-Pierre liked it or not.

Jaw tight, without a word Jean-Pierre walked to the car while Guillaume retreated to a safe distance away to wait. His bodyguard checked the outside and undercarriage carefully, then peered into the interior before opening the door. He popped the hood and checked inside it.

A minute later the engine started. Guillaume tensed, but nothing happened.

Jean-Pierre emerged, leaving the engine running. "All good."

Guillaume walked past him to the car. "Get that drone in the air."

"Already done."

"Good. Tell me if they find anything." He slid behind the wheel, buckled himself in and started around the side of the house.

The instant he cleared it, his vehicle's Bluetooth system signaled a call. He hit accept without looking, expecting it to be Jean-Pierre about the drone. "Yes?"

No one answered. But a classical song came on the car's radio.

He frowned, glanced at the display. He didn't like classical. "Hello?"

A chill ran up his spine as he read the words on the screen.

"Ride of the Valkyries," by Wagner.

He slammed on the brakes, his heart rocketing into his throat. The bitch was still alive and trying to fuck with him.

****

Satisfaction pumped through Chloe when the Audi suddenly slammed on its brakes partway down the driveway. The vehicle's side windows were tinted enough that she couldn't see inside, but God, she wished she could see Dubois' expression.

That's right, you bastard. I'm coming for you.

Except he was too far away, because earlier security

personnel movements had prevented her from getting to the correct spot. She needed to get closer. It was just her and Heath now, the others were waiting in vehicles, ready to extract them once she detonated the device.

She crept over the crest of the hill on her belly, ignoring the pain shooting through her hip and arm as she urged the vehicle forward.

Come on. Just a little more.

The remote she held only worked within a specific range, and Dubois was sitting just outside it. She thought of Fleur and the hundreds, maybe thousands of faceless women Chloe couldn't save.

Valkyrie justice was the only way. *Her* particular brand of justice, delivered in a searing ball of fire with the bomb she'd planted in the dead of the night while her team assisted.

A hand grabbed her ankle. Chloe froze and looked back at Heath.

"Drone," he whispered, face grim as he moved only his eyes upward.

She followed his gaze, lying perfectly still, and sure as hell, a drone was flying toward them from the house. *Shit.*

She flattened herself against the ground. They were pinned in place for the moment. Their camouflage-pattern clothes would help hide them in the grass. But if that thing had thermal imaging on it, they were screwed. The rest of the team had left the area to avoid detection, and was too far away to back them up.

"Three armed men inbound," Heath said.

Chloe's gaze snapped back to the house. Three men were sprinting across the lawn, heading in their direction, two holding pistols and one carrying a rifle.

Hell.

"Let's go." Heath grabbed her hand and pulled her to her knees, letting go when she winced. "We gotta move," he said, putting his rifle to his shoulder.

He was right. "Go. I'll be right behind you."

He cut her a suspicious look. "Not moving until you do."

Her gaze strayed back to the Audi, pulled there with a force too strong to resist.

"No. We gotta go. *Now*," Heath snapped.

She was torn. Torn between escaping the men running toward them so Heath wouldn't be in danger, and Dubois sitting right there, so close to the trigger point.

"*Chloe*."

The Audi suddenly started reversing.

No!

Bracing for the pain, she shoved to her feet and started running toward the Audi. Pain ripped through her hip, radiating down her thigh with each step.

"Chloe, *no!*"

Heath's shout sliced through her, the anger and horror in his voice spurring her on. She blocked him and the pain out. She had to kill Dubois. His men weren't within firing range yet. There was still time to get within range, hit the detonator and then take out the men coming after them.

Her left foot landed on a rock. She hissed in a breath as she slipped. Fire shot through her hip, buckling her leg. She rolled at the last second, taking the hit on her right side and automatically curling to absorb the impact.

The detonator bounced out of her hand and tumbled down the incline.

She shoved up on her hands just as a rifle cracked behind her. Heath firing. And when she looked up at the Audi, she simultaneously realized two things.

It had stopped.

And Guillaume Dubois was staring right back at her through the windshield.

Chapter Twenty-Seven

*I*t can't be.

But he couldn't deny what he was seeing with his own eyes.

Gabrielle. She was here. Still alive, lying prone on the ground as she stared back at him some thirty yards or more away, that stupid fucking song still paying over the radio.

Valkyrie.

She'd leaked his activities to Vienne. She'd destroyed his family, killing his brother and turning his wife and children against him. Faked her own death. Now she'd come to kill him.

Rage blasted through him, so hot and powerful it stole his breath. This bitch had ruined him. She'd come to kill him but now he would put her in the morgue for real.

He threw the transmission into drive, cranked the wheel to the right and slammed his foot down on the accelerator. The Audi fishtailed around, spewing gravel behind the rear tires as he raced toward the grassy incline.

Gabrielle rolled to her side and pointed a pistol at

him.

Bang! Bang!

He jumped as two rounds hit the windshield in front of his face almost simultaneously. But they didn't penetrate.

She dragged herself to the side and went for the front tires next. The car didn't react.

He watched in satisfaction as she jerked her gaze up to meet his through the cracked windshield. *It's bullet-proof, bitch. Just like me.*

Smiling, Guillaume gripped the wheel tighter, pinned the accelerator to the floor and sped right for her.

"NO, DAMMIT, NO," Chloe breathed.

She dropped the useless pistol, her eyes darting to the remote lying in the grass down the incline.

It was her only hope. Five yards away, but it seemed like a thousand. And Heath was still firing at the onrushing men.

An anguished cry ripped from her as she dove for it. Pain tore through her left hip and arm like fire. Her vision swam, nausea roiling in her stomach as the sound of the Audi's engine grew louder, almost screaming in her ears along with the gunfire being exchanged in the background.

She could hear the rapid rounds hitting the windshield in a staccato rhythm. Heath, screaming her name as he fired, trying to save her.

Her groping fingers met plastic.

She grabbed the remote, rolled to her stomach, caught sight of Dubois through the windshield as her thumb moved to the button. He was too close now. She'd be caught in the blast wave.

But this was the only chance she had to survive.

"Game over, asshole," she grated out.

Meeting Dubois' maniacal stare through the ruined

windshield, she covered her head with her arms, opened her mouth to save her eardrums, and pressed the button.

****

"Goddamn it, Chloe, *move!*" Heath roared, firing at the Audi as he ran toward her. She was lying flat on her stomach on the grass, hadn't moved even though death was racing right at her.

Blood roared in his ears, his heart in his throat. He'd had no choice but to take down the men coming at them. But Dubois' car was fucking armored and then some. Nothing Heath did was even slowing him.

He watched in horror, totally helpless as the bastard sped at her.

A split second later, a deafening boom split the air. The shockwave knocked him off his feet, punched the air from his lungs as the Audi exploded in a ball of fire, launching off the ground.

And as he watched, Chloe flew backward and hit the ground on her side.

Stunned, Heath threw his rifle aside and shot to his feet, tearing over the damp grass toward her. "Chloe!" He screamed it, terror and anguish streaking through him.

Fuck, fuck, she'd been way too close to the blast, and she wasn't moving.

His lungs heaved, his thighs burning as he sprinted for her, praying. *Please be alive. Please, God, I need you to be alive.*

Behind her at the foot of the slope, the Audi was a twisted mass of blackened steel, completely engulfed in flames. The stench of burning metal filled his nose, the heat scorching him as he approached Chloe.

He skidded to his knees at her side, raking his gaze over her as he took her face in his hands. "Chloe. Chloe, sweetheart, can you hear me? If you can hear me, open your eyes and look at me." Her carotid pulse was strong. She was breathing. But she wasn't responding.

He checked her neck and spine, looked for signs of internal bleeding, then ripped his phone from his pocket and called Trinity. She was the closest one to them. "We need a medevac chopper at the estate," he ordered her. "Dubois is dead, but Chloe was hit in the blast wave." His voice turned ragged. "She's unresponsive."

****

Clipped voices. Strange, unintelligible syllables. Cold. Pain.

A constant, distant thudding in her ears. A rhythmic pulsing. Then hands touching her.

Agony forked through her skull. She screamed but it was swallowed by the heavy weight pressing her down, down, into the blackness. She instinctively fought against the blackness, afraid it might drown her. But the dark undertow was too strong. It sucked her under, swallowing her in its crushing depths.

Pain began to register. Sharp twinges radiating through her head and along her spine, pulling her up from the darkness.

"Chloe? Can you hear me?"

A low, quiet voice. Familiar, yet far away. And the pain was getting worse, making her want to curl into herself and sink back into the blackness.

"Hey. Firecracker, can you hear me?"

Her eyelids fluttered. She tried to open them, only to slam them shut when a blinding white pain stabbed through her skull.

Warm fingers curled around her hand. "Squeeze if you can hear me."

Summoning her strength, she squeezed.

A sigh of relief gusted against her forehead. "Thank

God."

She licked her dry lips. "Heath?" she whispered, then wished she hadn't, the spike of pain threatening to split her skull open.

"Yes. I'm here," he whispered, his voice rough. "Don't try to talk. You're in the hospital. You're hurt, but you're going to be okay."

Battling through the pain, she forced her eyes open. He was leaning over her, a big, blurry shadow in the darkened room. Trying to see him made her dizzy. Her mind was fuzzy, confused. She squinted, blinked to see him better and her vision cleared enough for her to see his big, relieved smile. "Hi."

"Hi," she whispered back, wincing.

"You've got a grade three concussion and some internal bruising, but no fractures."

Dubois. She'd been inside the blast radius when she'd detonated the bomb. "Is he dead?" she managed.

"Yes. You got him."

She sagged into the bed, a torrent of emotions slamming into her. Fleur had died because of him. And she and Heath almost had too.

A blinding rush of tears flooded her eyes. They leaked past her clenched eyelids, spilling from the corners of her eyes down her temples and into her hair.

Strong arms slid under her, warmth surrounding her as Heath's lips spoke against her ear. "It's all right. I'm right here, and you're gonna be okay."

More pain streaked through her left arm as she reached up to embrace him, her palms resting on his broad back. The tears kept coming no matter how hard she tried to stop, the sobs jerking her, hurting everything so bad she feared she might throw up.

Heath stayed like that, holding her without moving her. Soothing her and protecting her from more pain.

"I'm s-sorry," she choked out.

"Shhh. It's okay."

No, it wasn't. She'd almost gotten him killed today, too focused on killing Dubois. She didn't deserve him. "N-no. S-sorry."

"I know. But I'm still here. And I forgive you, but only because you're still alive. I love tacos even though they fall apart, remember?"

Another time that might have made her smile a little. But she hadn't taken his feelings or safety into consideration. Had never thought what seeing her die in front of him would do to someone like him.

Out of words and in too much pain to talk anymore, she absorbed the comfort he gave and focused on regaining the control she prided herself on. When the tears finally stopped and the jerky hitches of her chest and shoulders stopped, exhaustion tugged at her.

Heath eased up enough to smooth a thumb across her damp cheek, his beautiful blue eyes brilliant even in the dimness. "What's your pain at on a one-to-ten scale?"

No point in lying. She wanted to cut her own head off just to escape it. "Twenty."

He winced. "Ouch. I'll call the nurse. They gave you something in your line a while ago. For now, just close your eyes and lie still."

She was only too happy to comply.

Medical staff came in. She grudgingly answered their questions in French, using as few words as possible, wishing they'd just shut the hell up and go away because her head was seriously going to explode.

Finally, she and Heath were alone in blessed quiet. He leaned down to kiss her forehead. "Sleep now."

She let it take her, stealing her away from the pain. When she woke next the pain was better, her skull no longer threatening to split apart. She was tender all over, not surprising given what she'd survived. Heath fed her some broth and crackers. "There's someone out in the hall waiting to see you," he told her. "You up for a short visit?"

"Sure."

He went to the door and an unfamiliar man walked in. Tall, graying hair, but built as solid as Heath, with piercing, silver eyes. "Hi, Chloe. I'm Alex Rycroft," he said, stepping close to her bed.

"Oh, wow. Hi," she blurted, automatically holding out her hand.

His lips twitched as he shook it, his grip warm and firm. "I've heard a lot about you."

"All good things?"

"Mostly."

"I uh… Thanks for cleaning up the mess I made."

"Messes," he corrected.

Her face flushed hot. "Um, yeah. Thanks."

He nodded, amusement lurking in those silver eyes. "Still working on this last one, but I wanted to come and thank you in person. Dubois has been on our radar for years and I was starting to think we'd never get him. So, thank you."

"Believe me, it was my pleasure." Though she wasn't feeling quite so perky about it at the moment. The only reason she wasn't being arrested was because various intelligence agencies had wanted Dubois gone, and Rycroft was once again working his magic on her behalf.

"Oh, I know it was," he said with a slight grin before sobering. "Regarding how your real name got leaked, we still don't have any leads. And we're not sure exactly how much he knew about you. The good news is, we think only Dominic knew and not his brother. We're trying to isolate who fed Dominic the intel. Once we know that, we'll work backward and find the source. It may just be the break we need to expose the dirty players within the Valkyrie Program." He turned to Heath. "I'll see myself out. If you need anything, let me know."

"I will, sir, thanks."

"Just Alex. I'm retired, haven't you heard?" he said with a wry grin, and left.

"Wow," she breathed when the door shut behind him. "Alex Rycroft."

Heath laughed. "Never thought you were the type to get star struck."

"I'm not, but…" She gestured to the door. "Alex Rycroft." After everything she'd heard about him from Megan and Trinity, she felt like she'd just met a living legend.

A soft knock sounded, then the door cracked open and Megan appeared there. "Hey, you're awake."

"Barely." She put on a wan smile for her friend, who crossed to the bedside to grasp her right hand. "I just met Rycroft. He came to thank me for killing Dubois. I said it was my pleasure."

Megan shook her head at Chloe, then gave Heath a sardonic look. "Told you she's a bad influence." She scolded Chloe. "Look what you got poor Heath into now."

"I know." Killing three men to cover her while she selfishly went after Dubois. She rolled her head to see him. "I already apologized." His gentle smile told her he really had forgiven her. Even if she didn't deserve it, she had it nonetheless. The thought of him leaving shortly hurt worse than all of her other injuries combined.

Ty came in next with Amber and Jesse. Then Trinity.

The eldest Valkyrie strode over to stand next to the bed, her shrewd blue eyes studying Chloe. "Those are some amazing shiners you've got there," she murmured.

Yeah, her eyes were getting more and more swollen every minute, it seemed. "You gotta get Rycroft to clear Heath," she begged. "I forgot to ask him." He might lose his security clearance because of her. Might lose his freaking job and never get hired again because of what he'd been forced to do today to protect her. "I dragged him into it, and he had no choice but to take out—"

"Quiet. You're supposed to be resting, and I'll do the talking right now."

Chloe shut her mouth, her pulse elevated. With her declared dead she'd thought getting Dubois at his country estate would be a walk in the park. In, boom, out, without any snags.

She'd been wrong. She was currently paying the price for that decision. She wouldn't allow Heath to pay as well.

"We've handled things with the authorities for now, but this is way beyond my scope. Rycroft is doing what he can, but this is gonna leave one hell of a paper trail. There's no way we can hush everything up completely. There are already rumors flying about who targeted Dubois and why. His death is already all over the media."

So his daughters would know what he'd done too. Chloe was sorry for that. But not for killing that bastard. "And Heath?"

Trinity folded her arms, amusement glinting in her eyes. "He's been cleared."

Chloe exhaled in relief, then shot Trinity a scowl, although it was hard to say if she pulled it off with her swollen eyes. "Why didn't you just lead with that?"

"Because I like a bit of suspense. Keeps things interesting." She slanted a look at Heath, then back at Chloe. "Speaking of interesting, I talked to the doctor in charge of your case. You're going to be on reduced activity for a while—"

"As in, *severely* reduced," Heath added.

"—so once he releases you, which will likely happen in the next twelve hours, you're coming with us to the UK."

"I—"

"Chloe?" Trinity put a hand on her arm. "You're coming." She squeezed, released and straightened. "Now.

Everyone out except Heath." She took Megan by the shoulders, spun her to face the door, and pushed. "Go. Out."

Megan made a disgruntled sound and did as she was told. "Jeez. Bossy."

Ty clapped a hand on Heath's shoulder as he smiled at Chloe. "You guys need anything, give us a shout."

Heath waited until they were gone before coming to sit in the chair at the side of her bed. "Nice to have friends, huh?"

"Yes." Surreal, but nice. And even nicer to have friends with connections in high places, to pull strings behind the scenes and take care of pesky things like criminal charges and revoked security clearances.

He laid his forearms on the bed and set his chin on top of them, watching her. "You look like hell, firecracker."

She made a face. "Feel like it too." She reached for his hand, the feel of his long fingers curling around hers soothing her on the deepest level. "So you still have the contract in Syria?"

"Unfortunately."

"When are you supposed to leave?"

"Two days."

Her heart lurched. Only two days, and he'd be gone.

She held his hand tighter, fighting a war within herself. She'd been trained not to rely on anyone. Not to need anyone. But she needed Heath, and was afraid to let him go. She wouldn't beg him, however. A woman still had her pride, concussed or not. "Will you come with me to the UK before you fly to Syria? If I promise not to blow anything else up while you're there?"

Heath laughed softly as he picked up her hand and kissed the back of it, gazing into her eyes. "I don't trust that promise for a second. But I'd go anywhere to be with you, firecracker."

Chapter Twenty-Eight

Her target wasn't going to show.

Eden waited at the hotel bar, nursing the watered-down gin and tonic she'd ordered half an hour ago. He wasn't coming. Either he'd gotten suspicious that something was up, or he'd blown her off.

Disappointing, but it came with the territory. There was always another time. Another way to kill a target.

She gave it another ten minutes before calling it a bust. As she slid off the barstool to grab her purse, her eye caught the breaking news story being broadcast on the TV behind the bar.

Wealthy Paris businessman and philanthropist killed at his country estate.

Guillaume Dubois' face came on screen.

She hid a smile. *Well, well.*

Eden paid for her drink, scanned the bar one last time, then headed back to her room upstairs. Once there she ditched her heels, stripped off the skin-tight black cocktail dress and splurged with a nice, hot soak in the tub. Why not? It had been a hell of a week and she rarely stayed in a place this nice. She'd been following the same man for nearly a month now, working her way deeper and deeper into his inner circle.

Wrapping up in a hotel robe, she decided to spoil herself again and ordered a hot fudge brownie sundae with a pot of tea from room service. While she ate it, she opened up her laptop to check for messages. One caught her eye immediately. From the sender she only knew as "Bam Bam".

Not sure if you're still out there. But if you get this message... We got him, and the women are safe.

Next to it were two links. One detailing how a group of migrant women were found and rescued from the hold of a ship in Le Havre a few nights ago. The other was a story about Dubois.

A rush of triumph made the hair on Eden's arms stand up. She opened the link and scanned the story with eager eyes.

Guillaume Dubois was one of France's wealthiest men, well known for his charitable donations to various causes.

"Yeah, and most of that money came from selling women," she muttered under her breath, disgusted.

In a shocking act, he was murdered early this morning on his estate in Normandy when his vehicle exploded with him inside it.

"Beautiful."

Three of his security guards were also killed in the brazen attack. *This is the second tragedy to hit the Dubois family in recent days. Guillaume's younger brother, Dominic, died in an explosion in his Paris home last week. Police say the murders are connected, and the deaths have rumors about the brothers' possible link to organized crime buzzing.*

"About fucking time someone saw the truth." She clicked on the photos showing Dubois' country manor, then zoomed in on the one showing the burned-out wreckage of his car. It was nothing but a heap of scorched and twisted metal.

Both Dubois murders bore the hallmark of a pro. Eden was almost positive the woman she'd been in contact with was a fellow Valkyrie.

She smiled as she typed back a response to the message, then paused. For a moment she considered writing more. A clue that a fellow Valkyrie would understand, just in case. It had been many years since she'd seen any of her sisters. Eden wished she could see them again. Feel like she belonged again.

In the end, she decided against it. Shutting the laptop down, she leaned back against the nest of pillows behind her and polished off her sundae, already pondering how painful a death befitted her next victim.

****

"Whoa." Chloe couldn't wipe the grin off her face as Megan drove them up the long driveway toward the manor house. As threatened, Trinity had put her and the others onto a private plane and flown them here to the UK as soon as Chloe had been released from the hospital.

Laidlaw Hall was like something out of a movie, and even the sunglasses she had to wear because of a new sensitivity to light couldn't dull the color of the stone in the evening light. Warm, honey-yellow, almost glowing against the emerald green of the perfectly manicured lawns and shrubs out front.

"I know, isn't it gorgeous?" Megan's voice was filled with pride. "It's not even mine, but it still feels like home."

They passed the gatehouse where she and Ty lived, and headed for the main house. A man came out of the house and down the front steps to meet them, a white-and-brown dog at his side.

"There's Marcus."

Heath's arm was solid across her shoulders, keeping her tucked into his side. He wasn't too happy about her being up and around yet, but she'd wanted the hell out of the hospital, even if she had a constant, splitting headache. The meds they'd given her had helped a bit, though she was still dizzy and the ringing in her ears hadn't stopped. All in all, she was lucky to be alive, let alone without serious internal injuries or brain damage.

"Go slow," he warned, reaching in to help her out of the backseat. "Easy does it."

She scowled but did as he said, grabbing his shoulders when she stood because the ground seemed to move under her feet.

"You good?" he asked, those piercing blue eyes assessing her expression.

"Yeah." But she was so damn glad to have him beside her.

He wrapped a steadying arm around her waist and she leaned into him as they slowly walked to the stairs. Megan made the introductions. Heath shifted his hold on her to shake hands with the master of the house, then Marcus focused on Chloe.

"Welcome, Chloe." He had a cool accent, and his dark eyes seemed to see through the tinted lenses of her shades. He had burn scars visible around his left eye and in patches where his dark beard hadn't grown in on his cheek, jaw and neck, and he walked with a cane.

Megan had said he'd been wounded in an explosion in Syria. But Chloe had to wonder if he was truly okay with having her here, knowing she specialized in the kind of weapon that had taken so much from him. "Thanks. Good to be here."

"The others are inside. We've got your room ready for you." He turned smoothly and made his way back up the steps. "Karas, come." The dog jumped up and trotted after him.

A woman emerged through the darkened opening of the front door. Shorter than Megan with a slender build, Asian features. She smiled at them. "I'm Kiyomi. Nice to meet you both," she said, offering her hand.

"You too," Chloe replied, shaking it. The woman was tiny, her fingers so slender Chloe was afraid to squeeze too hard, but the proud posture and the steel in those dark eyes told Chloe all she needed to know about Kiyomi's inner strength.

Amber and Jesse were inside waiting for them. "Hey, you made it. And look at you, walking around on your own power already," Amber said.

"It's cuz I'm indestructible," Chloe answered with a grin. She wanted to lie down, and Heath would probably make her soon, but she also wanted to get the lay of the land here and be brought up to speed on what was happening.

"Ty and I'll grab your bags," Jesse said, heading for the Range Rover.

Meanwhile, Megan led them up a wide staircase to the second floor. "Here's your room," she said, opening the second door on the right side of the hallway.

Everything about this place was amazeballs. Old, custom woodwork, fancy oil paintings on the walls, and her room was... "Wow." She gazed around her in amazement. "Are you serious? I get to stay here?" It was fancier than the nicest hotel she'd ever been in. The king-size, four-poster bed had a deep red satin spread on it.

"I always thought it looked like the inside of a brothel," Marcus said wryly from the doorway, "but I'm glad you like it."

Megan swatted his shoulder and spoke to Chloe. "I figured if anyone should have the Crimson Room, it was you."

"Oh my God, is that a *fireplace*?" She pulled off her sunglasses, squinted as the light streaming through the window hit her sensitive eyes, shooting off a spike of pain in her skull.

"Yep. Wood's already laid in there if you want a fire later."

So cool. A fire crackling away, Heath and her alone together in this gorgeous room all night… Would be downright romantic if she wasn't recovering from an acute concussion and a couple of bullet wounds that prevented her from enjoying Heath the way she wanted to.

He squeezed her good shoulder gently. "You guys hang out for a bit. I've gotta get my flights figured out."

Once he left, Chloe sat on the bed, fatigue pulling at her. Megan folded her arms and cocked her head, her sister mimicking the pose beside her. Their coloring was slightly different, but some of their features and their body language were uncannily similar.

"When's he leaving?" Megan asked.

"Tomorrow. Not sure what time. He has to report to his station in Damascus by the morning after that." Sadness spread through her at the thought.

"But you're together, right?"

"Sort of."

"Whoa, wait." Amber frowned at her. "Sort of?" She looked at her sister before focusing back on Chloe. "Pretty obvious to everyone how he feels about you. You're not into him?"

Oh, she was into him. Way into him. "It's…complicated."

Megan snorted. "Girl, who do you think you're fooling? It's always complicated, especially with us, but you can make it work if you want to."

Chloe waved a hand, her cheeks heating. She hated talking about this stuff in front of people. "We haven't talked about it. I don't know what he wants."

"What do *you* want?" Amber countered.

Things that scared her. "Really not in the mood for this right now. Can we talk about something else?"

"No," the sisters answered at the same time, but then Amber reached into her pocket and pulled out her phone just as a soft knock sounded on the door.

"Come in," Megan called out.

Kiyomi poked her head in. "Just came to check if you needed anything," she said to Chloe.

"Yeah, come on in here." Chloe waved her in while Amber read whatever was on her phone.

Then Amber's thumbs got busy typing something. "There's a message from the woman you were in contact with." She held out the phone so they could all see it.

Good work, Bam Bam.

"Bam Bam?" Megan asked with a laugh, raising an eyebrow.

She shrugged. "I thought it fit."

"Oh, it fits." Her friend studied her for a moment. "You need to lie down."

"I will. Right after you guys bring me up to speed with everything going on."

In the end they compromised. Chloe climbed into bed while the others gathered around for a short meeting. The list of remaining Valkyries was depressingly short, meaning there were hardly any of them left alive.

Priority one was locating them as soon as possible and trying to bring them in. Priority two was setting up a private WITSEC-style program for them that had already been started, funded with money skimmed from criminal organizations and former targets that Amber had skillfully invested on their behalf.

And thirdly, they were going to find out who was hunting them. If Rycroft's team found the source responsible for leaking intel on Chloe to Dominic Dubois, it would be a huge break.

"I'm so down with that," Chloe said, wiggling her foot restlessly under the covers. She was all fired up, ready to kick some ass, pain or not. Those assholes had forced them to become weapons, and then thought they could dispose of them like used TP when they were no longer needed and posed a potential threat to expose their dirty deeds? Hell to the no. Someone was going to pay.

"By the way, I have your file if you're interested in seeing it," Amber said.

"What file?"

"Your personnel file that I hacked from the Valkyrie database before they shut it all down."

Chloe's eyes widened. "Are you serious? What does it say?"

"I'll send it to you."

"No, just tell me the highlights." Reading would just strain her eyes and make her head hurt worse.

Amber half-smiled. "All right. Let me go grab Lady Ada."

"Who's Lady Ada?" she asked the others in confusion as Amber left.

"Her laptop," Megan answered. "She's extremely protective and possessive of it, so never ever touch it unless she gives you permission."

Huh. "Okay."

Amber walked in with her laptop open, and shut the door. "All right, the highlights on Chloe Wilson. Your real name was Elizabeth Marie Connors."

It was? How in hell had she forgotten her own damn name? The cadre had done a good job of wiping her memories clean.

"And you were born in Nebraska."

"Nebraska…" A sudden barrage of images flashed through her mind. Fields of tall, green cornstalks, and others of golden wheat shimmering in the summer sunshine. Of passing by acres of them in the front passenger seat next to her mom, windows down and the wind blowing in their hair as they sang to something on the radio.

She hadn't remembered the memory until just now. It made her smile even as a sharp pain pierced her.

"Your birthday's July twenty-eighth," Amber continued. "Your parents never married. Your mom got pregnant in junior year of high school. That same fall your father left town to go on a college football scholarship and never came back."

Her dad had been a football star? "She never talked about him, even when I asked," Chloe murmured, fascinated and a little sad. "All she ever said was that she'd loved him and hadn't wanted to hold him back." It made so much sense now. Her mom had set him free and taken on all the responsibility of being a single parent to keep her.

It put a lump in Chloe's throat. Her mom had struggled so much to take care of her on her own, keep enough money coming in to feed and clothe her and keep a roof over their heads. She'd deserved so much better than dying a slow, painful death from cancer.

Amber continued scanning the file for a moment, then looked up with a smirk. "Says here you showed a remarkable penchant for disobedience and destruction when you were first put into the program."

Megan chuckled. "Yup. You're looking at the class rebel right there."

Amber kept reading. "That's it, really. Specialized in explosives and demolitions, tested for ADHD and found to be on the spectrum…"

"I remember when they diagnosed me," Chloe said. "I was relieved that there was a reason why I couldn't sit still or focus for long when I was younger."

"It explains a *lot*," Megan remarked.

"You must have figured out how to manage it, or they wouldn't have graduated you," Kiyomi pointed out.

"Oh, it's still there," Megan said with a twinkle in her eyes. "She wouldn't be Twitch without it."

Amber closed the laptop. "So yeah. That's you."

"Thanks for telling me," Chloe said. "And I gotta say, it's so cool to be here with you guys. To be part of this. It's been…hard to be so isolated for so long."

The others nodded, expressions suddenly serious, a little sad. "I know," Amber said. "But you're not alone anymore."

"That's right, because we're family," Megan added, looping one arm around her sister's shoulders and the other around Kiyomi. "Skeletons and all."

It was more than Chloe had ever imagined having. Enough to make her throat tighten. "Cool. But we're gonna need a code name to call ourselves."

The others all stared at her. "What?" Megan asked.

Chloe waved a hand, frowning. "You know, a moniker. Something awesome." Valkyries was obviously no good, though she was damn proud of having earned the title. And her mark, now ruined. Bastards.

"Uh, okay…" Amber looked at Megan and Kiyomi. "Any ideas?"

"Renegades," Megan suggested.

"It's been done to death," Kiyomi said. "Needs to be something more original."

"How about the Dysfunctionals," Amber said, her voice dry.

"That fits," Megan agreed, "but it also sucks."

Amber scowled and pushed her sister's arm off her. "Hey, it's a million times better than *Renegades*."

"Bitchilantes," Chloe blurted with a flash of triumph.

Three pairs of eyes fastened on her in silence.

"The Bitchilantes," she repeated with a nod, glancing around at them eagerly. Oh, come on, it was perfect. "Vigilantes, but bitches."

Megan busted out a laugh and shook her head as the

others grinned. "Well, it fits. And it has a definite ring to it."

Hell yeah, it did. "Yeah? Are you all cool with it?"

"Sure. Bitchilantes it is," Amber agreed as Kiyomi nodded.

A brisk knock on the door made Chloe sigh even as a smile spread across her face. "That'll be Dr. Killjoy, coming to crash the party." She was looking forward to it. And to being alone with him as soon as possible. She had things she needed to say to him in private.

The door opened to reveal Heath, and her pulse skipped. "Hate to end this deep and no doubt meaningful discussion early, but the patient needs to sleep."

"Told ya," Chloe said.

"We'll let you rest up, then we can visit more later on if you're feeling up to it." Megan led the others out of the room and shut the door.

Chloe didn't plan on leaving this room until morning. She wanted to maximize all her remaining time with Heath. Alone.

She took the opportunity to admire the view as he crossed to the bed, trying to memorize everything about him and block the stab of pain in her chest that his imminent departure caused. "Got your flights figured out?"

"Yeah." He slid under the covers and laid on his side facing her, propped his head on his hand and curved his free one around her waist. "Rycroft's going to fly me to Frankfurt in the private jet, then I'll hop a flight to Damascus."

"What time do you leave?"

"Oh-four-hundred."

Her heart sank. Their time together was coming to an end way too soon, each second slipping away far too fast. She wrestled with her thoughts, the chaotic tumble of emotions. They hadn't known each other long. Would she look stupid and desperate if she told him she wanted to keep this going? If she told him… "Heath—"

"I don't wanna go." He slid his hand up her side to cup her cheek, his eyes intense. "I want to stay right here with you, but I have to finish my contract and be there for my guys."

She leaned into his touch, relief and gratitude swelling inside her. "I understand. And you wouldn't be my sexy Boy Scout if you dodged your responsibilities. But I… You really mean a lot to me." It was hard for her to say, made her feel horribly vulnerable and exposed.

"You mean a lot to me too." Heath searched her eyes. "Enough that I want a firm commitment from you before I leave."

A burst of hope popped in her chest. She was all ears. "What kind of commitment?"

"I'm falling so hard for you. I want to be in on the rest of this mission you're undertaking. Since I can't do that yet, I want to know that you'll wait until I can."

The thought was both terrifying and exhilarating, but she was falling hard too. "You're asking me to wait for you?"

"Yes. And in the meantime, we'll talk as much as we can." His fingers curved around her nape. "I don't want to lose you, firecracker."

Her heart swooned and rolled over. That was the most romantic thing anyone had ever said to her. Having an incredible man like Heath want a future with her was unreal. "I don't want to lose you either."

He smiled, taking her breath away. "You won't." He touched his forehead to hers. "Now say you'll wait for me."

She didn't even have to think about it, just nodded. "I'll wait." He owned her heart already.

Then his mouth was on hers, a slow, tender vow.

Tears pricked her eyes. She willed them away, focusing on him. "I would so do you right now if I wasn't concussed," she complained.

His eyes lit with silent laughter. "Or have gunshot wounds and blast injuries?"

"Or those." The timing sucked.

"Hey, I wanted to give you something to remember me by while I'm gone. Something you can look at to remind you that I'm coming back for you." He half-rolled away from her, drew something out of a pocket and turned back to her.

Chloe blinked at the knife. A custom KA-BAR with two little green feet on the blade, along with the motto *That Others May Live.* She took it from him, unable to help the goofy smile on her face.

"I've carried it with me since my first tour," he told her. "You can think of me whenever you throw it."

The sweet, ridiculous gesture made her laugh softly, even as her heart squeezed hard enough to make her eyes sting. She couldn't believe she'd found him, only to be parted from him so soon. She was going to miss him so much. Three months? It was going to feel like a damn decade. "You sure know the way to a girl's heart, Barrett," she said, setting the knife aside.

"Yeah, well, I was fresh out of Symtex," he said dryly.

"My romantic Boy Scout." She looped her arms around his neck and pulled him in for another kiss, sealing their pledge. "I'll wait for you." As long as it took. "And when you're done, you know where to find me. Because you're mine."

"I am." He kissed her again, whispered against her lips. "And I'd find you again no matter where you were."

279

Chapter Twenty-Nine

Damascus

Nine weeks later

Where the hell was she?

Heath frowned in frustration as he checked his phone one last time on the way to the shower. He'd just come back from yet another bodyguard stint that had taken him to three of the most dangerous cities in Syria. Once he'd arrived back here at the compound, he'd finally been able to check his messages—only to find he didn't have any.

It had taken him all of four days to decide he hated it over here and never wanted to come back. This would be his last contracting job. He missed his family and was homesick, but not for Connecticut. Because his home was wherever Chloe was. Being apart from her for so long had made this stint way harder than any he'd done.

He'd called and texted Chloe half a dozen times over the past few days, but he hadn't heard anything back.

He'd even resorted to reaching out to Ty, to see if his buddy or Megan knew where she was. The answer hadn't been comforting.

The team had gotten a potential lead on Eden last Monday night, and Chloe had flown to Russia with Trinity to follow up on it. That had been four days ago. No one had heard anything from them since, and it was making him crazy.

What if something had happened to her? What if she was in trouble? What if she hadn't gone looking for a Valkyrie at all, but something even more dangerous, like one of the people suspected of hunting them from within the Valkyrie Program?

It had been more than two months since he'd last seen her at Laidlaw Hall. It felt like a year. They'd spent the holidays and Christmas apart. They'd sent each other gifts, and one of his had been wrapped with a card bearing the warning: *Do Not Open 'Til Christmas. I Mean It.*

The entire crew had been back at Laidlaw Hall for Christmas, including the three Valkyries currently based in the States, who'd flown in to spend the holiday with their new sisters and significant others gathered at their base. They'd included Heath in their Christmas dinner via video chat, and he'd finally been able to open his gift from Chloe. It included a whole bunch of junk food, including energy drinks, a taco kit, and a paper Christmas cracker.

The cracker had given him pause.

Is it safe for me to pull this thing apart? he'd asked Chloe, only half-joking.

Everyone had laughed, and he'd been relieved when nothing had exploded when he'd opened it and dutifully put the paper crown on his head while he ate his lukewarm meatloaf and instant mashed potatoes while the others enjoyed their home-cooked British turkey dinner around the huge antique table in the formal dining room. They'd even had Yorkshire puddings without him, damn them.

Up until this past week he and Chloe had talked pretty much every day on the phone or via video chat. God, he missed her. Missing her was a physical ache in the center of his chest that never went away. He was dying to hear from her, couldn't wait until this contract was up in another month so he could go be with her.

He loved her. She was it for him. He wanted to finish this damn job and start a new chapter with her, make a life together going forward. Be with her through whatever crazy shit she got herself into.

That made this radio silence from her even tougher. Trouble didn't find Chloe, she went looking for it with a single-minded determination that put him in a cold sweat whenever he thought about it. He should be with her right now, making sure he was there to guard her while she was off doing…whatever it was she was doing.

He hadn't seen her coming. She'd blown his world apart, turned everything upside down, and it wouldn't be right again until they were together.

One of his fellow security contractors called out to him from down the hall of their barracks. "Barrett. Package arrived for you. I put it on your bunk."

"Thanks, man." He ran the towel over his damp hair and turned right down the corridor that would take him to his room. At least at this facility the chow was decent, and everyone got their own room.

Deep in thought about Chloe, he typed out another text to her as he entered his room.

Haven't been able to reach you in a few days. I'm back at base now. Just let me know you're okay.

He almost put *Love you* at the end, then held off. He hadn't told her yet, but only because he didn't want to scare her off. When he told her, he wanted it to be face-to-face, not in a text.

He damn near jumped a foot when something whizzed past his head and hit the back of the door with a loud thud.

A knife. *His* knife.

He gaped like an idiot at the hilt of his custom KA-BAR sticking out of the wood for a split second before snapping his head around to look across the room and—

His heart seized, then did a slow roll and swelled to twice its normal size, threatening to split his ribs. *Jesus.*

Chloe reclined on her back on his bed, all healed up, wearing cargo pants, a tight T-shirt, and a shit-eating grin. "Hey, handsome."

The floor seemed to tilt under his feet. He smiled so wide his face hurt. "Oh my God." He pounced on her, her happy giggle warming his insides as he flattened her beneath his weight on the bed and dragged her into a full-body hug.

Burying his face in the crook of her neck, he breathed her familiar scent in then exhaled, all but shuddering in relief, his heart about to explode. She was here. She was really *here*. "God, what are you doing here?" he rasped out.

"Thought I'd surprise you." Her embrace was fierce, her lips next to his ear. "Are you surprised?" The husky edge to her voice wrapped around him like a caress.

"Yes." He couldn't move. Couldn't bear to let her go, even for a moment.

"Our lead in Russia disappeared in the Crimea. We lost the scent and couldn't turn up anything else to go on, so I decided screw it, and flew here this morning. Why, were you worried about me?"

"I always worry about you. You make me insane. I missed you so damn much." He levered up on his forearms to stare down at her, hardly able to believe he wasn't dreaming as he drank her in. He shook his head, overcome by the gut punch of emotion. "I'd almost forgotten how beautiful you are."

Her cheeks flushed but her eyes sparkled. "You trying to seduce me, Barrett?"

"Not yet. But I'm about to."

She grinned. "You sure you're okay with this? I'm told me being in here is against the regulations."

"I'm *so* okay with it," he said, and brought his mouth down on hers. He couldn't get enough of her. Had gone way too long without being able to hold her, touch her.

He got her naked, peeled off his shirt so she could touch him and got busy reacquainting himself with her delectable body. Her scent. Which spots made her shiver when he kissed them, which ones the stroke of his tongue would make her moan. He worked her up until she was squirming restlessly, then slid down and pushed her thighs apart.

"Heath."

"Stay still," he ordered, gripping her hips as he stared at the luscious flesh between her thighs. He kissed her. Savored her with soft flutters and caresses of his tongue until she was panting and gripping his hair, straining against his mouth.

Her hand flashed out and stopped in front of his face, a condom she must have brought with her in her palm. "Hurry."

He ditched his pants and underwear, sheathed himself, then draped her legs over his shoulders. Holding her gaze, he set his thumb against the swollen bud of her clit as he moved into position and eased forward.

They both groaned as her heat clenched around him. Heath shuddered, grabbed a fistful of her hair and kissed her as he began to thrust, rubbing her inside and out until she came apart around him with the sweetest cry. He swallowed it eagerly, framed her face between his hands and drove deeper, faster. Pleasure detonated inside him, wringing him out and leaving him helpless in her arms.

Easing her legs down alongside his body, he gazed

down into her face, unable to hold the words back a moment longer. "I love you. I love you so damn much." It was such a relief to say it. Holding it inside these past months had been tough.

Joy and surprise lit her eyes. "I love you too." Her cheeks turned pink at the admission, as if she was shy about saying it. "You made it impossible not to."

He grinned, at peace and fulfilled in a way he'd never imagined was possible. "How long do I have you?"

Her gaze turned speculative. "How long do you want me?"

"I was thinking forever."

A slow, satisfied smile that made his heart hammer. This woman was his, and his alone. "I've got a reputation for danger. Think you could handle me for that long?"

"Yeah, firecracker, I think I could."

She reached up to stroke her fingertips down the side of his face, her expression adoring. "I think you could too."

Catching him off guard, she hooked a leg around his and flipped them over, putting her on top and reminding him that he would never know what to expect from her. But he wasn't complaining. Her naked, luscious body was on top of him, and she'd just agreed to be his.

"You like keeping me on my toes, huh?" Life with her would have its ups and downs and more than its fair share of danger. But it was worth it, because she was worth everything. And life with her would never be boring.

"You know I do." She smiled down at him, her eyes gleaming with mirth and an unholy mischief he recognized all too well. "Stick with me, babe. It'll be a *blast*."

—The End—

Dear reader,

Thank you for reading *Explosive Vengeance*. I hope you enjoyed it. If you'd like to stay in touch with me and be the first to learn about new releases you can:

Join my newsletter at:
http://kayleacross.com/v2/newsletter/

Find me on Facebook: https://www.facebook.com/KayleaCrossAuthor/

Follow me on Twitter: https://twitter.com/kayleacross

Follow me on Instagram: https://www.instagram.com/kaylea_cross_author/

Also, please consider leaving a review at your favorite online book retailer. It helps other readers discover new books.

Happy reading,
Kaylea

Excerpt from
Toxic Vengeance
<u>Vengeance Series</u>

By Kaylea Cross
Copyright © 2020 Kaylea Cross

Chapter One

Sevastopol, Crimea

Serving platter in hand, Eden paused by the kitchen doorway to survey the elegant dining room beyond the threshold. The place was unbelievable.

Over the course of her career she'd conducted all kinds of missions in various places, but none of them as over-the-top as this. It was ostentatious. The cutlery was gold plated, and the enormous crystal chandeliers hanging over the thirty-foot-long mahogany table each cost as much as a high-end luxury sports car.

At the middle of the table, a peacock preening in the midst of the dinner guests, sat the man she was here for.

Target acquired.

Notorious Turkish arms dealer Serkan Terzi. He was the guest of honor tonight, wined and dined in the utmost luxury by a Russian admirer he sometimes did business with. Weapons and drugs, mostly. Sometimes people—vulnerable women and girls.

She had crossed paths with him before, when he'd been on the perimeter of her radar during previous ops. Through her handler, the U.S. government had sent Eden to eliminate various targets, men who posed a risk to national security. But never Terzi himself.

Since he bought U.S. weapons and materiel, and the government wanted the business bad enough to overlook him, he'd been left alone. Even though he sold those same weapons to criminal groups and terrorist organizations in Syria because it fed his bank account, posing a direct risk to American interests and personnel there. Because money meant everything to those in power.

But the rules were about to change.

The Valkyrie Program had been scrapped, and the handler she'd kept infrequent contact with since had gone silent several weeks ago. Eden wasn't sure if Chris was dead or not. Either way, she was on her own now. And that meant she no longer had to stay within the parameters imposed on her for so long. It was incredibly freeing to do things her way.

"Sonya, are you finished serving the prawns?" a woman asked in clipped Russian.

Staying in character, she turned to the head of the catering company hired for this event and put on a smile. "Yes, I was just headed back into the kitchen to get the next platter."

The woman gave her a stern look and strode off to check on another server. Eden bustled back into the kitchen to get another silver tray of hour d'oeuvres. She'd set up a fake ID for this background weeks ago before applying to the catering company, because the host was every bit as cagey as Terzi, and had his security vet each catering employee's credentials before granting them access to the estate. Luckily her credentials were impeccable, thanks to help from her former handler.

For all his brash arrogance and illusions of being untouchable, Terzi had proved frustratingly difficult to isolate. She'd been trying to get to him for almost three months now, and tonight was the best shot she was going to have.

Out in the dining room she circulated among the guests, keeping careful watch of who was here and where everyone was positioned. Her light-brown complexion and eyes made her stand out somewhat amongst the crowd, so she needed to otherwise make herself as unnoticeable as possible in her black uniform. Terzi was still at the table, now sipping on a flute of champagne, all smug and feeling invincible.

Eden would make sure he found out otherwise tonight.

His chief bodyguard was positioned in the far corner of the room, keeping watch. Two weapons were hidden in shoulder holsters beneath his custom-tailored suit jacket, and another in an ankle holster made visible by the slight bulge every time he took a step. The host's security was more discreet, stationed throughout the house and dressed in formal wear. Eden had memorized their placements earlier, as well as their schedule during previous recon of the estate over the past two days.

She wasn't worried about the tight security. She'd killed in front of an audience before and no one had ever been the wiser. All she had to do was deliver the fatal dose and disappear before they sealed off the mansion to question the staff. Once she did that her ID would be burned, but it didn't matter.

She had several points going in her favor tonight. The number of guests and staff would make it easier for her to slip out unnoticed in the ensuing chaos. And Terzi had a fondness for marzipan she was about to exploit to the fullest.

She stayed as invisible as possible throughout the first three courses. After the main meal was served, while everyone relaxed around the table with another round of drinks, she got busy in the kitchen gathering the tools of her trade.

When she got the cue from the head of the catering company, she picked up the tray and followed another server bearing a tray of cocktails into the dining room. Several others were already there pouring tea and coffee for the guests, along with serving different kinds of dessert.

Eden kept her expression neutral as the server with the cocktails moved around the table and stopped at Terzi. He smiled up at her, taking the Amaretto Sour and saluting his host.

Eden waited until he'd taken a large sip before offering the guest beside him an exquisite, handmade marzipan fruit from the plate she carried. Terzi's gaze cut to the pretty little morsels, a smile spreading across his face.

Certain of her mark, Eden lifted the tray to avoid another server passing by and quickly placed the laced marzipans in her clenched fist on the plate. Deftly turning it as she positioned herself beside Terzi again, satisfaction punched through her as he took four of them.

The dosage was tricky. He needed to eat at least two of them for it to be fatal, and she didn't want to make it too obvious that it was poison. Better if it seemed like food poisoning at first, or a reaction to his blood pressure and heartburn meds. The cocktail would help. It was fortunate that Terzi had a weakness for almond-flavored things, disguising the scent of the cyanide.

Lifting the tray as she moved to the next guest, she "accidentally" knocked the final laced marzipan off the tray. As soon as it hit the floor another server swooped in to pluck it up and discard it, allowing Eden to move to the next guest without fear of poisoning them.

A few minutes later as she made her way to the other side of the table, she cast a surreptitious glance at Terzi out of the corner of her eye. He'd only eaten one marzipan and already looked ill.

He was sweating lightly, frowned as he put one hand on his protruding stomach. Dabbing at his face with his linen napkin, he reached for his Amaretto Sour and took another gulp. Then he picked up a second marzipan, paused to examine it, and popped it into his mouth.

Excellent.

She was headed through the kitchen doorway when

she heard the first indication of alarm. At a sharp gasp and a cry, Eden ducked around the doorway into the kitchen.

Hidden from view, she glanced back in time to see Terzi lurch from his chair. He made it two steps before doubling over and vomiting all over the priceless Persian rug beneath the dining table. People gasped and shoved from their seats as security moved in.

Time to go.

A thud sounded somewhere behind her as Terzi hit the floor in the other room. She pushed her way through the flurry of people moving around the busy kitchen. She didn't have to see Terzi to know what was happening. He'd be convulsing now, helpless as his body struggled for oxygen it could no longer absorb, foaming at the mouth even.

Good. Bastard deserved to die in terror.

Three more servers were bringing fruit trays down the hallway when she got there. Security agents rushed past them, faces grim.

Eden gave them blank looks and moved out of their way, staying in the periphery. As soon as they were past her, she rushed down the hall, heading for the powder room she planned to escape from.

Ten feet from her goal a man stepped out of the doorway and stopped, blocking her way. Strong hands shot out to wrap around her upper arms.

She wrenched free and reached for the weapon at the back of her pants, then froze when she looked up into his face. Shock blasted through her as she stared up into a pair of stormy gray eyes she never thought she'd see again.

WHAT THE *HELL*?

For a moment Zack was too stunned to speak. He'd convinced himself it was his mind playing tricks on him again when he'd spotted her going into the kitchen earlier. Had convinced himself that it couldn't be her. Because he'd been imagining seeing her everywhere for months and never found her—in hotels, train stations, airports...in his dreams.

Yet here she was. Nina. Standing right in front of him after all this time.

"What are you doing here?" he blurted, concerned and still struggling to process everything. Finding her here and now was way too damn suspicious under the circumstances.

Her expression closed up, and she looked at him like he was a stranger. "You need to get out of my way," she said in a clipped voice, those unforgettable honey-brown eyes filled with resolve. That look said either he moved, or she'd make him.

Before he could respond, more shouts came from the dining room. Someone yelling for security to lock down the place. He had no doubt they wanted Nina. And that if they caught her, they would kill her.

He focused back on her, the hard set of her features, and made a snap decision. It meant breaking his cover, but he was willing to pay the consequence to get Nina out of here. "If you want to live, come with me now." Grabbing her arm, he turned them and began leading her down the hall.

She was stiff at first, so stiff he tightened his grip, then she relented, jaw tense.

He dragged her through one of the side doorways just as more security agents rushed in through another. Zack glanced around the brick courtyard. They were already locking the estate down. His car was parked out on the road but they'd already closed the main gate.

He released her arm but snagged her hand to make it look like they were a couple, and held on tight in case she had other ideas. Once they were clear, he was going to get some answers. "We're gonna have to scale the wall."

She didn't say a word, just hurried toward it with him.

Twenty feet from the eight-foot-high structure, she broke free of his grip with a practiced move that took him off guard, and ran toward it. He watched, stunned, as she jumped up to catch the top, then nimbly swung over it and dropped down on the other side like a pro. Zack quickly followed suit, half-expecting to have to chase after her when he landed.

But she was standing there scanning the road instead. "We're clear, but we need to hurry."

The juxtaposition between this tough, capable woman and the one he'd thought he'd been falling in love with was jarring. Just who the hell was she, really? Not the flight attendant she'd pretended to be when they'd met in St. Petersburg ten months ago, that much was clear.

And he was really, *really* concerned that she might be a whole lot worse.

"This way." He grabbed her arm again, his mind still reeling, and hurried them to his car. Cops had been stationed near the mansion for extra security. They were just coming down the road as he pulled away from the curb and got them away from the estate. But he wanted answers, and he couldn't hold back for another second.

"Who are you?" he demanded, a sinking feeling taking hold in his gut.

The night they'd met in St. Petersburg he'd been posing as an American businessman trying to get in with an arms dealer. He'd seen her sitting at the hotel bar in that tight skirt suit uniform, and her welcoming smile had made his brain short-circuit. Her cover story had checked out, and he'd been so sure the attraction was mutual that he'd invited her to be his date to an event with the arms dealer the following night.

Throughout all their time together she'd never done or said anything to make him suspicious that she wasn't who she claimed to be. Not once, for that entire three-day weekend they'd been glued to each other, and then every time they'd met afterward over the next seven weeks.

Until he'd woken alone in that Moscow hotel the last time and found the note she'd left, leaving him bewildered and crushed. Now it all made a horrible kind of sense, and he was a fucking idiot for ever falling for her ruse.

"My name's Eden," she said quietly.

He shot her a sideways glance as he sped down the darkened street. She looked the same as Nina had, but there was a hard edge to her now that hadn't been there before. He had no idea if she was telling the truth or not, but he'd be a fucking idiot to trust one word that came out of her mouth. A mouth he'd known intimately not too long ago, and still dreamed about it moving over his skin.

"Did you kill Terzi?" He couldn't believe he was asking that, but it was impossible to ignore the evidence before him. Because this was the *second* time the man he'd been trying to gain the trust of had died of probable poisoning while she was around.

She didn't respond. And that was all the answer he needed.

Goddammit. He bit down hard to stifle the expletive that threatened to burst out of his mouth. She'd used him to get an intro to her previous target. Had made him think she felt something for him. But he'd been a means to an end, nothing more, and now she'd just fucked-up a five-month-long sting to nail Terzi and his inner circle.

But then why spend all that time with him after the job was done in St. Petersburg? Why pretend she'd felt something for him for so long? Unless she'd been hoping to kill someone else he was connected to, and when she decided he was no longer of use, she'd ghosted on him.

"Who are you, really?" he ground out, pissed off at himself as much as her.

Her gaze was fixed on the side mirror as he drove. "Just drop me off at the next street."

"No way. I have to take you in." His CIA contacts

would want to question her—right after he did.

She snorted. "That's not happening."

Anger punched through him, surprising him with its force. "Oh, it's happening." He turned right at the next light and sped through the light traffic. He wanted to get her some place safe so they could talk in private, find out what the hell was going on and who she was working for. "In the meantime, you need to explain what—"

He broke off at the sound of the door opening, gaped in astonishment as Nina/Eden dove out onto the road and rolled away from the car.

"Jesus Christ!" He hammered the brake, wrenched his gaze up to the rearview mirror as "Eden" rolled to a stop on the pavement behind him, then popped up like a seasoned stuntwoman and darted for the sidewalk.

Struggling to recover from his shock, Zack threw the car into park and jumped out to chase her. He bounded over a hedge and tore after her, his shoes pounding against the pavement. Just as he rounded the corner he caught a flash of her as she veered from the sidewalk back toward the road, then lost sight of her in the traffic waiting at the light.

Cursing under his breath, he searched frantically left and right as traffic passed by. Where the hell was she? She couldn't have gone far.

He glanced back at his vehicle—

Just in time to see her hop into it and drive away.

Swearing, Zack whipped around and raced for the car, urgency screaming through him. He couldn't lose her. Not after all this time, not after what she'd done. But his efforts were useless. Within seconds she'd blown past him and had vanished from sight.

"Gotta be *shitting* me," he muttered, pulling out his cell phone to report it, even as he knew it was a waste of time. By the time anyone located his car, she would be long gone.

Who the hell was she? Who had sent her after Terzi tonight?

Whatever the answers, there would be hell to pay for what she'd done tonight. Zack had to find her and bring her in before she got herself killed.

End Excerpt

About the Author

NY Times and USA Today Bestselling author Kaylea Cross writes edge-of-your-seat military romantic suspense. Her work has won many awards, including the Daphne du Maurier Award of Excellence, and has been nominated multiple times for the National Readers' Choice Awards. A Registered Massage Therapist by trade, Kaylea is also an avid gardener, artist, Civil War buff, Special Ops aficionado, belly dance enthusiast and former nationally-carded softball pitcher. She lives in Vancouver, BC with her husband and family.

You can visit Kaylea at www.kayleacross.com. If you would like to be notified of future releases, please join her newsletter: http://kayleacross.com/v2/newsletter/

Complete Booklist

ROMANTIC SUSPENSE

Vengeance Series
Stealing Vengeance
Covert Vengeance
Explosive Vengeance
Toxic Vengeance
Beautiful Vengeance

Crimson Point Series
Fractured Honor
Buried Lies
Shattered Vows
Rocky Ground

DEA FAST Series
Falling Fast
Fast Kill
Stand Fast
Strike Fast
Fast Fury
Fast Justice
Fast Vengeance

Colebrook Siblings Trilogy
Brody's Vow
Wyatt's Stand
Easton's Claim

Hostage Rescue Team Series
Marked
Targeted
Hunted
Disavowed

Avenged
Exposed
Seized
Wanted
Betrayed
Reclaimed
Shattered
Guarded

Titanium Security Series
Ignited
Singed
Burned
Extinguished
Rekindled
Blindsided: A Titanium Christmas novella

Bagram Special Ops Series
Deadly Descent
Tactical Strike
Lethal Pursuit
Danger Close
Collateral Damage
Never Surrender (a MacKenzie Family novella)

Suspense Series
Out of Her League
Cover of Darkness
No Turning Back
Relentless
Absolution

PARANORMAL ROMANCE
Empowered Series
Darkest Caress

HISTORICAL ROMANCE
The Vacant Chair

EROTIC ROMANCE (writing as *Callie Croix*)
Deacon's Touch
Dillon's Claim
No Holds Barred
Touch Me
Let Me In
Covert Seduction

Printed in Great Britain
by Amazon